BLOOD & BONES: DEACON

Blood Fury MC, Book 4

JEANNE ST. JAMES

Jeanne
ST. JAMES

Acknowledgements:

Photographer/Cover Artist: Golden Czermak at FuriousFotog

Cover Model: Joe Adams

Editor: Proofreading by the Page

Beta readers: Whitley Cox, Andi Babcock, Sharon Abrams & Alexandra Swab

Blood Fury MC Logo: Jennifer Edwards

Warning: This book contains explicit scenes, some possible triggers and adult language which may be considered offensive to some readers. This book is for sale to adults ONLY, as defined by the laws of the country in which you made your purchase. Please store your files wisely, where they cannot be accessed by under-aged readers.

———

Keep an eye on her website at http://www.jeannestjames.com/ or sign up for her newsletter to learn about her upcoming releases: http://www.jeannestjames.com/newslettersignup

Join her FB readers' group for all the inside scoop here: https://www.facebook.com/groups/JeannesReviewCrew/

———

Blood Fury MC, Blue Avengers MC and Dirty Angels MC are registered trademarks.

Character List

TO AVOID SPOILERS THIS LIST ONLY INCLUDES THE
CHARACTERS MENTIONED IN THE PREVIOUS BOOKS

BFMC Members:

Trip Davis – *President* – Son of Buck Davis, half-brother to Sig, mother is Tammy, Runs Buck You Recovery

Sig Stevens – *Vice President* – Son of Buck Davis, mother is Silvia, three years younger than Trip, helps run Buck You Recovery

Judge Scott (Judd) – *Sgt at Arms* - Father (Ox) was an Original, owns Justice Bail Bonds

Deacon Edwards – *Treasurer* – Judge's cousin, Skip Tracer/Bounty Hunter at Justice Bail Bonds

Cage (Chris Dietrich) – *Road Captain* – Dutch's youngest son, mechanic at Dutch's Garage

Ozzy (Thomas Oswald) – *Secretary* – *Original* – manages club-owned The Grove Inn.

Rook (Randy Dietrich) – Dutch's oldest son

Dutch (David Dietrich) – *Original* – Owns Dutch's Garage, sons: Cage & Rook

Dodge – Helps manage Crazy Pete's Bar

Whip – Mechanic at Dutch's Garage (formerly known as the prospect Sparky)

Rev (Mickey) – Mechanic at Dutch's Garage (formerly known as the prospect Mouse)
Shade – works at Tioga Pet Crematorium (formerly known as the prospect Shady)
Easy – works at Tioga Pet Crematorium

Stella – *Trip's ol' lady* - Crazy Pete's daughter, owns Crazy Pete's Bar
Autumn (Red) – *Sig's ol' lady* – Accountant for the club's businesses
Cassidy (Cassie) – *Judge's ol' lady* – Manages club-owned Tioga Pet Crematorium

Former Originals:

Buck Davis – *President* – Deceased
Razor Stevens – *VP* - Deceased
Ox – *Sgt at Arms* – Deceased
Crazy Pete – *Treasurer* – Deceased
Tin Man (Tinny) – Deceased

Others:

Henry (Ry) – Judge's son
Daisy – Cassie's daughter
Jemma – Judge's sister
Syn Stevens – Sig's sister
Saylor – Rev's sister, Judge and Cassie's house mouse
Lizzy/Billie/Angel/Brandy – Sweet butts
Max Bryson – *Chief of Police* – Manning Grove PD, Bryson brother
Marc Bryson – *Corporal* – Manning Grove PD, Bryson brother
Matt Bryson – *Officer* – Manning Grove PD, Bryson brother

Adam Bryson – *Officer* – Manning Grove PD, Brysons' cousin, Teddy's husband

Leah Bryson – *Officer* – Manning Grove PD, Marc's wife

Tommy Dunn – *Officer* – Manning Grove PD

Teddy Sullivan – Owner Manes on Main, Adam Bryon's husband

Amanda Bryson – Max's wife, owner Boneyard Bakery

Carly Bryson – Matt's wife, OB/GYN doctor

Levi Bryson – Adopted son of Matt & Carly Bryson (birth mother: Autumn)

Prologue

NOTHING STAYS THE SAME

DEACON STOOD ON THE PORCH, watching the plain tan four-door sedan turn into the driveway. Without a word, his father and mother left him there as they went out to meet the dressed-up woman climbing out of the driver's side.

They exchanged words Deacon couldn't hear. Though, he wanted to. He wanted to know what was being said between the three of them and how it would affect him.

His mom had said his Aunt Trixie and Uncle Ox had gotten into trouble and were in jail, so his cousins now had nothing and no one.

Deacon didn't know much about his aunt and uncle because his mother didn't want anything to do with her brother and his wife. He'd heard his parents talking about them in the past, and the word "trouble" always came up. Along with some other words he wasn't allowed to say unless he wanted to be grounded.

So, he didn't really know his cousins—the ones who no longer had parents to take care of them—even though they hadn't lived far away at all.

He was only told this morning, while he was eating his

Corn Pops, that his cousins, Judd and Jemma, were coming to stay with them.

People, who were practically strangers, were coming to stay in their house.

When his mother told him that, he dropped his spoon into his cereal bowl and splashed milk onto the kitchen table. He quickly used his napkin to clean it up before his father saw it. But Deacon said nothing until he was told he'd have to share his bedroom with Judd.

"What? Why?" How was that fair?

His mother had narrowed her brown eyes on him. "Because they have nowhere else to go except into the system. And we only have three bedrooms in this house. One needs to be for Jemma. That means you'll have to share yours with Judd."

"Why can't they go into the system?" He didn't want to share his room with anyone else. He didn't want to share his parents with other kids.

He was happy the way things were.

And, anyway, Judd wasn't even his age. He was like a million years older. Why would the teenager want to share a bedroom with a ten-year-old?

"Because despite the way my brother lived his life, they are family," his mother said. "They didn't choose this, they are victims of circumstance."

Whatever that meant.

Deacon jutted out his jaw and pounded his fist on the table, making the cereal bowl jump. "But I don't wanna share my room!"

Deacon's heart began to thud as his father took three long strides over to him and cuffed him upside the head. "Boy, you have everything. They have nothing. You will share your room, your toys and everything else you have with your cousins. And I don't want to hear a word about it.

They've already been through enough and they don't need to hear you whining like a damn crybaby."

"But Dad—"

"Not another damn word about it, boy. They're coming here because we're all they have. What if it was you, huh? What if something happened to me and your mother and no one gave a shit enough about you to take you in? You'd end up in some foster home and probably spend the rest of your life in and out of the system. They've had no guidance in their life. They need that and a roof over their heads. And we're going to provide it."

Deacon's bottom lip had trembled as he stared at the sweetened yellow puffed corn floating in the lukewarm milk.

But now, not even an hour after choking down the last of that soggy cereal, he stood on the porch and watched as his cousins got out of the back of the car and, when the woman popped the trunk open, his father grabbed two small garbage bags from it.

They didn't have suitcases? That was all they had?

As his mother reached to pick up a five-year-old Jemma, Judd pushed past her, grabbed his sister and lifted her up instead. Jemma clung to her sixteen-year-old brother with her tear-stained face buried in her neck.

Why was she crying? She was getting her own damn room. Unlike Deacon. And his room wasn't even big enough for two beds.

His father, carrying the black plastic bags, headed toward the house.

Judd stood in the driveway, his sister in his arms, staring at Deacon's father's back, then his gaze landed on Deacon. He couldn't tell if Judd was mad or sad, or what, because the kid's expression never changed.

It remained blank.

His mother wrapped an arm around Judd's shoulders and steered him toward the house. She said something to him, but Judd didn't respond. He just walked, holding on to Jemma tightly. Like he was afraid someone would steal her from him.

Just like he was about to steal Deacon's room. Deacon's life.

As his father climbed the porch steps and passed him, he muttered, "You better drop the attitude, boy. I can see it on your face and so can they. You might not have asked for this, but neither did they. I'm sure they would've been happier staying where they were, not getting uprooted like this. So, you better think twice before you say something stupid to either of your cousins, you hear me?"

Deacon couldn't unglue his gaze from those two cousins, who were approaching *his* house. Neither of them would even be fun to hang out with. Judd was too old. Jemma too young.

"You hear me, boy?"

"Yes," he forced out between clenched teeth.

His dad gave a sharp nod and went inside, the springs on the wooden screen door squeaking as it slammed and bounced against the frame behind him.

Deacon spread his feet wide and crossed his arms over his chest, refusing to move out of their way as they stepped onto the porch.

His mother released a disappointed sigh as she went around him, but Judd stopped right in front of him. He waited until Deacon's mother went inside, then his cousin, much taller than Deacon, said, "Think I wanna share a room with a spoiled, snot-nosed shit like you? You think I got a choice to be here? I'm only doin' it for my sister, that's all." Judd leaned down and sneered right in Deacon's face. "So, get the fuck over it, twerp. What's mine is mine and now what's yours is mine, too. Get used to it. Now, get the fuck outta my way."

Deacon stared at him for a few seconds longer. Then he

moved, but not fast enough. Judd clipped Deacon's shoulder as he pushed forward, knocking Deacon to the side.

Judd paused in front of the door and said over his shoulder, "You do anything bad to my sister, I'll beat the shit outta you."

"You touch me and I'll tell my Dad."

"Then he'll beat the shit outta you, too. Your pop told me he's glad I'm not a pussy boy like you." Judd jerked open the screen door and carried Jemma inside.

Before the screen door slammed shut, he saw Jemma's face peek out from Judd's neck and she stuck her tongue out at Deacon.

Deacon rubbed at the burn in his eyes and the sting in his nose. He tore down the porch steps and out to the shed, where he grabbed his prized BMX bike, which he refused to share, and hopped on it. He pedaled until he couldn't pedal anymore, until his lungs were burning and he lost track of time.

By the time he got home, it was dark and past his curfew. After he put his bike back in the shed, he came around the corner of the house to find his father waiting for him on the porch in the rocking chair. Rocking and waiting. Probably getting more ticked by the second.

His dad was usually fair, but Deacon knew he not only broke the rules, but missed dinner. He'd also somehow torn a hole in his new jeans, so now his mother would have to repair them.

"I'm sorry, Dad," he mumbled as he slowly climbed the porch steps.

His father stopped rocking and got to his feet. "Yeah. You're going to be."

The sound of his father's belt being unbuckled made him freeze.

"Go to your room and wait for me there."

Deacon flicked his eyes up to his father's. "Is Judd in there? You gonna let him watch?"

"He's going to see what happens when he doesn't follow the rules. Just because he's sixteen doesn't mean he'll get away with pulling stunts like this. You know the rules. You broke them."

Deacon began to tremble as heat filled his cheeks. "But Dad!"

His father slid the belt from the loops of his jeans. A familiar sound that made the hair on the back of Deacon's neck stand. "One more word and I'll add another six on to the six you already earned. You don't disrespect me, your mother, your blood or this house. And you did all of that today. Now go."

Deacon blinked quickly and wiped away the tears that were already starting to fall as he jerked the screen door open and ran inside.

———

DEACON WINCED as he pulled his PJ bottoms up over his still stinging butt.

Judd sat on Deacon's bed, his back against the head-board and his ankles crossed as he studied him.

The whole thing had been embarrassing. Not only because his butt had been exposed as he kept his feet on the floor and his hands planted on the bed while his father struck him with the belt, but because he had let a few whimpers escape and he couldn't stop the tears.

All with his cousin, who was a stranger, watching.

But his father used Deacon's discipline as a warning to Judd. Letting the older boy know that he needed to keep in line, that he wouldn't tolerate Judd becoming like his father, Ox. He would respect the law and his family. He would become a productive citizen and not some out-of-control convict.

Now it was just the two of them in Deacon's room. And Deacon had nothing to say. All he wanted to do was climb into the bed Judge was settled on and pull the covers over his head.

But he had a feeling he wouldn't get to sleep in his own bed tonight. Someone would be sleeping on the floor in the sleeping bag that was rolled up against the wall. Of course, it would be him.

Judd had already staked his claim on Deacon's comfortable bed. And if they got into a fight about it, his father wouldn't hesitate to come back into that room and dole out some more "respect."

"You picked a hill not worth dyin' on, kid."

Deacon sniffled and wiped the back of his hand under his running nose. "What's that mean?"

"Means you just need to not do stupid shit and if you do stupid shit, you need to know how not to get caught."

"And you're going to show me how not to get caught?"

"You bet I am and for that, you're gonna be my bitch 'til I'm old enough to move out."

"What does that mean?"

"Means when I need you to do somethin' for me, you're gonna do it. And you ain't gonna whine like a little pussy about it, got it?"

Deacon nodded, though he wasn't quite sure if he "got it." But if there was a way to avoid the belt, Deacon was on board with that.

Judd grinned. "If you haven't figured it out yet, kid, I'm takin' the bed. And that sweet little BMX bike you rode off on? That's mine, too, 'til I get a set of wheels."

"But—"

"Did you enjoy pullin' your pants down in front of me and gettin' hit with that belt?"

"No."

"Then you stick with me, kid. Watch, listen and learn."

Watch, listen and learn.

He could do that if it helped him avoid his father's belt or a cuff upside the head. Or even getting grounded.

So, maybe his cousins moving in wouldn't be such a bad thing.

As long as he got his own bed back.

Chapter One

FINGERS WORKED his hair and pulled at his scalp.

She was probably being rougher than she needed to be as she braided it. On purpose.

Because he was leaving.

And she was pissed.

It had been hot and wild, but it was time for him to hit the road.

He was supposed to leave two days ago, but a couple of extra nights couldn't hurt when the pussy was wet and willing.

Her bare perky tits pressed into the Blood Fury MC's colors inked into his back. His looks got him loads of willing pussy. His cut and tats got him dirty pussy. And not the kind of dirty that needed a shower. Though, afterward, they'd both need one.

But the kind of pussy who weren't looking for a husband or a boyfriend, usually because they'd just scraped one off, or a man scraped them off. Instead, they wanted a man who knew how to use his dick and tongue. And use them well.

Tina finished braiding his mohawk before securing the end with a hairband, and then pressed herself harder against his back, sliding her hands around to his pecs and down, tweaking the barbells in his nipples.

"Never met a man so into piercings," she purred.

Deacon remained sitting on the edge of the bed, his eyes focused on his clothes piled on the floor. He needed those to escape. But he couldn't make a move while she held tightly onto his barbells.

"Yeah," was all he answered. He wasn't there for deep conversation. In fact, he hadn't picked her for talking at all. What he had been there for was over.

It was time to jet.

"Do you have to go so soon?"

Soon? He'd been there too long already. She was starting to get clingy. While the pussy had been great, it wasn't one he'd want to revisit.

"Gotta work." And that wasn't a lie.

"What do you do?"

Fuck. He'd found her on Tinder, not eHarmony. She needed to learn the unspoken rules of a hookup app.

"I'm a pimp."

Her hands dropped suddenly, like his skin had burned her, and her tits disappeared from his back. "What?"

"Yeah. This was a job interview. Thought you knew that."

"Bikers are pimps?"

"Yeah, we got a whole stable of bitches. You did alright. You interested? You'd draw some decent money. You work enough johns in a night, you could make enough scratch to start an IRA."

He heard a sharp intake of breath behind him, then winced when she shrieked, "Get out! Get the fuck out of my bed! Get the fuck out of my house!"

That was one way to get cling-free.

He quickly got to his feet, yanked on his clothes, shrugged on his cut and shoved his feet into his boots, not taking the time to lace them. He'd do that when he got outside.

Before walking out of the bedroom, he tossed over his shoulder, "Guess that's a no?"

Tina was sitting on her bed, the sheet now wrapped around her, pointing toward the door. "Get out! Before I call the cops."

Deacon shot her a smile, gave her a chin lift and did what he did best...

Got out while the getting was good.

———

"Four fuckin' days."

He lifted one eyelid and stared at his giant of a cousin who was filling the doorway of Deacon's office.

He had his feet kicked up on his desk with his ankles crossed, his arms crossed over his chest and he'd been trying to take a little snooze. He guessed that wasn't going to happen any time soon. He reluctantly lifted his other eyelid.

Judge apparently had a burr up his ass today.

Deacon just might be that burr.

"Last I checked there are seven days in a week, not four. Learn to count, cuz."

Judge took a step into the office and shoved Deacon's feet off his desk. "Four fuckin' days to do a job that shoulda taken two."

"Got sidetracked."

"Yeah, like normal. By pussy."

"It was decent pussy." Otherwise he would've been home a day earlier.

"Glad you were havin' fun while my ass was back here takin' our business seriously."

"Hey, I got the job done and the money should be hittin' our account any day now."

Judge only grunted.

His cousin and business partner couldn't argue that because it was true. They were getting a nice little chunk of change for Deacon finding a fugitive out in the boonies of northern Pennsylvania. The skip had been hiding out in a hunting cabin in the woods, where cell phone coverage was sketchy, and the neighbors consisted of mostly white-tail deer, black bear and squirrels. And a few backwoods rednecks.

Despite that, Deacon managed to track down the bail jumper, get him cuffed and deliver him to the nearest police station for the bondsman to come haul his ass back to Jersey.

It actually only took him a day and a half. But Deacon wasn't bringing up that point right now. Not when he had a scowling giant standing a couple feet away from him.

Fee-fi-fo-fum.

"What's up your ass anyway? Is Cassie findin' herself unsatisfied with your baby carrot cock and forcin' you to fuck your Fleshlight again?"

"Got nothin' to do with Cassie."

"Then, why you bein' a dick?"

Judge planted his knuckles on Deacon's desk and leaned over until they were face to face. "'Cause I can."

"Whatever. Be Mr. Grumpy McGrumpFace all you want. I still *wuv* you." He puckered his lips and made kissing sounds at Judge. "You need a hug?"

"Need you to take your fuckin' job seriously."

"This ain't a job, Judge. It's my business, too."

"Then fuckin' act like it!" his cousin bellowed.

Justice, his American Bulldog, got up from lying at Deacon's feet to come around the desk. He nudged Judge with his nose.

"Jussie don't like you yellin', just sayin'."

"Then stop makin' me do it."

Deacon's cell phone rang and vibrated at the same time.

Unknown Number popped up on his screen. He snagged the phone off his desk and put it to his ear. "Deacon Edwards, skip tracer extraordinaire and all around awesome badass."

He grinned as Judge rolled his green eyes.

"This Justice Bail Bonds?" the male with a heavy accent on the other end asked.

He sat straight up in his chair. "Yeah, it is."

"This is Anthony Bianchi from Bianchi Bail Bonds..."

"Okay?" Deacon hit the speaker button on his phone and placed his cell on the desk so Judge could listen, too.

"From Philly," the man finished.

So, *that* was the accent. Fucking Philly. He hated that city. It was almost like Jersey, but way worse. It was Jersey's sweaty armpit.

Even so, the guy was acting like they should have heard about Bianchi Bail Bonds. Like they were famous or something.

"Yeah, so..." Deacon prodded.

"Yeah, so got ya numba from anotha bondsman. He said you're good at trackin' down these fuckwads when they skip."

Well, that sounded like a glowing review. His eyes met Judge's. "Yeah, I'm good."

"I need betta than good."

"I'm *betta* than good," Deacon repeated with a smirk.

There was a pause on the other end of the call. "You makin' fun of my accent?"

He nodded while answering, "Nope. So, what d'you need from us?"

"Got a skip that might end up in your area. This guy's a real piece of work, though. Domestic abuse. Sexual assault. Attempted murder. How tha fucka got bond, who fuckin' knows. Probably some asshole judge who's worried about tha man's reputation ratha than the victim's right to live without *fea*."

Fea? Deacon rolled his eyes. *For fuck's sake*, fear.

This dude was worried about victim's rights? He was making scratch off that "fucka."

"Also, tha asshole's got no problem with witness intimidation."

"So, he's dangerous," Deacon concluded.

"That's what I'm sayin'," Anthony said. "He's been in and out of jail, likes to use and abuse women. Sweet talks 'em for a while, gets in good with 'em, then *boom*, runs up their credit cards, wipes out their bank accounts, and's got no problem thinkin' he's a man by makin' a woman do what she don't wanna do. I got two sistas, I don't got time for that kinda trash, hear what I'm sayin'?"

"Yeah, I hear you," Deacon muttered. He didn't have time for that kind of trash, either. Jemma might be his cousin, but she was more like a sister to him and he wouldn't want a man doing that to her. Or any other woman.

"Anyhow, he's bad fuckin' news. That means if you take this job and you see 'im, you gotta watch yourself. Make sure you got protection. I wouldn't put it past 'im to take a shot at ya. I wouldn't put it past him to take out tha woman. Which is why I'm callin' ya." The man hacked a couple of times, not bothering to cover the phone when he did so. "Last woman he fucked up and drained dry is now up near you in Mansfield. Probably tryin' to hide out 'til the trial. But now the mothefucka's probably lookin' for her to either *convince* her to drop the charges or make her *disappea*."

Like swim with the fishes type of disappearing?

"You notify Mansfield PD?" Deacon asked him.

"Yeah, first call I made."

"They probably don't have enough people to sit on her full time."

"That's why you were my second call."

Deacon could hear the unspoken "dumbass" on the end

of that. "Wouldn't it be smarter to get her a damn bodyguard?"

"Prolly, but that ain't my problem. My problem's findin' tha fucka and deliverin' him to the court and gettin' my fuckin' money back. I'm a business, not a babysitta. The victim has to look out for her own ass. It was her fault for gettin' involved with this putz in tha first place."

So, Bianchi was saying the victim pretty much deserved what she got. *Fucking great.*

"She the only victim involved in his current case?"

"Yeah. He did a numba on her, and guess she wasn't gonna take it lyin' down."

"Good for her," Deacon muttered.

"Not so good for her, if this whacko finds her."

"He got connections? Like, does he have the assets to take out a hit on her?"

"Nah. He's just a broke-ass losa. Gets his jollies from breakin' women, physically and financially."

"So, what are you askin' me to do?" Deacon asked, scraping a hand down his beard.

"Snag his ass and hold 'im for me."

"You sure he's comin' up this way?"

"Nope. But if I can find the victim, so can he."

"She aware he skipped?"

"Don't fuckin' know. Again, not my problem. That's tha DA's problem."

The District Attorney for the City and County of Philadelphia probably had way bigger problems and cases than one domestic abuse incident. Their office was most likely overwhelmed.

"So, ya interested?" Bianchi asked.

Deacon met Judge's eyes. His cousin gave him a slight chin jerk.

"Depends on what it's payin'," Deacon said after a few seconds.

"I'll give ya ten."

A measly ten percent? Deacon shook his head and laughed. "Then no, ain't interested. 'Specially if this asshole's violent."

"Twelve then."

"No."

"Whadya want? No guarantee he's headin' up your way."

"Right, that means I might be wastin' a lot of time sittin' on the vic if he decides to go underground and forget she ever existed."

"Got a feelin' he won't forget her. He's tha kinda dick who don't like a bitch gettin' tha better of 'im."

"Yeah?"

"He might go underground, then pop up like a weasel when she least expects 'im, slice her damn throat and then go back into his hidey-hole. He's tha kinda dumbass who thinks if there's no witness, tha charges will be dropped."

"Again, sounds like she needs a bodyguard. Not my area of expertise."

"And again, that's her problem, not mine."

Judge blew out a breath and shook his head.

Deacon was sure his expression matched Judge's annoyed one. This guy was a total fucking asshole. But, in truth, the man was right, his job had been to provide a bond for a criminal. That was it. He wasn't a crusader of justice.

But then, neither was Deacon or Judge.

He pursed his lips and considered what the job may be worth. "Twenty-five percent."

"*Cazzo!* I'll find someone cheapa."

"You get what you pay for, Bianchi. You get fucked if he's not captured. Somethin's better than nothin', right?"

Through the phone, Deacon heard fingers drumming against what he figured was a desk, so he stayed quiet and waited.

"Twenty," Bianchi countered.

"Twenty-five. Last chance or I'm hangin' up. Don't got time for these fuckin' games." He needed to stare at the back of his eyelids soon. Bianchi was interrupting his nap.

"All right. You drive a hard bargain. Twenty-five."

Deacon smiled up at Judge. His cousin didn't return that smile. "Email us the bond, docket, photos, any info I'm gonna need." He rattled off the business email address. "Soon."

"Gonna get it to ya in the next half hour."

"I'll be in touch if I got any questions. You find him first, let me know." Deacon ended the call before getting a response. He leaned back in his comfy office chair and folded his arms behind his head. "What you thinkin'?"

Judge shook his head. "Just wonderin' what pussy you're gonna fall into while in Mansfield."

"Don't be a hater. Not ready to settle down like you, old man."

"Then hopefully you're wrappin' it tight when you go divin'."

"Also not makin' the same mistake you did. Learned from you to never trust a fuckin' woman." He grinned. "'Cept for Mom. I trust her."

"Maybe you shouldn't," Judge threw at him as he walked out of Deacon's office.

"What does that mean?" Deacon yelled.

Judge paused right outside the door. "When she used to tell you all the cookies or pie were gone? She was just savin' that shit for me."

"Bullshit."

"Keep tellin' you, I was the son she never had." A snort came from down the hall.

Justice sat down next to him and whined. "Guess you're gonna be hangin' with Bubba Grump for a few days. I got some scratch to make." The bulldog laid his head on

Deacon's lap and turned his chocolate brown eyes up at him. "Would take you along if I could, believe me. You can hang with *ya sista*. And Daisy." He rubbed Jussie's head. "And make sure you take a huge shit in the giant's boots. I'll give you extra treats when I get back if you do."

Chapter Two

HE KNEW this wouldn't be an easy job. Not after reading all the documents Bianchi emailed him about William Warren. Then he did some online searches of his own. Turns out, the man was nothing but a menace to women.

Hell, he couldn't even call Warren a man. A real man didn't do what he did to women. How he kept getting sprung from the slammer to do it again baffled Deacon.

Warren had to be one slick fucker. Charm the women, be real sweet to suck them in, then slowly drain them financially dry. He did it in several ways. Borrow, beg or steal a credit card, a debit card, or get access to a bank account. Steal any hidden cash from purses, sock drawers or jugs full of change. Any way he could put his hands on a woman's snatch to get access to her scratch, he did it.

He was good at coming up with excuses to get them to "loan" him money. He was also good at making them feel guilty. He was even better at getting them to fall for him, so he had access to "pick their pockets" right in front of their face.

A master manipulator and a crafty con artist. He was

the kind who worked harder on his con simply to avoid getting an actual job.

From what Deacon could tell, Warren picked women who were younger, maybe newly on their own, and much more impressionable. Not women who were more seasoned against assholes like him, but who would more than likely buy into his bullshit without a lot of hassle.

Warren was also the type of man who ended up being a "hard lesson learned" for those ladies. One they would vow never to make again. He took pleasure out of teaching women that lesson, both financially and physically.

From the rap sheet Deacon read, the man was always on the move. Once he hit a victim in one area, he moved to the next. He had no roots, no hometown. No base to go back to. He could move anywhere to find his next target. Deacon couldn't find any close relatives, except a father who was in a federal prison out in Oregon. And the man had been there for a long time, since Warren was a kid. Deacon found out Warren's father had murdered his mother. Afterward, no one came forward to claim the four-year-old and he ended up in foster home after foster home.

Having a shitty home life wasn't any excuse for what the man did to women.

Deacon saw pictures of Warren's latest victim, which were taken at the hospital. Reilly Porter's beat-down had been brutal. Clicking through the evidence photos attached to the email Bianchi sent had made him grind his molars until they almost cracked. His hands clenched so tightly into fists, his fingers had locked up.

He only needed a few minutes alone with Warren to teach *him* a lesson.

The only picture of Reilly where her face wasn't distorted from bruising and swelling, possibly even broken bones, was a driver's license photo. He did a few social media searches and couldn't come up with anything online.

It seemed she had deleted all her public profiles. Deacon didn't blame her if the crazy motherfucker was looking for her.

The victim was smart to leave where she'd been living and working to disappear. Online and offline. However, it wasn't fair to Reilly that she had to hide because of this asshole.

So, Deacon was determined to snag the fucker. Plus, twenty-five percent was a nice chunk of change. How that fucker came up with the ten percent plus fees Bianchi charged Warren to bail him out on a million-dollar bond, Deacon needed only one guess.

Another woman Warren conned.

Because he doubted Warren had that kind of cash lying around, nor did he have any assets for collateral. No, this was the type of guy who always used someone else's money. Another unsuspecting victim, who would eventually find herself financially devastated.

He had to assume for a man to do this on a regular basis, Warren had mommy issues.

As Deacon glanced up the paved driveway that disappeared up the mountain and into the woods, a chill shot down his spine. He knew in his head the driveway did not lead up to the Shirley compound, but it still felt too much like déjà vu.

That night up on that mountain last November was a night he did not want to relive any time soon. Or ever. It left invisible scars on most of them.

His problem right now was that he couldn't simply head up to the address Bianchi gave him. Only one mailbox stood where the road met the driveway, which meant only one residence was at the top.

That also meant he couldn't watch the house from a distance, which was his original plan. Now he had to come up with another tactic, other than setting up camp in the woods. Because that was not happening for twenty-five percent.

And, as it was early April, the weather could go either way. A snow storm one day and a warm spring day the next. During this time of the year, Mother Nature tended to be bipolar. Which was one reason he was parked along the road in his Ford F250 pickup instead of sitting on his sweet Harley Low Rider S.

He rolled down the driver's side window, put his binoculars to his eyes and peered up through the trees, which had already started to bud.

"Christ," he grumbled. He still couldn't see shit. Whoever owned the house at the top wanted privacy. Which was also evident by the two stone pillars at the bottom that were connected with an electric gate.

Not to mention, the nice "no trespassing" sign. Not the plastic red and white one purchased at the local hardware store for about a buck. This sign was carved out of wood and expertly stained. A high-class way to say "keep the fuck out."

Whoever lived up there had some scratch because he doubted a double-wide was parked at the top. Simply paving the length of that driveway alone would cost more than one of those tornado traps.

It seemed Reilly had some sort of "connection." And not of the broke-ass kind of association like Warren.

After getting the address, Deacon had done some digging and the property appeared to be owned by a company. R. Ackerson, LLC.

Sounded like Reilly had friends in high places. If so, maybe she could afford a bodyguard to keep her safe. Because Deacon's sole purpose of being parked at the bottom of a mountain outside of Mansfield, Pennsylvania, was to find and capture Warren, then deliver him to Bianchi.

That was it.

Nothing more. Nothing less.

He was not a bodyguard. He was not a babysitter. He was not a hero.

Well, the last one could be debatable.

He'd been known to be like Superman in bed.

He grinned.

Right now, he needed to reevaluate his plan. He'd go into town, casually ask questions, possibly show pics of Warren, and find a motel to set up his "base." And maybe he could find a woman to warm his bed and help him keep an eye out. It always helped to create some networks in town.

———

HE WAS HUNGRY. He was thirsty. Even a bit horny.

It was quite possible he could scratch all those itches in the bar he just walked into.

Not exactly a dive, but it wasn't some kind of stuffy martini bar, either. It was casual, served good homemade grub and cold beers. At least, that was what the cashier said at the local dollar store after Deacon showed her the picture of Warren and got an answering shrug. Then he'd asked her where the locals went to unwind.

Turned out to be a locally-owned sports bar, the Mill Creek Bar & Grill. It wasn't the type of establishment that would need to hang a sign stating, "No Colors Allowed," but he left his cut in the Ford anyway. But then, he never wore his Fury colors while hunting a skip.

Potentially, doing so could make his club a target. Instead, he wore a pair of worn Levi's, his BFMC belt buckle, his boots and a plain off-white thermal since the night had gotten a bit nippy.

Conveniently located a couple of blocks down from his motel, he left his truck there and walked.

He kept his head on a swivel while he hoofed it down the sidewalk, on the off chance he'd spot Warren. He had burned that fucker's face into his memory. He also made sure to wear his black paracord bracelet since he had nowhere to hide cuffs or zip strips on him to secure a fugitive. Like a Boy Scout, being a bounty hunter, it paid to be prepared.

Most fugitives weren't going to stand there and wait for their captor to find something to secure them with. They would go into fight or flight mode. Not simply get on their knees and interlock their hands behind their heads like a good little boy or girl.

And Deacon sure as fuck wasn't running after anyone and preferred not to get into a damn scuffle, if he could avoid it. His face was too pretty to risk getting fucked up like that.

When he walked inside the bar, the building was bigger than what it appeared since it was a lot deeper than it looked on the outside. An oval-shaped, double-sided bar sat lengthwise in the middle of the space. Along the sides in that front area were high tables. The back was more of a dining area, which was pretty full for the time of night. But then, there were different types of sports being shown on big screen TVs hanging along the walls. Whether those games were live or taped, Deacon had no clue. He wasn't into sports except for the NFL. He was a Steelers fan since he'd grown up watching all the games with his dad. However, at the beginning of April, football was a distant memory.

He spotted an empty stool down at the other end of the bar and made his way to it, scanning the patrons sitting around the bar and surrounding high tables as he went.

None of the patrons looked like Warren.

He doubted the fugitive would just be chilling in a bar,

drinking a beer and eating fried mozzarella sticks, anyway. But, *hey*, the dude could be so whacked that he didn't care who saw him.

He settled on the stool, ignored the male bartender three customers down and caught the eye of the female one across from him. He gave her a crooked smile and a chin lift. She immediately broke away from the woman she was talking with and hurried over, throwing a cardboard coaster onto the bar top in front of him.

She leaned over just enough to give him a nice peek at the top curves of her tits, which were stuffed into a bra a size too small. Her tight tank top, which advertised the bar and grill, also did nothing to hide her assets.

The redhead—definitely not a natural red like Autumn —knew how to make good tips.

"Hey." Her husky voice swept over him.

"Hey." He took his time scanning the overflowing flesh to let her know he appreciated what she was generously sharing.

Her tongue swept over her bottom lip. "What are you in the mood for?"

Heh. "What's worth havin'?"

Her lips curled up at both ends. "Depends. Are you hungry... or thirsty?"

He raked his gaze over her face, then continued down her chest. "Both." She wasn't bad. About a strong seven on a scale of one to ten.

Her blue eyes sparkled at his answer. She fingered the drink coaster, circling it with the pointed tip of her long, red-painted fingernail.

"Well," she said softly, "got a good local IPA on tap. We also serve a mean anus burger."

Deacon blinked. "What?"

The bartender smiled. "What? Are you asking what's on the Angus burger besides cheese?"

That was not what he was asking, but he would go with that. "Sorry, didn't catch your name."

She shoved out her chest and her hand at the same time. "Oh, I'm Bambi."

Bambi. He shook her extended hand. She scraped her nails along his fingers when she released it.

Deacon glanced around for a pole. Nope. No pole. No stage. He was still sitting in a local bar and grill. "Well, hey, Bambi, I'm Nick." The name he always used when he was out hunting.

"Well, Nick," she purred. "You can have whatever you want on that burger."

"Can I now?" he purred back.

"Bambi!" came a bellow from the male bartender.

Bambi made a face and shrugged. "So, a beer and a burger?"

"Yeah, sure. I like my burger warm and pink in the center."

"I'll get that order in for you and be back in a sex with your beer... *sec. Oops.*" She put her fingertips over her mouth and giggled.

Deacon checked out her ass as she moved down the bar. Yep. Definitely a solid seven, maybe teetering on a seven and a half.

It looked like his thirsty, hungry and horny problem might all be solved in one shot.

His gaze raked over the patrons eating at the tables toward the back. No Warren, of course. No surprise.

Bambi was back in a flash, setting a pint glass filled to the brim in front of him. "I started a tab for you, Nick." She tilted her head. "I don't meet too many guys up here with a pierced nose. Besides your left nostril and right ear, what else do you have pierced?"

He lifted his beer to his lips, "That's a secret I only share with a select few," and took a long sip.

"I have a feeling it's more than a *select few*," Bambi answered. "But how does one get on that list?"

"It's a rigorous process." He hid his grin behind the beer.

Bambi rolled her eyes. "I doubt that. I'll go check on your burger."

As she went to move away, he reached over the bar and grabbed her wrist, pulling her back. "Hey, before you do that, got somethin' to show you."

Her eyes lit up. "One of those secret piercings?"

"Not yet." He slipped the picture of Warren out of his back pocket and placed it on the bar, tapping the photo with his finger. "Seen him in here recently? Or even around town?"

She picked the photo up to study it and pursed her dark red lips. "He doesn't look familiar."

"You sure?"

"He's pretty cute. I'd remember him."

Fuck yeah, she'd remember him. He left a lasting impression with women. And not a good one.

She lifted her gaze back to him and tilted her head. "Why are you looking for him?"

The lie—the one he used in most circumstances—slipped easily off his tongue. "He's an old high school teammate of mine. Another buddy told me he was back in the area, but I can't find him."

She squinted at him. "Teammate?"

He puffed his chest out a little. "Yeah, football. Star quarterback of my alma mater." The only time he'd ever touched a football was when him and Judge had tossed one around in the backyard as kids.

With her bottom lip caught between her teeth, she stared at him for a moment, her eyes raking over his chest and shoulders. She glanced at the picture again. "I can ask Danny. And some of the staff in the back."

Deacon shot her a mega-watt smile. "That would be great. And really appreciated."

"There are ways to show that appreciation," she whispered, tucking the picture into the front pocket of the black apron wrapped around her waist. She gave him another smile and a wink as she turned. "I'll bring your burger and make sure it has a warm, pink and *juicy* center just like you asked."

Normally, with a woman dropping sexual innuendos like that, his dick would be starting to pay attention. Surprisingly, his wasn't. Which meant, he needed to decide whether Bambi was worth pursuing or not for tonight.

Not even ten minutes later, she returned. A plate containing a burger and fries in one hand, a squeeze bottle of ketchup in the other. She placed it in front of him and then slipped the photo and silverware wrapped in a napkin out of her pocket, putting them next to his plate.

"Danny hasn't seen him. Neither has anyone who works in the back."

"Thanks for checkin'." Deke unwrapped the napkin. "You know what? Give me another napkin. And a pen."

One of her dark eyebrows lifted, but she snagged another napkin from under the bar and pulled a pen from her apron.

When she put the napkin down on the bar top, she kept a tight grip on the pen. Did she want him to wrestle it from her?

He grinned. "If I give you my number, can you call me if you see him?"

Those fingers loosened up quickly. "Sure."

He accepted the pen from her. "But promise not to say anythin' to him. Wanna surprise him." He scribbled down the number to a burner phone he bought earlier in the day and handed her the napkin.

Her eyes flipped from the number to him. "Can I call you for anything else?"

"Depends on what you got in mind." He popped a fry into his mouth.

Her voice got low and husky. "I have a lot of things in mind."

His dick might have twitched the tiniest bit on that. Maybe he should get her number, too. "What time do you get off?"

"Depends."

He cocked an eyebrow. "On?"

"Well, my shift ends at midnight. But how soon I *get off* will depend on you."

Heh.

Too bad she didn't have any good info... Getting an invite to her bed would only take care of one need, not the need for information.

And it was only the first night in town, too. He had no idea how long he'd need to stay. He didn't want to hook up with some chick who might get bent if he didn't want to spend a second or third night with her. That could get messy.

He needed to weigh the pros and cons on boning Bambi.

As she waited for his answer, her attention was pulled toward the front of the bar when the door opened.

He glanced in that direction, too, just in case it was Warren.

It was not.

Fuck no, it wasn't.

It was someone much better looking than Warren. The blonde walking in was teetering on a ten, unlike Bambi.

Suddenly the bartender was off his radar and the newcomer landed right in the center of it.

The woman wore a gray pantsuit with pinstripes and a light pink V-neck blouse under the jacket. The pants fit so they accentuated her long legs. The spiked heels made her appear taller than what she was, but, from what he could tell when she took long strides around the bar, she wasn't short. Those long legs could wrap around his waist and hold him hostage.

Her blonde hair was up in a bun, so that meant it was long. How long, he wasn't sure, but long enough to fist. It wasn't a severe bun, but a loose one, so if you just pulled a couple pins from it, it would fall around her shoulders.

Bet she didn't have a name like Bambi.

"Hey, Reese! Busy day?"

The blonde's gaze sliced right through him, not even hesitating on him for a second as it landed on Bambi. "Crazy."

"Your regular?"

The blonde nodded and blew right past him to a table in an empty back corner. She put an oversized, expensive looking black leather bag on the seat next to her and pulled out a laptop, setting it up on the table.

It looked like she just stepped out of some big city, not someone who walked into a local bar and grill in a small town in northern PA.

He did his best to concentrate on his *soon-to-be-cold* burger and fries. Unfortunately, his burger was not warm and pink in the center. It was brown. Overdone. Not juicy. *Fuck.*

Suddenly, his meal wasn't as interesting as the blonde who sat by herself.

Confident. Independent. Most likely with a spine of steel. A *take-no-shit* type of woman.

While it shouldn't be, his dick was way more interested in the blonde than the bartender. But he doubted he'd be able to sweet talk her into taking him home for the night.

No, a woman like her would need to be handled with

more finesse than Deacon had. Or... he could play the bad boy angle. Some women like to get nasty in the sheets for one night with a man who normally wouldn't be her type.

The one good thing about those women were they usually weren't clingers. They got their thrill, then couldn't wait to scrape off the man. Were afraid of being seen with him. They had one type who was good enough to stand by their side, another to scratch the itches the first type couldn't.

Deacon was the second type.

Maybe he should let it be known he was available to be that for her for a few hours. He'd love for his dick to scratch a few of her itches.

Deacon turned on his stool to keep one eye on her while he sipped his beer and popped a few more French fries into his mouth.

When he took a big bite from his burger...

The burger shot its load, causing a wet plop to land on his chest.

"Fuck," he muttered, putting the burger back on the plate and staring at the mess that was spreading even wider on his shirt. The grease was soaking into the cotton and would be a bitch to get out.

A giggle had him looking up.

"A little club soda will fix it." Bambi lifted a *gimme-a-sec* finger. Not even a minute later, she came around the bar with a glass of club soda and a handful of napkins.

She put the glass down and when he held out his hand for the napkins, she shook her head. "I got it."

She forced her way between his thighs, until she was standing wedged between them, dipped the napkin in the glass, then began to rub at the stain.

"Well, one place where you have piercings is no longer a secret. Or should I say two?"

The spot over his nipple was now drenched and it was

hard to miss not only the hard tip, but the titanium barbell running through it.

He looked over Bambi's head as she continued to rub, making sure to flick his barbell as she did so, and met the blonde's gaze. She was watching them, her expression blank.

He gave her a half-smile and her eyes quickly dropped back to her laptop.

He continued to stare at the woman as Bambi finished molesting his nipple, while he wished it was the blonde instead.

Yep, that woke up his dick.

He pulled his attention from the blonde, put it back on Bambi and grabbed her wrist. "Think it's fine now. Gonna rub a hole in my shirt."

"I just wanted to make sure it didn't stain."

"My shirt's now soaked."

Bambi leaned in and whispered, "So are my panties."

He tended to have that affect. "What's she drinkin'?"

The bartender's brow dropped low and she stepped back, giving him some breathing room. "Who?"

"The woman you called Reese."

Bambi's head spun back toward the blonde, then back toward him. "Why?"

"Wanna buy her a drink."

"That won't get you anywhere with her. I don't think she likes men."

Interesting. "Know that for a fact?"

"No. I just know that she always comes in here alone. She eats and drinks alone. Leaves alone. A few men have tried picking her up and all have failed."

Fuck yeah, he liked a challenge.

Bambi plucked at the barbell she could see through his damp shirt. "But, honey, you've got a sure thing right in front of you."

Deacon jerked his chin toward the blonde. *Reese.* "What's she drinkin'?"

Bambi frowned. "A vodka tonic."

"Get her another one and put it on my tab."

Her face got hard and she stepped back even further. "I guess you don't want me calling you later."

"Only if you see William Warren."

Bambi leaned in and warned, "She's not going to want you."

That was yet to be determined.

"You know what? Get her that vodka tonic and get me a beer. But deliver my beer to her table."

"I hope she chews your balls off and spits them out," Bambi sneered as she moved away from him.

He glanced down at his thermal. The mess was gone but his shirt still had a huge wet spot. He could hit the head and hope they had hand dryers. Then take a detour on his way back to his spot at the bar.

Chapter Three

Reese glanced up from the brief she was writing when Bambi set down her grilled chicken salad. She also placed another vodka tonic and a pint glass of beer next to her laptop.

She never ordered a second drink. She only allowed herself one with dinner and that was it. And she certainly didn't drink beer.

"I didn't order another drink, Bambi."

"You didn't, but a guy at the bar did."

Reese frowned. "What guy?"

Bambi turned to point but dropped her hand. "He was sitting at the bar. I'm not sure where he went. I hope he didn't skip because he didn't pay his tab yet."

"Well, tell him thanks but no thanks."

"I told him you wouldn't want it, but he didn't believe me. I also told him you don't like men."

Reese blinked at that last statement. She didn't bother to address it with Bambi, as they weren't friends. What Reese liked and didn't like wasn't anyone's business besides the person who joined her in bed.

Though, it had been a long time since she'd gotten

naked with anyone. Most of the men she met were clients and she didn't sleep with clients, even if they tried. It was unprofessional and could get messy. She also didn't want to stain her business like that. She'd work too damn hard to get where she was and she wasn't going to destroy all her effort just to get some satisfaction between the sheets.

And, anyway, a vibrator usually did the trick just as well, if not better. No one knew where her clit was better than her.

She reluctantly admitted that the man sitting at the bar had made her pussy twinge the slightest bit. But only because he looked like a bad boy who could get nasty between the sheets.

However, if he was the one who bought her the drink, he was sniffing up the wrong tree. Reese had no time for bad boys. Not even for a quickie. That type was usually self-absorbed and definitely didn't know where her clit was.

A clearing of a throat had her glancing up from her forkful of salad to realize the server had disappeared and the man Bambi had been hanging all over at the bar had taken her place.

His voice was like warm, smooth bourbon when he stated, "I ordered you a drink, but it looks like she also brought my beer over here by mistake."

Sure she did.

Starting at the top, she took her time inspecting him, not bothering to hide that fact. His dark blond hair reminded her of something a Viking would wear. It was shaved clean on the sides and was long at the top because he had it French braided in the shape of a mohawk. She'd never seen anything like it on a man before, but somehow it fit him.

His searching eyes were dark, most likely brown. He had a thick but well-trimmed dark blond beard. His left nostril was pierced with a small hoop. His right ear the same. Even though he wore a long-sleeved thermal, she could guess he was tatted up since tattoos covered his hands and forearms and disappeared under the sleeves where they were pushed up to his elbows. Both arms and hands, not just one.

His shirt was still slightly see-through where Bambi had enthusiastically "assisted" him with his spill. And because she could see the outline of a barbell through one nipple under that damp cotton, it wasn't hard to make out the shape of another barbell piercing in the other. Especially since both of his nipples were hard nubs pressing against the soft cotton.

He had one side of the thermal tucked in and the other side pulled out, giving her a view of his bulky square belt buckle that consisted of four letters—BFMC—attached to a wide black leather belt. His jeans were clean, but worn, and fit him very, *very* well.

Where he stood, she could see his pretty long legs—the man was maybe six foot or so—and his black leather lace-up boots.

When she was done assessing him, she lifted her gaze, taking a last sweep of his narrow hips, his broad shoulders and chest. "No, Bambi told me you told her to bring it here."

"Then she was confused."

Reese tilted her head as she stared up at him. It was almost impossible to tell but the very corners of his mouth were tipped up. This man thought he was slick.

Problem for him was, she was slicker.

"Bambi's good at her job. She rarely gets an order wrong."

"Must eat here a lot."

"The food is good, the service is good and usually people leave me alone."

"I'm botherin' you."

Not posed as a question, Reese didn't take it as such. She just lifted her eyebrows at him, waiting for him to take the hint and mosey away to someone more interested. Like Bambi.

He didn't.

Ignoring him, she took another bite of her salad and washed it down with a sip of her vodka tonic. When she was done with that, he was still standing there, now with his thick arms crossed over that broad chest of his, bunching up his biceps under the off-white thermal.

If he was trying to impress her, he was failing. A few tattoos, piercings, some muscles and a stubborn attitude did not do it.

"I'm Nick, by the way."

She stabbed at her salad with her fork. "I really don't care."

That answer right there would have most men giving up, maybe even getting pissed because she spurned their advances, and walking away.

Not this one. He actually widened his stance. Maybe to give the big balls he must have some room.

"I'm in town lookin' for a friend."

A friend. Sure. A one-night-stand, more like it.

"Apparently, I didn't make it clear the first time, but... I really don't care. I have work to do, so if you'll excuse me..." She shoved another forkful of lettuce into her mouth.

She refused to look at him, because the longer she did, the better he looked. Things had been stressful lately and her mind kept going in directions it shouldn't.

Like having a quickie with a tattooed, cocky, bad boy.

Her office was only two doors down from the Mill Creek Bar & Grill, but then, if they went there, he would know who she was and where she worked. If she was going to have a fling, she'd rather it be anonymous.

She groaned and downed the rest of her vodka tonic. What was she thinking? Not straight, apparently.

She had work to do and needed to concentrate. She also

needed to think about the vibrator at home in her bedside drawer and not the man who still stood at her table, too stubborn to give up.

She shoveled another forkful of salad into her mouth and went back to typing up the brief she needed for court tomorrow. If she ignored him long enough, he might simply go away.

And take that temptation along with him.

She almost cried in relief when he finally turned.

Damn, he had a nice ass, too.

No, Reese. No. Bad boys equal bad news.

"Hey, don't forget your beer," she called out and pushed the full pint glass to the other side of the table. "And the vodka tonic, too. I don't accept drinks from strangers, and I don't want you wasting your money."

He hesitated and glanced over his shoulder at her, his expression as hard as stone. "Why? 'Cause you don't think I have much?"

"I don't care if you do or don't. Not my business."

Nick nodded and picked up the beer but left the drink where it sat. With a jerk of his chin, he said, "Have a good night."

Unfortunately, it wouldn't be a good night. It would be a long, shitty one since she was behind on her cases. Having to deal with her sister's mess, on top of everything else, had put her at a disadvantage with her workload. While her sister depended on her to fix her mess, so did Reese's clients.

Dealing with clients paid her bills, dealing with Reilly cost her time and money.

She sighed, staring at her now empty glass. Her gaze slid to the full one the man named Nick left behind.

She hated herself a little as she lamented how it would simply go to waste if she left it there. But she also worried that drinking a second drink while she was only eating a salad might get her a bit loopy. She still had a bunch of paperwork to do for her case tomorrow, so she needed to be sharp.

She looked up from the vodka tonic to the man who once again sat at the bar. Watching her.

Her. Not Bambi, who was flitting behind the bar near him, trying to get his attention.

She sighed again and reached for the drink. She lifted the glass in the air toward him as a silent thank you.

With a grin, he lifted his beer and chin toward her in answer.

Then he turned and went back to eating what she could only imagine was a very cold burger and fries.

She went back to working on her brief while she finished her dinner and drink. The next time she looked up, he was gone.

———

STANDING in the shadows right outside the Mill Creek Bar & Grill, he felt like a stalker. He remained out of view of the blonde who exited and headed the opposite direction of where Deacon waited.

He'd been out there for a good half hour.

He knew better than to wait. In truth, he knew he had no shot with her.

But still...

Something about her made his blood hum and his balls tighten.

Why he was leaving behind available pussy to chase unavailable pussy, he didn't know. He must have lost his fucking mind.

Thrill of the chase, maybe.

More like stupidity.

Even in those heels, she had no problem navigating the badly lit sidewalk past the front of the bar, across the opening of a dark alley and onto another sidewalk. Two doors down, she paused, dug in that huge black bag of hers and pulled out what, even in the limited light, he could see was a set of keys. She disappeared out of his view when she went inside whatever business was there.

He waited a few seconds before following the same path and stopping at the corner of the one-story brick building she had entered. The business she had disappeared into had two picture windows with the blinds closed and a solid painted wood door in the center.

He dug his cell phone out of his back pocket, hit the power button and lifted it to read the carved wood sign hanging next to the door.

Law Office of Reese Ackerson, Esquire.

Law office. Esquire.

Her being an attorney wasn't surprising. The way she dressed, her confidence, her no-nonsense attitude fit most attorneys he knew. She seemed slick and smart, too.

"Reese Ackerson," he said under his breath.

Ackerson.

He quickly scrolled through his phone and pulled up a document, searching it until he found what he was looking for. For the reason that last name sounded familiar.

R. Ackerson, LLC.

He frowned. Could it be one and the same? Was this the connection Reilly Porter knew? The person who was hiding her?

To be positive, he would need to follow her from her office to see if she drove back to that house up the mountain.

But he was already pretty fucking sure.

The town wasn't that big and whoever owned that house had scratch. Successful attorney type of scratch.

And the way she looked, acted and dressed screamed successful. It wasn't an act, but the real deal.

Tucking his phone back into his pocket, he tried the door handle. But as expected, it was locked. And from what he could see between a slight gap in the blinds, the front office was dark.

Which meant she went somewhere toward the back. Alone.

Right now she was probably kicking off her heels, pulling the pins from her hair, and removing her jacket. Maybe even unbuttoning the first few buttons on her blouse.

He dropped his head. "Fuck," he muttered. What he thought would be a random stranger, now might not be. She might be connected to the victim of the fugitive he was looking for.

That could be good. Or bad. Apparently, he hadn't made the best impression. Or any impression at all.

She had been immune to his charms. *Hell*, he hadn't even had a chance to fully turn on his charms. She had shut him down and out immediately.

But having a common goal—which was helping Reilly Porter stay safe by catching Warren—could get his boot in her door.

Door. Sure.

But for now, she was locked inside her office and he was locked outside. He needed to figure out a way to approach her if she really was the one living up on that mountain. Even if she wasn't, it seemed she would know who was, unless there was another R. Ackerson in the area.

He needed to decide his next step. Wait for her until she comes back out and try talking to her? Or go get his truck and follow her home to make sure the house on the mountain belonged to her?

The way she responded to him inside the bar made that an easy decision.

Keep his distance until he no longer could.

REESE GLANCED in the rearview mirror. It was after eleven and the mountain road she lived off of normally didn't get a lot of traffic, even during daylight hours. To have someone following her, not only in town, but out of it, wasn't a normal occurrence.

And right now, anything out of the ordinary in her life shouldn't be taken lightly.

Once the victim advocate had contacted Reilly about her abusive ex-boyfriend skipping bail and disappearing, Reese's life became a whirlwind. While she went and "saved" her sister—*again*—she had her administrative assistant cancel all her appointments and delay all her court appearances since Reilly's well-being became priority number one.

She rushed down to Philly and picked up her sister from a friend's house, where she'd been hiding out.

She told Reilly to only bring a couple of bags because they didn't have time to pack up her whole apartment and get her moved. Instead, Reese paid a moving company to box what little Reilly had and put it in a storage unit, rented under her corporation's name.

Reese tried to think of every connection that would link her and Reilly as sisters. Having different last names helped. But still, she had hoped she hadn't missed anything so that abusive asshole could find her younger sister and finish the job he had started. Which was her being almost beaten to death.

But now, being followed late at night made the tiny hairs on the back of Reese's neck stand. The last thing she wanted to do was draw Billy Warren right to where she lived. Which was Reese's home and Reilly's current safe haven.

Instead of pulling into her driveway and opening the

electric gate, she drove right past her own property with her heart thumping in her throat.

All she could see of the vehicle, which stayed about a quarter mile behind her, were headlights. That left her with no description to even give police.

In reality, she could simply be feeling a little paranoid.

More like a lot.

However, Billy Warren was not just an asshole, but one of epic proportions. He used his bad boy charms to suck women in and then took advantage of them by stealing their money before abusing them.

That made her think of the man she met earlier. Nick could be cut from similar cloth and Reese wasn't interested in finding out. It had been best just to ignore him earlier.

Both she and Reilly really needed to swear off men for a while. Apparently, they both sucked at picking good ones.

She pressed her foot harder on the accelerator, giving the BMW X6 a boost of speed. Unless she did a U-turn, there really wasn't much in the area where she was headed, except for state game land. No lights. No help. Nowhere to lose a tail. And worse, spotty cell phone coverage.

Civilization was behind her and the dark, uninhabited woods in front of her. Again, a reason why she was suspicious of someone driving behind her.

She had loved living out in the middle of nowhere... until now.

Damn it.

She reached into her leather tote bag and dug for her phone. Once she located it, she tried unlocking it using her fingerprint, but it dropped from her shaky fingers.

"Shit!"

She couldn't risk pulling over to find it. Instead, keeping one eye on the road, she leaned over and felt around the floorboards as far as she could reach. Hopefully it didn't fall between the seat and the center console. Every time it did that, it took forever to fish it back out. And that would be impossible to do while she drove.

A flash of movement on the road caught her eye and she jerked up in her seat in time to see a deer bounding across the narrow roadway. She slammed on the brakes, her seatbelt locking, and jerked the wheel, attempting to miss the animal.

Her vehicle skidded just enough to catch the loose stones on the edge of the road, ripping the steering wheel from her grip. Closing her eyes, she braced as the front end of her BMW kissed a tree. Luckily, not hard enough to set off the airbags, but enough to stop the vehicle's forward motion.

And her escape.

"Shit!" She slammed her hand on the steering wheel in frustration, unlatched her seatbelt and began to frantically search for her cell phone. Headlights lit up the interior of her X6, but not enough to make it easier to find her phone.

Scrambling, her fingertips touched something familiar near her foot and she grabbed her phone. Unlocking it quickly, she lost her breath when she realized what she feared was true. She had zero bars of cell phone coverage.

"Damn it!" Tossing the useless phone onto the passenger seat, she yanked her tote bag from the passenger side floorboard, where it had fallen in the minor fender bender, and once again dug inside it, searching for the next best thing besides her phone.

A sense of calm came over her as soon as her fingers wrapped around it.

Trying to keep her wits about her, she went to put the vehicle in reverse to see if she could get it free from the slight ditch and tree. But before she could, the vehicle which had been following her parked right behind her. Its front end tight to her back bumper.

Effectively trapping her.

She couldn't go forward or reverse.

She was stuck.

She was at the mercy of whoever was rushing up to her vehicle. With the mystery vehicle's headlights blinding her, she couldn't see who it was since it was only a dark figure on the move.

If she couldn't flee, she needed to fight.

She inhaled a deep breath, slowly released it and tried to slow both her racing heart and mind. She'd taken self-defense classes in college a long time ago and tried to remember some defensive moves.

Moves she should've taught Reilly.

Dig fingers into his eye sockets, stomp on his foot, knee him in the balls, jam his nose into his brain with the heel of her palm. Scratch, bite, kick. Do whatever was needed to escape.

Since her vehicle was pinned in, locking the doors was useless. She needed to immobilize her attacker and then, if needed, escape in his vehicle.

She could do this.

She should've bought a gun after what happened to Reilly. She'd have no qualms shooting that motherfucker dead since he deserved it.

Better yet, she could say shooting his ass was in self-defense. Then Reilly's nightmare would be over, and her sister could live her life without fear—

The man grabbed her driver's door and Reese prepared herself as it opened.

"You o—"

Shoving her arm out and pressing the button at the same time, she made contact.

"*Fuuuu*—"

The man immediately dropped to his knees, but the contact was broken between him and the stun gun, which meant he'd be back on his feet again sooner than she could flee.

"Get back!" she screamed at the collapsed man. "Or I'll tag you again." She pressed the button on the stun gun and heard the sharp crackle and saw the spark arc between the tips. The noise alone should scare someone off. But somehow, she needed to get to his vehicle without him taking her down first.

"Fuck," came out in a groan from the heap on the ground. "Fuck! What the fuck, woman?"

Reese blinked. The voice sounded familiar.

Sort of.

She reached behind her and grabbed her cell phone, hitting the power button to illuminate the human heap, who was clutching his chest.

"Fuck! You shocked me right in the fuckin' nipple and lit up my barbell."

What the hell was he doing following her?

"Who are you?" she screamed. "Why are you following me?"

"I'm..." He groaned, rubbing his chest. *Fuckin' shit!...* Nick."

"Did Billy Warren send you?" She hit the button on the stun gun again making the electrically-charged sound which could make most assholes pucker.

He lifted a hand in the air. "Don't fuckin' hit me with that again. Jesus. I think you fried my nipple off."

"Answer me!"

He grabbed onto her open door and began to pull himself up.

She pressed the button again on the stun gun and jabbed it in his direction.

He let the door go and stumbled back, falling on his ass. "Christ, woman!"

"I'm calling the police."

"The fuck you are. There's no fuckin' coverage out

here." He kept rubbing at this chest. "Goddamn it. I might be maimed for life."

"Answer my question. Did Billy Warren send you?"

He got onto his knees and pushed himself to his feet, this time at a safe distance from her car. "No. Put that damn thing down."

"Fuck you. You don't tell me what to do. I want to know why you're following me. Start talking or I'm going to shove this against your balls and make some fried oysters."

His hand automatically covered his crotch and he took another step backwards, almost tripping again. He caught himself and lifted a palm out. "Christ, give me a sec to unscramble my brain." He blew out a breath, ran both hands down his face and then stared at her. "Was comin' to make sure you were all right since you hit a goddamn tree."

"I hit the tree because of you!" she shouted.

"You hit the fuckin' tree 'cause you swerved to avoid that damn deer!" he shouted back.

"I wouldn't have had to avoid the damn deer if you weren't following me."

He shook his head. "For fuck's sake," he muttered. "Put that thing down and I'll explain."

"No. I have no idea who you are and why you're here. This is staying in my hand while you explain. Start explaining and quickly."

Chapter Four

DEACON MIGHT HAVE to blow his whole load right there on the side of the road. In the dark. In the woods. He would need to reveal why he was in town and who he was. He wasn't thrilled about doing it. But if the woman who just shocked the shit out of him was R. Ackerson, then, if anyone should know the truth, it would be her.

He winced. His nipple still felt as if it was on fire.

"You live back there?" He tilted his head in the direction from where they came. He figured he'd been made when she blew right past her own driveway.

"First of all, why would I ever tell you where I live? And secondly, you're supposed to be explaining, not asking me questions."

"I need the answer to my question first."

"So you can use that information against me?"

"Yeah, just like a fuckin' lawyer does," he muttered.

Her mouth dropped open, then it snapped shut. "How do you know who I am?"

"Just puttin' the pieces together."

"What pieces?" she asked, her eyes narrowed on him. He couldn't see the color since the only light came from the interior of her fancy BMW *whatever-the-fuck-it-was.* But he had noticed they were green when he talked to her back at the bar.

He had plenty of time to check her out while she checked him out. In those few minutes when he stood by her table, she had assessed him thoroughly and also made a judgement about him because of his looks.

He couldn't admit he followed her back to her office because that might shut her down before she even opened up. He had to choose his words carefully.

And stay clear of that fucking stun gun.

"If you live in that house up on that mountain, then I'm looking for the woman staying there. Reilly Porter."

Her grip tightened on the stun gun which she still held out in front of her, probably in case he lunged at her.

He would love to lunge at her, grab that fucking thing and whip it out into the woods.

"I have no idea who that is," she lied.

If he didn't know better, he might believe her. But she was a lawyer and lawyers could lie their asses off and sound believable.

But then, so could he.

"She's hidin' out on a property owned by R. Ackerson, LLC. A company owned by you."

She stared at him, her face a blank mask. She was checking to see how confident he was on his information.

He couldn't be one hundred percent sure Reese Ackerson was R. Ackerson, but his gut instinct told him she was. It wasn't a common last name, and there was no other reason to be traveling that dark, desolate mountain road late at night unless she lived on it.

"How do you know my name?"

"Bambi called it out when you walked into the bar."

"No, my last name."

Blood & Bones: Deacon

"I asked Bambi." If she was going to lie, so was he. Singed tit for tat.

"Before or after you approached my table?"

Fuck. "Does it matter?"

"Did you know who I was before you approached my table?" she asked in a commanding voice. Probably the same one she used in the courtroom. The "tell me the truth or else" tone. It was actually kind of hot.

But for that question, he had no reason not to tell her the truth. "No."

She thought he approached her for a reason other than he had. The plain truth was he thought she was hot and was hoping to get her naked. At the time, that was all it was. Purely sexual interest, not a damn thing more. He had no idea she had any connection to Warren.

"Why are you looking for Reilly Porter?"

"Ain't actually lookin' for her. Lookin' for the man who might be lookin' for her."

She tried to hide the worry in her face, but failed. Her lip curled into a sneer when she spat out, "Billy Warren."

"Yeah." Too bad all women didn't have that reaction to Warren. If they did, they'd save themselves a world of hurt.

"Why?"

If she knew Reilly, then she knew why. "He's on the run."

"I know."

"Was asked to find him if he shows up here in Mansfield."

"Why?"

"'Cause I got a business not too far from here findin' assholes like Warren."

"What kind of business?"

Was he being cross-examined on the witness stand? "I'm a bail bondsman."

"So, you bailed that asshole out of jail?"

"No, I'm also a skip tracer and licensed bounty hunter. Bianchi Bail Bonds in Philly bailed him out. Now they're lookin' for him and contacted me."

"Why do they think Billy will come up here?"

He leaned closer, but kept out of arm's length. "You know why."

Her lips flattened out. She dropped the hand holding her stun gun into her lap and closed her eyes. "Fuck."

"Bianchi thinks because of Warren's history, he's gonna come up here, look for Porter and finish what he started so she can't testify against him."

Her eyes popped open. "You just confirmed my fear. But I was hoping no one could find her up here."

"Well, you were fuckin' wrong. Bianchi figured it out, so expect Warren to be able to also."

"Shit." She chewed on her bottom lip.

"Is she a client?"

Her brow furrowed. "No."

"Who is she to you?"

She grimaced. "My sister."

"Is she alone up there in that house?" If so, that would not be good.

The women had different last names, one of them could be married or divorced. There could be other adults up there with Porter. Or worse, kids who could be at risk.

She dropped her head and rubbed at her forehead, her long hair hiding her face from him. She had taken it down after she went into her office. She had also shed her jacket and opened a couple top buttons on her blouse.

She had done exactly what he had fantasized about. But, unfortunately, he was dealing with reality right now, not his imagination.

"How do I know you are who you say you are? How do I know you're not here on behalf of Billy to use me to get to my sister? I want proof of who you are. Some sort of ID."

If he showed her that, she'd find out he'd lied about his name. *Shit.*

"I can show you my badge." He rarely carried it but he had it with him in his truck.

"That won't tell me shit. You could buy one on eBay."

That was true. His badge didn't have any identifying info on it. It only stated he was a Fugitive Recovery Agent, unlike some law enforcements' which included a badge number to identify the pig wearing it.

It would be hard to pull anything over on the woman sitting before him. She wasn't stupid. She had knowledge of the law. She was also aware of the dire situation she and her sister were now in.

She would be very cautious.

As she should be.

He sighed. He needed her to trust him, to get access to her property, so he could set up there to keep an eye out for Warren. If the man knew enough to come to Mansfield, he'd have the exact address of where Reilly was located.

"Gonna be completely honest with you if you're completely honest with me." When she didn't respond, he prodded, "We got a deal?"

"So, you've been lying."

Christ. "No, wasn't lyin' when I said I'm here to capture Warren, if he shows up, and deliver him to Bianchi. I am a licensed bail bondsman and bounty hunter. We can help each other."

"How?"

"Give me access to your home and I'll help keep your sister safe."

Her gaze raked over him. "How are you going to keep her safe?"

He did the same to her. "How are *you* gonna keep her safe?"

Her jaw shifted. "I'll move her somewhere else until the trial."

"Won't be a trial without a defendant. You should know that. So, I gotta catch that motherfucker first."

Her head lifted and she stared straight at him. Even in the limited light he could see her eyes were hard and determined. "Then, we'll just have to draw his ass out."

Then, we'll just have to draw his ass out.

He wanted to smile at that but didn't. Instead, he said, "Gonna check the front of your Beamer and see if it's drivable. In the meantime, put that fuckin' stun gun away. Then I'm gonna follow you home."

"You still haven't proven to me who you are."

"For fuck's sake," he muttered, digging out his wallet. He found a business card and handed it to her. She used the light from her phone to read it. "Anyone can get business cards printed. I want to see an actual ID."

He pulled out his driver's license and held it out to her, but when she reached for it, he tightened his hold. She tugged at it and he finally let go. He went to the front of her vehicle, using the light of his cell phone to inspect the damage.

Luckily, it appeared drivable. It would need some minor bodywork, definitely a new front grill. Maybe even a bumper and new radiator. But for now, she could limp it home.

"Your name isn't Nick," she called out.

He flashed the light under the front, searching for any antifreeze leaks. It seemed dry.

Yeah, she could at least drive it home. He'd follow her, get her secured in her house with her sister and then they could have a real discussion instead of one alongside a dark road.

He walked back to where she sat and finally answered her. "It is and it isn't."

She rolled her eyes. "Which is it?"

"If you gotta know—"

"I do."

"It's my middle name. I use it when I'm out huntin'."

"Hunting fugitives."

"Yeah."

"When you're not out *hunting*, do you go by Deacon?"

"Deacon, Deke, dick. Depends how pissed the woman is who's sayin' my name."

"If a woman is calling you a dick, then she must have a good reason."

"Won't argue that."

She held out his license between her index and middle fingers. They were long and slender. Her long fingernails were painted, but unlike Bambi's, Reese's weren't as brightly colored and didn't have such sharp, pointy tips. They looked more conservative.

Like how she dressed. Professional. Put together. Classy.

Not Deacon's normal target when it came to one-night-stands.

Though, the few women he'd known similar to Reese were more conservative during the day and went buck wild at night when they could let loose and put their hair down, just like Reese had done.

He'd also met a few who were frigid bitches. Nothing warmed them up or made them happy. They just needed to spread their misery to others.

He wondered which one Reese was.

He slid his license back into his wallet. "Trust me now?"

"Oh, yes. A hundred percent now that you showed me a driver's license which could also be fake. Sure, come on back to my house and hang with me and my sister."

Deacon considered her for a moment, then shrugged and shoved his wallet back into the rear pocket of his jeans. "Fine. On your own then. Tell your sister good luck."

He gave her a two-finger salute and spun on his boot heel to head back to his truck.

Fuck this. He'd head back to his motel, get a good night's sleep, call Bianchi in the morning and tell him to find someone else to capture Warren. Deacon got into his truck and started it.

Her driver's door still hung open. So, he waited a minute, just in case she changed her mind on being difficult and actually wanted his help.

No skin off his nose if she didn't. His wallet just wouldn't be as fat.

When her BMW's door slammed shut and her reverse lights lit up, he put his own truck in reverse and backed up enough to be able to pull around her.

And that was what he did. With no reason to stay, he continued down the road in the opposite direction of town, hoping to come across a pull-off where he could swing a U-turn easier in his truck than the narrow area where they'd been sitting.

That wasn't the only reason, but that was what he told himself.

With a quick glance in his rearview, he made sure she got her cage out of the ditch and back on the road. The last thing he saw was her taillights as he drove around a bend.

"Good fuckin' luck," he muttered into the dark interior of his Ford. "You're gonna need it."

He found a pull-off not a quarter mile later and swung his truck around, not rushing to return to town. Nobody was waiting for him in his room and it was too late to find someone to keep him company.

He could call Bambi, but she hadn't been thrilled about him blowing her off for Reese. And he wasn't in the mood to sway her otherwise. He wasn't in the mood to grovel for a little pussy.

His fist would be simpler and cause zero complications.

His fist also wasn't stubborn. Unlike blonde lawyers.

He took his time driving back through the game lands to avoid wildlife darting across the road, but it wasn't a four-legged Bambi which had him slamming on the brakes.

No, it fucking wasn't.

It was a white BMW stopped alongside the road. There must have been more damage than he originally thought.

Shit.

There wasn't a lot of room where she had pulled off since the road had no shoulder. The only good thing was the road wasn't highly traveled so it should be pretty safe to leave it where it was until a wrecker could come and get it.

However, now she had no choice but to accept his help. They were still a couple miles from the bottom of her driveway, and she wasn't hoofing it that far, then climbing that mountain in her heels.

Though, he could see her trying simply to spite him.

He stopped his pickup next to her cage and powered down the passenger side window. The interior of her vehicle was dark, but he could see a figure sitting in the driver's seat, her forehead pressed to her steering wheel as she gripped it with both hands.

"Yo!" he yelled out.

She slowly lifted her head and turned to face him. If she refused to roll down her window and talk to him, he was driving away.

It would serve her right.

If she wanted to be goddamn difficult, so could he. Again, he wasn't going to grovel for pussy, and he wasn't going to do the same to help this woman.

But she was smart. She knew she needed help, she just didn't want to accept it from him.

He grinned but quickly smoothed it back out when she finally rolled down the window.

"Wanna lift?"

"Calling a tow truck."

"You got coverage?" She didn't have coverage. He didn't even have to look at his own phone to know that they still had zero bars.

It took her a few seconds to admit, "No."

"Get in. I'll take you home and you can call once we get there."

"I don't know you."

He jerked his chin up at her. "Deacon Edwards, owner of Justice Bail Bonds out of Manning Grove." He left off the "badass bounty hunter" bit because he didn't think she'd appreciate that right about now.

"I read all that. That's not what I meant."

He twisted his head and looked around, making a point. "Anyone else out here gonna help you? Or are you gonna hoof it the two miles back to your house, not countin' that long-ass driveway, in those neck-breakin' shoes of yours?"

"You noticed my shoes?"

"Hard not to." Made her legs look as long as her damn driveway.

"I'm not sure if I want to leave my vehicle here."

"Do you have a choice?"

She didn't answer.

"Got good insurance on it?"

Of course she did.

"Get in," he said more firmly. "Last time I'm askin' before I drive the fuck away and leave you sittin' here in a broken-down vehicle in the dark on a desolate road with no cell phone coverage."

"That wasn't a question, that was a demand."

"Yeah, a demand to get your head outta your ass. Here's a question for you: Want my help or not? You got thirty seconds to decide."

She powered her window back up and he started to count off those thirty seconds in his head.

A few seconds later, the BMW door opened, and she climbed out. Standing next to her vehicle, she leaned back in and gathered her belongings.

Deacon pursed his lips and studied her ass as she did so. Even in the limited light, those suit pants not only made her legs look long, but they also made her ass look edible. He wanted a bite of that perfect peach.

He wondered if she did squats or some such shit.

He quickly averted his eyes as she turned with her arms full. He didn't want to be tagged again with that stun gun, which he was sure she was not leaving behind.

Reaching over, he opened the truck's door for her. "Got everything important, just in case you come back here and find that Beamer on blocks and stripped bare?"

Her eyes widened and she took a quick look back at her vehicle.

"Heard the bears around here are thugs. Probably make some good scratch sellin' off those rims."

She threw her stuff on the passenger side floor and climbed in. He held his breath hoping she didn't break an ankle climbing on the Ford's side rail with those heels.

Maybe he should've gotten out and helped her.

Fuck that. She probably just would've kneed him in the balls and screamed that she could do it herself because she was an independent woman and didn't need a fucking man.

Heh.

He already had a fried nipple, he'd like to keep his nuts where they belonged.

However, he did take the time to enjoy watching her pull herself into his truck and settle into the seat with a few soft grunts.

"You good?" He tried to keep the amusement out of his voice. He somewhat succeeded.

She stared straight ahead through the windshield. "Yes."

"Seatbelt."

She twisted her head towards him. "Can you put your seatbelt on, please?"

He grinned. "Got mine on. Waitin' on you."

"No, that's how you ask. You don't just throw out demands and expect it not to irritate people."

"Got it." He waited a second and then said, "Seatbelt."

He pressed his lips together as she growled a little and pulled the seatbelt down and across her tits, securing it in the latch.

When she was done, she asked, "Happy?"

"Not really, but it's a start." Fighting a grin, he put the Ford in drive and took her home.

———

REESE SET her stuff down on the kitchen counter. "My sister's probably sleeping. Let's try not to wake her, please."

"I'm not the only one who makes demands. Just addin' a please on the end, don't change it."

"It was a request, not a demand."

Deacon shook his head. "Lawyers. Always gotta deflect."

She watched the man wander from her kitchen and across her high-ceilinged great room. Her house was a contemporary A-frame and she bought it because of the enormous windows that faced the valley beyond. On a clear day, the view was amazing and endless.

From floor to ceiling, the room and its windows were two stories high, and the main floor, where they stood, had an open floor plan. The master suite was also on the same level with the same amazing view. She had three spare bedrooms on the upper level and another large open space took up the lower one. She had set up the lower level as a more casual space. A bar, large-screen TV with surround sound, a large sectional, a fireplace, a reading nook and more.

346

Unfortunately, she didn't have a lot of spare time to enjoy it. Most of the time, when she had a few moments, she took a glass of wine or a mug of strong coffee out on the front deck, kicked up her feet, and just listened to the rustling of the trees, or the many creatures scurrying through the underbrush and fallen leaves.

If she sat out there long enough, she sometimes heard coyotes or foxes, hawks, occasionally an eagle or two, and some other animals she couldn't identify. It was a good way to wind down at the end of a hectic day or to motivate herself for the busy one to come.

This house was supposed to be her sanctuary.

She mistakenly thought Reilly would be safe here, too. But now her sister's safe haven could be compromised.

Unfortunately, the only way her sister would be safe again was to make sure Billy Warren's ass was caught, he went to trial, was found guilty and then tossed into prison.

At least for a little while. Long enough, hopefully, that he'd forget Reilly when he got out. Reese knew that was wishful thinking. Men like Billy didn't stop until he got what he wanted. Which was her sister to pay for fighting back and getting him arrested.

When Reilly first called her three months ago while she was in the hospital, Reese had immediately gone down to Philadelphia to be with her. Her twenty-four-year-old sister had been a mess and Reese had a difficult time seeing the bruises, the cuts, the swollen lips and eyes. The cast on her arm.

Luckily, a neighbor in her complex had heard the racket and called the police. Other neighbors came out of their apartments and somehow pulled Billy off Reilly and held him there until the police arrived to arrest him and the ambulance arrived to transport her. She was grateful they got involved—which a lot of people didn't do anymore—and most likely saved Reilly's life.

When Reilly was released from the hospital, Reese tried to get her sister to come stay with her. But her sister was headstrong. And, of course, stubborn.

Because of that, Reilly didn't just lie down and take Billy's beating, which he thought she deserved. And that made it worse for her. She could've died, but then, if it was her in Reilly's shoes, Reese would've never given up fighting, either.

A woman fighting back, and not curling up in a ball, always made an abuser more determined to beat her down.

Reilly had worked hard for the money he stole and she didn't have a lot, so it had pissed her off when she found out Billy had somehow accessed her accounts and drained her dry.

After seeing Reilly in the condition she'd been in, Reese really wanted a few minutes alone with Billy Warren herself. Since then, she actually had dreams of coming face to face with him and hurting him as badly as he hurt Reilly. She would wake up in a sweat, every muscle tense and breathing heavily.

The man needed to pay for what he did.

But Billy wasn't in her house right now, another man was. Reese studied him standing at her windows and looking out into the dark night.

"Jesus fuck," he muttered.

"What? Did you press your nose to the glass and leave a smudge?"

"Bet this view's fuckin' awesome."

"It was the selling point," she murmured.

"House probably cost a fuckton of scratch."

She was not talking about her finances with a complete stranger. Or anyone, really. How much she made and what she did with that money was nobody's business.

She ran her gaze over him, like she had at the bar, and

once she was done, she turned her eyes to his reflection in the window.

He was watching her. She didn't care that he knew she was checking him out, just like she hadn't cared at Mill Creek Bar & Grill.

Men did it to women all the time and didn't think twice about how it made a woman feel. Turnabout was fair play.

"We got the same goal," he said, turning and planting his hands on his hips. "We both want that motherfucker caught."

Yes, she wanted that motherfucker caught. Though, she'd prefer dead. Unfortunately, Deacon probably needed him alive to collect his fee.

She slipped off her heels and moved barefoot across her plush carpet toward where he stood, his long legs planted apart. "We have the same goals."

"Just need to trust me."

Just that easy. "I don't know you, *Nick.*"

"Don't know you, either," he countered.

"You're not the one with the sister at risk," she reminded him.

He tipped his head. She found it fascinating that a man not only knew how to French braid hair, but could do his own. She could barely do her sister's when they were growing up.

"True. Wanna protect your blood. I get that."

She stopped only a few feet in front of him. "Do you have family?"

"Yeah."

She hated to admit it, but she found him fascinating. What he did for a living. How he looked. Even how he talked. His English was sloppy, but he didn't appear to be unintelligent.

Though, she really didn't know him. If she had to guess, he just didn't give a damn about what people thought of him. Even so, he probably had no problems convincing a woman to spend a night with him.

She also figured it would be one night only. He probably didn't get rejected often. And when he did, he most likely had no problem moving on to someone else.

"You'd do whatever you have to do to protect them, right?"

"Goes without sayin'."

Even if he was a player and not serious about women, her gut was telling her he was serious about his job. That alone could be to her and Reilly's benefit. "Let's catch the bastard."

Nick aka Deacon Edwards, owner of Justice Bail Bonds out of Manning Grove, smiled.

It was a hell of a smile, too. One that made her bare toes curl into her plush carpet and her nipples pebble just the slightest bit.

"What's the plan?" she asked. Since he had come to Mansfield, he had to have one already, right?

"Know this is gonna be hard for you, but you're gonna have to listen to what I say."

Yes, that was going to be difficult. "I'll do my best."

He shook his head. "No. Not your best. To keep you and your sister safe you need to fuckin' listen."

"I might have some opinions."

"No shit. Sure you're gonna have lots of fuckin' opinions. Try keepin' them to yourself."

"No promises."

He cocked a brow at her. "Want your sister safe?"

"Yes." She shouldn't have to answer that, but he was making a point, so she let him.

"Want that fucker caught?"

"Dead, actually, but caught would be my second choice."

"Then you need to listen."

"Sorry, but I can't just listen to a man and not have a say in things. If I have something to contribute, I'm not keeping it to myself. Now, let's hear this plan of yours."

He scraped a hand down his beard and her eyes followed it. She wasn't much into facial hair but his fit him. The piercings not so much. Most bad boy personas didn't have their nipples and nose pierced. She found that curious, but not enough to ask him why he had them done.

He might mistakenly think she was interested.

Right now, she needed to hear a solid plan. Her sister's safety was much more important than Reese's likes and dislikes when it came to men. So, she waited.

"Need to get your sister outta here. Somewhere safe. Somewhere not linked with you or any of your family."

"It's just us. Some distant cousins live in Florida."

"I probably got a place she can go. Where he'd never find her."

"Where?"

He shook his head. "Gotta work out those details first. Once she's there, I can set up here."

"In my house."

"Well, I can't sit outside your fuckin' house unless I sit in a goddamn tree stand. And I'm not some special ops guy on a covert mission, I'm just a fuckin' bounty hunter. I see my target, nab my target and deliver the asshole. Then collect my payment. You won't see me out in the woods with camo and war toys. You want that, you pay for it yourself."

He was kind of cute when he was annoyed. "Okay. We get my sister out and you in. What else?"

"You go, too."

"What?" She was not leaving a stranger alone in her house. "I'm not leaving. If I did, I couldn't go far, anyway. I have my practice—"

"Said you needed to listen."

Oh, yes, that was right, that was what he said. "And I

said I'd have opinions. One of them is this: I'm not leaving my home to go into hiding. I have cases I put off already that I need to deal with. Clients to meet with. I'm already behind enough due to all the nonsense this asshole caused."

"You go, too."

She pinned her eyebrows together. Did he not hear her? "No, if I go, and no one is coming and going from this house, that will look suspicious. I need to continue with my regular routine. And, anyway, if he was going to break into the house to get to Reilly, he'd wait until I left for the day, right?"

He didn't say anything. Because he knew she was right. Maybe that bothered him and, honestly, she just didn't care if it did.

"When I leave for the day, you can come in and sit on the house."

"No, I'm not comin' and goin'. If he ends up watchin' the house he'll see me and not approach. Once I'm settled in, I'm stayin' put and keepin' watch."

Shit. The man wanted to be in her house twenty-four seven. Even when she was home. She'd have no privacy at all. She didn't like that. Not one bit. But she also wanted Warren caught.

A little suffering on her part could be worth the satisfaction of catching that bastard in the end. "How long do you think this will take?"

"Have no fuckin' clue."

"Could it be months?"

"Hope to fuck not. He skipped less than a week ago. Thinkin' he went underground to regroup. Probably already figured out she gave up her job and apartment. Probably assumed she ran to family to hide. Also, since he was bonin' her, they most likely talked besides just fuckin' and he knew about you. At least knew your first name. Maybe even had an idea of where you lived."

Reilly did say in the beginning, her and Billy talked a lot. About her life mostly, not his. Always asking questions, trying to get in good with her. He drew her in by appearing to care about her life.

Not talking about himself, or his past, should've been a sign.

Reese sneered at the thought Reilly had been so gullible, causing Deacon to frown. "What's with your face?"

"The more I think about that asshole, the more I realize prison isn't good enough," she admitted.

"Probably won't get a lot of time inside, anyhow. Skippin' will add some time, but not enough."

"You didn't see my sister in that hospital."

"Saw the pics. Saw it was brutal. She didn't take him stealin' from her lyin' down. Don't know her yet, but if she's anything like you, she's got balls."

"You don't need balls to be strong."

Why did people, especially men, use the term "pussy" for someone weak and say someone strong "had balls?" Most women she knew were not weak and she assumed they all had vaginas. Like her.

Men who thought women were the "weaker sex" needed a lesson on how wrong they were.

Billy Warren had balls and he was just a weak little man who stole from women and then beat them up. Reese would love to remove those balls and hang them from the rearview mirror of her BMW. Or, *hell*, put them on a string and make clackers out of them.

She closed her eyes and blew out a breath. Getting pissed off right now wouldn't help. She needed to keep calm and collected and work out a plan with the man standing before her.

They had a common goal, she reminded herself. She needed to concentrate on that.

"I agree with moving my sister. If you have a place for

her to go that's safe, I'll pay for her room and expenses. But I'm going to continue to stay here and work in my practice. Then, whatever we need to do to draw that bastard out, we'll do it. You capture him and deliver him to wherever you need to deliver him to, and I'll try not to kill him first. But no promises."

"Gonna keep your deadly tendencies in mind. Just so you know, him turnin' up dead will cause a whole new issue. For you and your sister. He deserves to be in prison, not you. Remember that."

"And my sister did not deserve what he did."

"Not sayin' the fucker's gonna be delivered without a scratch."

Deacon grinned.

Reese grinned.

That admission warmed her up to his plan a little more.

"Now... Need a place to hide my truck. Need a place to lay down my head. Tomorrow mornin', gonna meet your sister. Also gonna make some calls about where she can go. And you call a tow truck."

He didn't need to tell her to call a tow truck. She bit back the response she wanted to give him and instead said, "I'll need to get a rental until my car is fixed."

"How 'bout you take my truck to and from your office? This way I don't gotta hide it and if I need to go somewhere in it, he might think it's you drivin'. Windows are tinted dark enough he won't know who's behind the wheel. It's no Beamer, but I'm sure you can suffer through usin' it 'til your cage is repaired."

Her what? "Cage?"

"Car," he corrected. "What time do you leave for the office?"

"I'm usually out of here by seven." Depended on how well she slept. If she was tossing and turning, she ended up getting up and going in early. Staring at her bedroom ceiling was not productive.

"Fuck," he groaned. "Okay, gonna head back to the motel and stay there for the night. At the ass crack of dawn, gonna grab my shit, check out and head over here. Need the code for your gate."

"And my alarm system."

"Yeah, and your alarm system. Gonna check that out tomorrow, too."

"You know something about alarm systems?" Was he a jack of all trades? Bounty hunter, bail bondsman, security guard, lady's man, and alarm system specialist? Maybe he could fix the leaky faucet in the downstairs bathroom, too, while he was squatting in her house.

"Nope. But you're gonna show me how yours works. It'll either help me or hinder me, we'll see. Wanna set a trap for the motherfucker but need to give that some thought. In the meantime, I'll settle in, just in case he shows up. Sooner I catch him, the sooner I'm outta your hair and the sooner your sister will be able to return home."

"In one piece."

"Yeah, in one piece." He grinned. "Figured that would be the most important part."

He moved past her, his arm close to brushing against hers. The room was plenty big enough, he could have easily given himself some space, but chose not to.

She assumed the interest he had for her back at the bar still remained. If he hadn't known her last name when he bought her a drink, he hadn't been making contact with her to find Warren. That meant he intended to pick her up, instead. Or try to, anyway.

He paused just past her, facing the opposite direction.

Reese held her breath, waiting for him to say whatever he was about to say.

But he said nothing.

A few seconds later he continued on toward the side door, where they had entered the house, the one that led to a stairway down to her driveway and his truck.

She remained facing the windows and as soon as she heard his hand turning the knob, she called out, "Deacon."

Without looking, she knew he hesitated when the door remained closed.

"Thanks."

"Thank me once that fucker's caught. Set your alarm system and get some sleep. And, Reese..."

"Yes?"

"You can call me Deke."

Deke. "You prefer that over dick?"

She smiled as she heard him open the door. Then it closed behind him, a low chuckle left in his wake.

Billy Warren might not be the only man in this plan who could end up being dangerous. But not for the same reason.

Chapter Five

DEACON SAT out on the deck with his feet kicked up on another nearby chair, balancing his steaming mug of black coffee on his denim-clad thigh. He could imagine having his coffee out here every morning. Or toking on a blunt while he contemplated life.

Now he was contemplating a stranger's life. At a quarter to fucking seven in the morning.

"Once the fog lifts, you can fully appreciate the view."

Deacon was already appreciating the view.

Just not of the valley. Of the blonde who stood at the deck railing, a travel coffee mug in her hand. She was once again professionally dressed, this time in another dark pantsuit, wearing another pair of crazy-assed high heels. Blood red, which were sexy as fuck.

Her makeup wasn't heavy. She had the skill to make it look natural for the most part. If it wasn't for the lipstick and mascara, he'd be wondering if she wore any at all.

The green blouse she wore this morning matched her eyes. However, even with makeup on, he could see the shadow of half-moons under them.

She'd gotten shit sleep.

He could understand that with the situation she and her sister were in. "She know I'm here?"

"Yes. She's in the shower now."

"She needs to pack. Soon as I make arrangements, want her moved."

Reese nodded and turned to look out over the deck, giving Deacon another great view. This time of her ass.

Her hair hung loose around her shoulders and he was drawn to the movement when she fisted a thick handful and held it to the top of her head, blowing out a loud, most likely frustrated, breath.

She was a woman who liked to be in control of her life and Billy Warren was fucking that up for her.

A few seconds later, she dropped her hair and turned to face him. "Where's she going? I want all the details."

Of course she did. He didn't expect anything less. "I'll give 'em once I got 'em."

She didn't like that answer but it was the only one she'd get right now. He didn't want to give her the exact details and probably wouldn't, just in case Warren got to her. If Reese didn't know them, she couldn't spill them, even if she was threatened.

He'd tell her that later. Once Reilly was settled somewhere safe. Then he could deal with Reese's wrath of not knowing where her sister was and avoid having her pull the plug on the plan before it even began.

Because he was pretty damn sure that was what she'd do.

She held out her hand and he stared at it for a moment before taking his time to raise his gaze. That blouse emphasized the dip of her waist and the curves of her tits, and revealed just a hint of cleavage. A delicate gold chain with a small green pendant—maybe an emerald—just kissed that cleavage. He wanted to plant his lips where the pendant rested and suck that spot.

He paused on her throat, where he could barely see the pulse under her smooth skin. When he lifted his eyes to her face, she had one eyebrow cocked and her lips pressed together.

Busted. He grinned because he really didn't care. He wanted her to know he was interested and didn't plan on hiding it. Just in case she decided she wanted to do something about her interest in him.

He would not say no if she wanted to take him down to the floor, sit on his face until it was soaked and then ride his dick until his balls were dry.

Fuck yeah, he'd be okay with that.

He wanted to see the flame in her green eyes burning so hot they were like her emerald pendant. Instead of the perfectly veiled expression she was giving him right now.

"Starting to wonder if my sister is safe here with you." She jiggled her outstretched hand. "I'll need your truck keys."

He dug into his jeans pocket. "Prefer a more seasoned woman who knows what she wants and ain't afraid to ask for it." He dangled the key fob off one finger, just out of reach.

"How about a woman who knows what she doesn't want and isn't afraid to make that clear?" She snagged the fob off his finger and clutched it tightly within her fist.

It sucked that the woman turned him the fuck on. Even if she was interested in him, she was the type of woman who wouldn't allow herself that. She'd only want a man who'd fit neatly into her life. One who she could control.

Deacon did not fit neatly anywhere.

And no woman had ever controlled his life.

Not one.

Even so, he'd love to smudge that perfectly applied lipstick and feel that long hair wound around his own fingers. He'd like to watch her let go of her tight-assed way, even for a few hours. He was pretty damn sure when Reese let loose... She. Let. Loose.

"My sister's only twenty-four and has proven she doesn't make good decisions, so please don't look at her like you're looking at me right now. I don't need her falling for another bad boy. She only got her cast off recently from what the last one did to her."

He'd never gotten to the point where he had beaten a woman. If one was pushing his temper, he simply walked the fuck away. If he got to where he needed to break a woman's face and bones, then there had to be a good reason.

Not because he was angry, but because he was trying to save his own life or someone else's. Kill or be killed.

That was the only reason he'd ever hurt a woman.

"Not lookin' for young and foolish. Would rather have someone who's aware she's making a bad decision and jumps in anyway, knowing the consequences."

As his words sunk in, her delicate nostrils flared, and a flush worked its way up her throat.

Oh yeah, he finally got a response. One she couldn't control. She probably hated that.

When he surged to his feet, she started and took a step back, pinning her ass to the deck railing. "Well, that person sounds foolish, too."

He stepped up to the rail and set his coffee mug on it, making sure he was close enough for their shoulders to brush. He turned his head just slightly since they were facing in opposite directions. "No more foolish than the person who denies what they want."

"Do you know what you want, Deke?" Her question came out huskily, which did all kinds of shit to him below the belt.

His blood was beginning to rush, and it wasn't from the caffeine. "Always."

"I'm not sure if that's true," she murmured. She moved away, giving herself space and breaking the moment. She switched back to her *all-business, no-nonsense* Reese mode. "I need to get to the office. Make yourself at home. Reilly has my number. Make sure she keeps me updated."

"Reese..."

She hesitated with her hand on the handle of the French door.

"Warren comes to your office, you call the cops. No hesitation. Bianchi put them on notice that he may be landin' in their town. They have his info. So, don't do anything rash."

"Like what?"

She knew exactly what. She wasn't stupid. She had the delusion that being difficult allowed her to keep the power. It didn't. "Like stun gun him. 'Cause the second you release that trigger, he's gonna get up on his feet and teach you a lesson you don't wanna learn. Promise you that." His jaw got tight with the possibility of her putting herself at risk because she was stubborn.

"I'm aware of what he's capable of. I saw it firsthand."

"Seein' it and havin' it done to you are two different things. You hear me?"

Her pretty mouth went tight. "I hear you." She went inside and closed the door behind her.

"Yeah, right." Deacon shook his head and turned to stare down through the woods. "Hearin' and listenin' are two different things, too."

———

JUDGE RELEASED A LONG, low whistle after Deacon punched the code into the alarm, unlocked the side door and let his cousin into Reese's house.

The bearded giant was there to pick up someone and at the same time drop off someone.

Deacon would've delivered Reilly to Manning Grove himself, but since Reese had his truck, he had no wheels. Instead, he asked Judge to do the swap. And bring him more clothes.

Judge had made it known he didn't like any of what was going on and Deacon didn't blame him.

Holing up in a house and hoping that some asshole fugitive showed up wasn't a normal job or a typical plan for either of them. It kept Deacon away from the office longer than Judge liked, putting more pressure on him to keep the office running.

But Deacon had his laptop and, *thank fuck*, the house had strong Wi-Fi and enough bars on his cell phone to make or take any necessary calls. He'd do what he could for their business from the house while he waited for Warren to show his face.

He had called Trip early that morning and asked him to arrange an exec committee meeting. When the Fury prez got everyone gathered around the table upstairs in The Barn, they called Deacon and put him on speaker phone so he could explain the current situation and ask the club for help.

Nobody was a hundred percent on board about bringing an outsider to the farm—especially a woman who was the possible target of a psychopath—but Deacon couldn't figure out a better way to keep her safe without isolating her completely.

Keeping her at The Grove Inn was brought up as a suggestion, but Ozzy was the only Fury member who stayed on that property and he wasn't always there.

Plus, he liked to get his drink, his high and his fuck on. He wouldn't be thrilled having to watch a female who none of those three things applied to. Oz wasn't a babysitter.

In the end, they decided, since Deacon's apartment was empty with him being in Mansfield, Reilly could stay there until Warren was caught. At least she'd be where someone would least expect, and they could set up some brothers to keep an eye on her on a rotating basis.

It was the best Deacon could come up with and no one had a better idea other than just walking away from this job.

And he wasn't ready to simply walk away yet, for reasons he didn't want to admit to them. Or one reason in particular.

When Justice and Jury pushed past Judge, Deacon immediately dropped to one knee, ruffling the dogs' ears and letting them lick his face. "It's only been a couple days, you beasts. Know I'm irresistible, but—"

A female voice came from the direction of the great room. "Are they staying?"

He rose to his feet and turned toward Reilly, who sat on the couch with two bags at her feet. "Just one. The other's goin' back with you two."

"I'm pretty sure my sister won't be happy about having a dog in her house."

Deacon wasn't *pretty* sure, he was *damn* sure. But he was doing this job *his* way, whether she liked it or not.

With a wagging tail, Jury ran over to Reese's younger sister and nudged Reilly's crotch in greeting.

"Justice is here for two reasons. To keep me company and he's got great hearin'."

Reilly petted Jury while doing the obligated baby talk when speaking to an animal with four legs and did the same with Justice when he rushed over to check out the *new-to-him* person, who might have treats. Though, he wasn't too disappointed because scratches were almost as good as a snack.

"Reilly, this is my cousin Judge. He's gonna take you back to Manning Grove and set you up in my apartment."

He and Judge moved to where she was sitting. Both dogs wore smiles as she lavished them with hugs and scratches.

Reilly pulled her attention from the dogs and let her gaze rake down Judge. "Damn, you're big."

"That's what she s—" Judge whacked his arm, forcing him to cut off the last word.

Reilly laughed and stood, facing them.

She was a beautiful woman just like Reese. She wasn't quite as curvy as her older sister, but she probably would be when she put on a few more years. Her face and body still showed her youth. The same with her attitude. She was much looser and more casual than her older sister. Deacon was happy to see she hadn't allowed her recent beat-down to take away her spark.

Earlier, Deacon's fury had been off the charts when she'd come downstairs for breakfast after Reese left. The first thing he noticed as they greeted each other was her long blonde hair was a touch darker than Reese's, but they had the same green eyes.

The biggest difference between the two sisters, besides their age—which was almost eleven years, he discovered last night—was the slice from her temple and down along her right eye to her cheek. The cut was freshly healed but a scar might remain. With the way Reilly kept pulling her hair forward to cover it, it was obvious she was very self-conscious about it.

Broken arm, broken nose, bruises, and a cut from an unknown object. Reilly told him she hadn't been conscious enough at that point to be able to identify what he hit her with. Which was probably somewhat of a good thing.

Later the pigs on the scene had found a glass knickknack which Warren broke against her head.

She also barely remembered her neighbors kicking in her apartment door and jumping on Warren to subdue him.

Thank fuck they did.

Thank fuck someone had enough balls to get involved.

"Got your shit packed?" Judge asked her.

Reilly sighed and glanced at the two small bags at their feet. "Everything I have with me. The rest is in storage down in Philly."

"Just need enough clothes to get you through the next week or so. The sooner this is over, the better for all of us." Judge shot him a look. "Nice digs."

"Not shabby," Deacon agreed.

"Got some scratch."

"She works hard for it," Reilly cut in. "Her ex tried to drain her dry, even tried to take this house, though he didn't pay a damn dime for it out of his own pocket."

Deacon's brow shot up. During his online search last night for everything he could find on Reese, he hadn't come across anything about her being previously married or currently divorced.

"He take the kids?" Judge asked, looking around. Probably checking for some sign of snot monkeys.

"You mean the one he had with another woman while they were still married? Yep, he sure got stuck with that one."

"Damn," Deacon whispered.

"Havin' a kid with someone other than your ol' lady is a good way to fuck up a marriage, I suppose," Judge said with a grimace.

"How he created that kid is another," Reilly said. She frowned and shook her head. "The Porter sisters apparently aren't the best at picking men."

"All right," Judge boomed, clearly wanting to avoid that topic of conversation. "Time to hit the fuckin' road." He turned to Deacon. "Like we talked about in the meetin', gonna keep someone in that apartment with her at all times. We ain't havin' another Autumn situation, that's for damn fuckin' sure."

"Yeah, think that's for the best," Deacon agreed.

Judge turned to Reilly. "Can't tell your sister shit about where I'm takin' you or who you're with. You got me?"

"Why?"

"Just trust us," Judge answered. "It's better for both of you if she don't know. Once that motherfucker's caught, we'll let her know where you're at, so she can come get you. But 'til then, silence is fuckin' golden."

"She's not going to like that. She has a thing about being in control of every situation."

Deacon snorted.

"Deke will handle it," Judge said, whacking him on the back. "He's got balls of steel, so he says, so it shouldn't hurt too bad when she kicks him in them."

Reilly grinned. "I know you're making a joke, but you don't know my sister."

Deacon rubbed at his singed nipple. Maybe he needed to wear a cup around the house. Just in case.

"He's dealt with difficult women before. Right, cuz?" Judge asked, a grin splitting his long bushy beard and mustache.

"My sister is the queen of difficult," Reilly warned.

"Deke's always loved a challenge." Judge snorted and shook his head. He quickly sobered. "Got all the shit you need to apprehend that fucker?"

"Yeah. With what I already had with me and what you brought, I should be good."

Judge nodded. "Try to get this problem settled quickly, yeah?"

"Yeah. Once you get her settled in, buzz me. Got an idea."

"Can't talk about it now?" his cousin asked.

"Wanna think it through a little more first."

"Gotcha." Judge picked up Reilly's bags. "Want me to leave Jury with you, too?"

"Nah. Daisy will miss her too much."

"She ain't the only one," he muttered. He gave Deacon a nod, then turned to Reilly. "Let's go. Gonna give you the low-down on what you're walkin' into before we get there. So there ain't any surprises."

He hadn't told Reilly she was going to be protected by an MC.

But then, Reese had no clue, either.

Hopefully, Warren would be in custody before she found out.

Chapter Six

REESE ENTERED the code to reset the alarm, set her tote bag on the floor and, with a relieved sigh, kicked off her high heels. Her feet were killing her. She was exhausted from working both a long day and night at the office, attempting to make a dent in the mountain of work she had. She hoped tonight wouldn't be like last night and she'd actually get some solid sleep.

This worry about her sister had been eating at her, not only causing her heartburn, but sleepless nights.

The recessed lighting in her kitchen was on, but dimmed low. It gave her enough light to navigate the open concept kitchen without stubbing a toe or bruising a shin. She didn't bother to make it brighter since she was fighting a lingering headache.

Beyond the kitchen, the great room was dark, except for the glow from the gas fireplace. Someone must have switched it on and forgot to turn it back off.

Had he left? Had he gone up to the spare bedroom she'd designated as temporarily his?

And was Reilly even gone yet?

The house was way too quiet. Something she was

normally used to, but right now, was unexpected since two other adults had been sharing the same roof when she'd left for work this morning.

She had texted Reilly's cell phone a few times throughout the day without a single response. One of the last things Deacon had said, before she drove away in his blacked-out Ford, was she should trust him to keep her sister safe.

Reese wasn't sure if she could do that. She didn't like leaving Reilly's safety in the hands of a stranger.

Billy Warren had done his best to break Reilly, but luckily, failed. However, Reese didn't want to risk him getting another shot at her sister and being successful. So, she really didn't have a choice in trusting the tattooed, bearded and pierced stranger. He was used to dealing with fugitives. Reese was not.

She spotted Deacon's business card sitting on the counter where she'd left it last night, plucked her cell phone from the side pocket of her large bag, plugged in his number and hit Send.

Before she could even put it to her ear, she heard the faint ringtone of *Bad Boys*, the theme song from the cancelled COPS reality show.

Which one was it? Was he the bad boy or was he the one chasing them?

Reese tilted her head and listened carefully to locate where the sound was coming from.

Her deck.

She ended the call before he could answer and headed in that direction. She had spotlights along the wrap-around deck, but none were on.

The glowing tip of a lit cigarette pinpointed exactly where he was.

She debated going into her room to change into something more comfortable before going outside, but she was afraid if she did that, she might just fall face-first onto the bed and never move until morning. And she really needed an update on Reilly.

She opened one of the French doors and stepped out onto the deck but immediately jumped and squeaked as a whitish creature rushed toward her.

"Hope you like dogs," came the low rumble.

It took a second for her heart to restart and her eyes to adjust to realize that, yes, it was a dog. Said dog nudged her hand, then gave it a lick.

Why the hell was there a dog in her house?

"I assume it's yours and not a stray that came wandering through the woods?"

"Yeah, he's mine."

"Is it housetrained?"

"Better than me."

Reese didn't doubt it. "Does it shed?"

"Only foo foo dogs don't shed. Real dogs shed." Deacon tucked the cigarette between his lips, dropped his booted feet from the railing and sat up. "And stop insulting him. Justice is a *he*, not an *it*."

"Justice," she murmured. That name was kind of cool. And fitting for a dog owned by a bail bondsman and bounty hunter.

"Yep. His sister is Jury."

Reese glanced around looking for another uninvited four-legged guest. "She here somewhere?"

"No. She's my cousin's dog. He took her back with him along with your sister."

He took a long drag on the cigarette, held the smoke deep in his lungs, then leaned his head back and blew it straight up into the air.

Her nose twitched. "When I said make yourself at home, I didn't mean bring your dog and tobacco."

He chuckled. It was low and it shot a whirlwind of

warmth through her, from her tight chest to her aching toes. But it did little to loosen up the stress balled inside her.

"First off, Jussie's a good guard dog and it'll help havin' him here. Got good ears and better nose, even sharper teeth. Better for protection than your damn alarm system."

"Well, he didn't even bark at me. In fact, he licked my hand instead of protecting his master."

"His master," Deacon repeated softly. "Kinda like that. But yeah, told him to chill when I saw my truck comin' up the driveway."

That made sense. "I also don't allow smoking in my home."

"Wasn't done. Second, ain't in your house. Sittin' outside. Third, this ain't a cigarette. Well, it is, but it ain't. I don't smoke tobacco."

He took another hit on the cigarette that apparently wasn't one. This time, when he let the smoke roll out of his open mouth and up into his nose before again blowing it out of his mouth up and away, she leaned in and took a deep inhale herself...

And coughed. "Is it smart to be stoned while trying to catch a fugitive?"

"Not stoned. Just takin' off the edge."

She wondered what edge he was on. The way he was sprawled out in the chair, he appeared pretty damned relaxed.

"Take a load off." He tilted his head to the seat next to him. Justice settled on the deck between Deacon's spread feet and hiked up a back leg to lick his balls.

Nice. He probably learned that from his owner.

"I need to change."

"Then go change, then come take a load off. Bet your feet are screamin' from bein' in those shoes all day." He shook his head. "What women suffer through to look hot."

"You don't like when women make an effort to look hot?"

"Love it. Appreciate all that you women suffer through to look good. Ain't necessary, though. If you got it, you got it. No man's gonna bang you just 'cause you're wearin' some spiked heels."

She fought the upward curl of her lips. "Thank you for that life lesson. I'll keep that in mind." She sat on the edge of the lounge chair next to him, shrugged out of her suit jacket and tossed it over the back of the chair.

"That's you relaxin'?" he asked, then took a short puff on the joint.

"If I go into my room to change, I'll end up out for the night. I want an update from you first." She stretched out on the lounger and tucked an arm behind her head, staring up into the night sky. The cloud cover wasn't too thick, so she could see a few stars past the tree tops.

A deep grunt had her turning her head toward him. He was holding out the joint to her.

She stared at it for a second, then lifted her gaze to his face. "Really?" In truth, she was tempted to take a hit just to get rid of her damn headache.

"Yep. Think you need it. You're wound a little tight."

She wasn't going to argue that. Ever since Reilly was born, Reese had been responsible for her. At ten going on eleven, she took care of Reilly as if she was her own. Because neither of their parents did.

She made sure her sister was fed and clothed her whole life. Reese put herself through college, then Reilly. She did her best to set her sister up for success. But Reilly was never as driven as Reese. She always looked at life through a different set of lenses than Reese did.

Reese shook her head at the offer. He shrugged and pinched out the end.

"I assume you took her somewhere safe."

"Yeah."

"I tried getting a hold of her several times today and she didn't respond."

"Judge probably took her phone."

"What? Why?" And who the hell was Judge?

"Warren might not be smart enough to track her phone, but you never know. And anyway, at her age, tough not to post every minute of her life online. We need to control that right now."

"Who is Judge?"

"My cousin. We run the business together. Also, a licensed bounty hunter. He picked her up since you had my wheels."

She had a local body shop tow her BMW this morning. She hoped she wouldn't be without her own vehicle for too long since she wasn't used to driving a full-size truck. Though, she appreciated the gesture. "Where did he take her?"

"Here's the thing..." he started.

Oh shit. Reese didn't like the sound of that already. "The *thing* is to tell me where she is. I need to know what's going on with my sister. And if you took her phone away, I need to have another way to communicate with her to make sure she's all right."

"You can go through me." It wasn't a suggestion, it was a directive.

One that Reese didn't particularly like. "I can what?"

"You heard me. Know you're not gonna like it bein' done like that, but it's the best way. The *only* way."

"That's not your decision."

"The fuck it ain't. It'll protect the both of you."

"How's that?"

"'Cause the less you know, the better for her. This is one time it's smart to be dumb. Trust me on that."

"I've had self-defense training. I'm ready for that

asshole." The satisfaction she would get while putting that abusing bastard in his place... She could almost taste it. That was what kept her up at night. And when she did finally sleep, that was all she dreamed about.

Revenge.

She'd never been a blood-thirsty person until she saw her sister lying in that hospital bed broken.

"That's cute."

"I kicked your ass," she reminded him.

He snorted softly. "You didn't kick my ass. You took me unawares. I was comin' to help you, not hurt you, and you used a fuckin' stun gun. Not even close to bein' the same as kickin' my ass. And, for fuck's sake, I didn't fight back. You're a woman. I don't hurt women. If you were a man and pulled that shit, I woulda been doin' more than just rubbin' my fried tit and cursin' you the fuck out."

She hated that he was right, but he was. And she understood the need to keep Reilly's location a secret. But not knowing made it feel like any control over her sister's situation was slipping from her fingers.

And she needed to hang on, even if it was only by her fingernails. "Well, at least tell me where to send money. I'll cover her expenses, of course."

"Think you're bein' slick."

Damn it.

"Will tell you this much, she's at my place. Since I'm here, it's empty. That's all you need to know. Not the location."

"She's there by herself?"

"Ain't by herself."

"Then, I have to assume she's with people you trust completely." She sure as hell hoped so.

"Yeah. Not just men, women, too. They'll take care of her. Promise."

Promise.

341

Could she trust him and his promise?

Simply trusting someone blindly, or a group of people, wasn't easy for her. And Reilly hadn't made the best decision when it came to allowing Billy Warren into her life.

Reese needed to help her sister make better decisions from here on out. Until she proved she was capable of making those decisions for herself.

"I put her through college so she could be smart. Make good decisions."

"Since when does college make people fuckin' smart?"

She hadn't realized she'd said her thoughts out loud. But, again, he was right. An education made a person more well-rounded, not necessarily smarter.

She only wanted the best for her sister. In every aspect of her life.

"So she could be independent." And not rely on any man. She hoped that a college degree would give her a good foundation to build a great life for herself. A better one than their parents had provided. Or not provided.

And it still could. Billy Warren was just a speed bump in Reilly's life. A speed bump Reese would like to demolish.

Being early April, the night air was cool, but comfortable. She wasn't sure if it was the pot she got a whiff of or the fresh air that was reducing the throb of her headache.

She was just glad it was almost gone.

She sighed and stared up into the sky again, getting lost in its vastness. "She's young. She still believes she needs a man in her life. She hasn't learned that lesson yet, though this situation should teach her. She thought she loved him. She didn't. She only liked the thought of him. Of taming a bad boy." She had no idea why she was telling him this. He probably couldn't care less about why her sister hooked up with Billy. She turned her head to see him studying her. "One like you. Tattoos, beard, even piercings. You probably ride a motorcycle, too, right? You fall right into the stereotype of the bad boy and think no woman can resist you."

He huffed. "Right. I'm totally fuckin' irresistible. 'Cept to women like you who think you're too good for a man like me. Think you're smarter, better."

This time he wasn't correct. She wasn't too good *for him*. She had enough experience to know a man like Deacon was simply not good *for her*. Just like Billy had been bad for Reilly.

"Believe it or not, I wasn't born with what I have. I worked hard to pull myself up from where I began, to build what I have, to create the life I now live. I learned never to rely on anyone but myself. Wanting a man and needing one are different. And if I want a man, it doesn't mean I need him to make me a complete person. I can do that on my own."

"Sounds lonely."

Some days it was. Very. But her previous attempt at not being lonely had turned out to be a disaster. Maybe not in the same caliber as her sister's attempt, but still...

It was one lesson she wouldn't forget.

NEITHER SAID a word for a few moments. Instead, the last two words he said hung between them.

She didn't deny being lonely. She didn't argue it, either.

Which meant it was true.

She shifted in her chair like she was ready to call it a night. She wasn't comfortable with that truth when it was put out there like it was.

But Deacon wasn't ready for her to walk inside and shut him out. She had given him a little glimpse of who she was and where she came from, but it wasn't enough. He wanted to hear more.

She probably wouldn't give him anything personal if he

outright asked. That would take some work and a bit of finesse on his part, but he was pretty damn sure when it came to her business, she'd be more likely to talk.

He had heard the pride in her voice when she mentioned working hard and creating the life she currently had. "Put yourself through school to become a lawyer."

"Yes."

"You a defense attorney?"

She hesitated, most likely because she was trying to figure out where he was headed with his questions. She'd be the type to want to be a few steps ahead. She didn't like situations where she wasn't in control. "Why? Do you need one? I'm not cheap."

What attorney was?

He chuckled. "Not yet. You do criminal defense, then." It would be nice to have a lawyer hookup in case he or one of his brothers got in a jam. Deacon bet Reese was on fire when she worked the courtroom. She would not let a prosecutor get the best of her.

Hell no.

She would take total command of that room and all eyes would be on her.

That thought made his dick twitch. He visualized her pacing back and forth in front of a judge and jury, machine gunning questions at a witness on the stand, making that person sweat bullets.

Suddenly his little fantasy changed into Reese wearing a sexy black leather outfit, spiked heels and carrying a long bullwhip, her cracking it at her opponent in the legal arena.

Fuck yeah. That dick twitch quickly turned into a half chub.

Some women dreamed of taming a bad boy. But some men dreamed of taming a powerful woman. Like Reese.

"No, I specialize in civil litigation."

His head jerked back. And he regretfully let that little

fantasy go. For now. He might continue it later in his room. "What the fuck is that?"

"Let's just say, I get paid to argue. And get my clients what they deserve."

He snorted. "You get paid to argue. Now there's a fuckin' surprise."

Was she smiling? If so, she was fighting it.

Life was too goddamn short to be so uptight and serious all the time.

"Basically, I handle civil lawsuits. I can be retained by either side. A lot of my clients are businesses, like a car dealership. But my strength is getting a suit settled before it even goes to trial. It saves my client money in the end, which they appreciate. Happy clients give me referrals."

"You're good at negotiatin'."

"Yes."

She probably negotiated her own divorce. "Your sister said your ex fucked you over."

He was sure Reese wasn't happy Reilly gave him that much. Even in the dark, he could see her frown and tense up. "He tried."

"You got to keep this house." It might not be in the suburbs of Philly where houses cost a fuckton of scratch, but it wasn't a shack. The gate, the long, paved driveway, the house itself didn't read middle class. It read "financially comfortable."

Whether that was true or not, whether that was only a false front, he couldn't be sure. But the little bit he knew about the woman sitting on the deck with him, he could tell she wasn't a poser. She wasn't living above her means. She appreciated everything she owned and didn't take it for granted.

This house was something she wanted, and she did what she had to do to get it.

Deacon liked that.

Determination and drive.

This woman had it oozing out of her pores. He didn't need to know her deepest, darkest secrets to figure that out. She wore that shit on her sleeve.

"Of course, I did. It's my damn house." She twisted on the chair and put her bare feet down on the deck. "I'm tired. I'm going to bed."

She was ready to bolt.

He leaned over and grabbed her arm, keeping her in her seat. "Hold up." She jerked her arm, but he tightened his hold.

"I'm not talking about my divorce," she snapped, using her free hand to rub at her temple.

"Got it. Sore subject."

"You're here for one reason. To catch Billy. That's it. Not to become my bestie. Not to share giggles and gossip."

She had walls up all around her. Like a fucking fortress. Deacon suddenly wanted to be the battering ram that knocked those fuckers down.

For fuck's sake, he should get his goddamn head examined. Too many women out there who weren't this difficult. Women like Bambi. Or Tina. Or any of the other women he'd scored with since he lost his fucking virginity at fifteen.

"You're right. You wanted to know my plan. Need to talk about that."

"Make it quick. I need to get an early start in the morning."

"You ever just take a break?" She went to get up again and he yanked her arm, pulling her back down. "Sit."

Her eyes widened, then narrowed on him.

"Got it. Here to deal with Warren, nothin' more. Let's talk about that for a second." The muscles in her forearm loosened a little, so he released her. "When I looked for your sister's social media, I found nothin'."

"That's correct."

"When I asked her about it this mornin', she said you made her take it all down."

"Yes." Her answer was short and clipped. Like her patience was at its limit.

It wouldn't take much for his to get there, too. "I need it back up."

"What?"

"I need at least one account up and also need access to it."

"Why?"

"We're gonna set a trap."

"A trap," she parroted.

"Yep." With a muscle popping in his jaw, he got to his feet, strode two paces away, then spun. His blood was pounding in his ears. "You know, told you that you needed to fuckin' trust me. Know that's gonna be hard for you. But this questionin' my every move is pissin' me the fuck off. I don't have to fuckin' help your goddamn sister, but I am. I'm puttin' my family at risk by hidin' her somewhere safe. I'd at least like a little appreciation for that. But if that's too hard for you to give, then I'll tell you where she is, you can go pick her ass up and you two can deal with Warren yourselves."

"Basically, you're telling me to trust you or fuck off."

"Not 'basically.' That's what I'm sayin'."

Reese slowly rose to her feet. He half expected her to head inside and slam the door behind her.

Instead, she moved to where he stood with his body tight as fuck. Not just from anger, but now from how close she was. Practically toe to toe.

So close, but still out of reach.

Even after smoking pot, he could detect her scent. It was faint, but it was there. His nostrils flared as he inhaled, trying to draw more of her in. His fingers curled into his palms in a desperate attempt not to grab her and do whatever was necessary to loosen her the fuck up.

Because if she gave him that shot, he was pretty damn sure he could pull that stick out of her sweet ass. Even if it was only temporary.

Fuck. He just needed a shot at it. At her.

Without getting his ass stun-gunned again.

She turned her face up toward his and said, "Explain the plan. I'm willing to listen. I'm willing to do whatever is necessary to keep my sister safe."

"And you," he added. It would be stupid for her to sacrifice herself for her sister's safety.

"My sister comes first."

"Judge is gonna get me her username and password to one of her social media accounts. We're gonna post like it's her postin'. Hopin' that fucker's keepin' an eye on her account, so the post I make draws him here. To this house. Not likin' that you're here, too. So, I need to make sure you keep your eyes fuckin' open. Every time you're walkin' anywhere, want your stun gun in one hand, your cell in the other. Pay attention, keep vigilant. Don't underestimate that fucker. He won't hesitate to use you to get info on your sister."

"When will you post it?"

With no argument coming from her, he relaxed a little. "Tomorrow mornin'. Soon as I get that info and we decide what we're postin' and on which account. Whatever she was most active on and, hopefully, one he knew about."

She nodded. "Instagram. Before I made her disable it, she was posting on it at least once a day."

Good to know. Thank fuck Reese was on board. "We'll use that one, then."

"That's how Billy found her. Reilly had mentioned he made a few comments on some of her pictures, then slid like the snake he is into her private messages and began working her." She squeezed her eyes shut and shook her head. "Stupid."

"We all do stupid shit, Reese. He's an expert at suckin' in women. She wasn't the first."

Her eyes opened and even in the dark, he could tell they'd become hard. "I want her to be the last."

"Can't promise that. Even if I catch his ass, he won't be locked up forever. He lives off women's hopes and dreams... 'til he crushes them."

She lifted her open hand in front of his face and squeezed it into a tight fist. "I would like to crush something on that asshole that has nothing to do with hopes and dreams."

Deacon grimaced and fought pinning his thighs together. "Yeah, well. This plan might work if you don't do anythin' stupid." He leaned in and whispered, "Don't do anything stupid, Reese. Let me handle that motherfucker, not you. Don't make me regret allowin' you to stay here."

Her spine snapped straight. "Allowing me."

"Yeah, you heard me."

"*You* allowed *me* to stay in my own house. You're almost as generous as my fucking ex by *allowing* me to keep the house I fucking paid for."

As she spoke, her voice had risen and the last part was shouted loud enough he swore he heard it echoed back at him from the woods. If there was any wildlife nearby, they probably all scrambled for cover.

"I'm going to bed." She headed toward the door, but hesitated with her hand on the door handle. "Oh wait. Am I *allowed* to do that?"

Without waiting for his response, she went inside, slamming the door shut. He remained outside, where he figured it was a bit safer for the moment. He tracked her as she went into the kitchen, snagged a bottle of wine and a wineglass, and hoofed it across the great room to a door on the other side of the house. From his exploring earlier when she wasn't home, he knew it was the master bedroom.

He heard that door slam, too.

Then he *allowed* himself to grin.

He was getting a taste of that, if it was the last thing he did. Having a night with her would be a good use of his balls one last time before she ripped them off.

Chapter Seven

REESE FROZE as she raised the coffee mug to her lips. She swallowed hard and, keeping her head locked forward, she followed Deacon with only her eyes as he entered the kitchen, wearing black boxer briefs.

Just boxer briefs.

Snug. *Very* snug. Boxer briefs.

The stretchy cotton hugged his early morning erection as he moved toward the side door, letting Justice outside. He left the door open a gap, turned and headed toward her next.

She lowered the mug a little more, made sure her mouth wasn't gaping open and then lifted her eyes, because...

Because that was the right thing to do.

Breathe, Reese, breathe.

Breathe.

Almost every inch of his muscular arms were covered in tattoos. That wasn't the surprising part since she had seen him with sleeves pushed to his elbows. But he had more tattoos covering the skin across his upper chest.

All in black and grey.

She already knew his nipples were pierced but knowing and seeing it in technicolor were two different things.

Very, very different.

Especially since the kitchen lights reflected off the shiny metal barbells. The fact that he let someone—most likely a stranger—drive a needle through the tips of both nipples was both fascinating and disturbing at the same time.

But seeing them now, in the flesh, made a few things on her body flutter. Like her heart, her stomach and... elsewhere.

His hair wasn't in its normal Viking-like braid. This morning it was pulled back into a sort of messy man-bun to keep it out of his face.

Without a word, he moved past her, where she leaned back against the island counter, and headed toward the coffeemaker tucked into the corner.

Since she normally lived by herself, out of habit she only made enough for herself. And she was on her second mugful.

He reminded her of a zombie as he pulled the empty pot from the coffeemaker, stared at it for a second, then slid it back into place. But as he did so, she got a good view of his back. But only for a couple of seconds before he turned and headed directly toward her.

She could only imagine her eyes were as big as saucers as he approached.

Before she could spit out, "What are you doing?" he'd pulled the mug from her frozen fingers and sucked down half of her fresh coffee. After he was done, he blinked once and handed it back.

She scrambled to grab it before it could fall to the tile floor and smash to pieces.

She stared into her now half-empty mug, wondering if she should finish the rest or dump it down the drain. Before she could decide, he reached down and scratched his balls.

Yes.

That was what he did.

In front of a complete stranger. Scratched his nuts like he had a bug infestation or something.

"Really?" She cleared her throat when her question came out more like a squeak.

He shrugged. "Told me to make myself at home."

Holy shit, his voice was rough from being unused and it made things she didn't want to identify skitter through every part of her body.

"I guess I should've been more specific." She shoved the mug into his chest and he grabbed it. "You can finish that. I don't take my coffee with someone else's backwash."

"If you're makin' more, like mine brewed strong."

Just then, the microwave beeped, and she ignored his coffee order to pull out her breakfast. She grabbed a spoon and stirred her hot cereal but planned to let it cool for a few seconds.

"Your coffee order is noted, but I don't take special requests. The coffee and filters are in the cabinet right above the coffeemaker. And so are the mugs. Feel free to use them."

Instead of heading in that direction like she expected, he reached around her, his bare skin brushing against hers, lifted the spoon from her steaming cereal and shoved it in his mouth. She wasn't sure if the face he made was because he burned his damn tongue or because of what it was.

He went over to the trashcan at the end of the island, lifted the lid and spat it out. "What's that shit?"

She smiled as she grabbed a clean spoon from the drawer, added a little raw honey to the cereal and gave it another good stir. "Ten-grain cereal."

"Feed that shit to the deer."

"I like it and it's healthy." She glanced down at his hard-on, which seemed to still be at full attention. Unless he was a show-er and not a grower. But if what she could see was everything he had to offer, it still wasn't bad.

"How long does that normally last?" She took another bite of cereal and tilted her head toward his crotch.

His hand automatically slid over his hard length as he moved around the kitchen. "Depends."

"On?"

"Pretty sure you can figure out how to get rid of a hard-on." He opened the fridge door and peered inside. A second later, he closed it and began to root through her cabinets.

She had no idea what he was searching for.

He pulled out a box of muesli cereal, made a look of disgust and muttered, "Christ. More deer food." He shoved it back into the cabinet. "Since you got my truck, can you do a grocery run?"

Oh sure, your highness, whatever you need. I'm at your service. "Make a list." Maybe she should dip her head and curtsey, too.

He grabbed the magnetic pad of paper and pen she kept stuck to the side of the fridge and began to scribble some things down. Admittedly, it was kind of cute because as he wrote, his eyebrows were knitted together, and his mouth was slightly parted. All he needed to do yet was stick out the tip of his tongue as he concentrated.

When he was done, he ripped the top sheet off and came over to hand it to her. At least it gave her something safe to look at besides his nipples or his waning erection. She skimmed it.

Eggs

Bacon

Donuts (cream-filled, Boston – OK)

Rocky Road ice cream

Beer (no shitty lite)

Cola (no diet)

JD (Jim Beam- OK)

Captain Crunch (not store brand)
Real milk (no fake shit)
Sour cream and onion chips (waffle cut)

When she was done scanning the list, she went over to the stainless-steel trashcan, pushed her foot on the pedal to raise the lid, crumpled it in a ball and dropped it in from shoulder height. The whole time his brown eyes followed her every move.

His eyebrows lifted as she jerked her foot off the pedal and let the lid slam, then brushed her hands together as if wiping off some dirt.

"That wasn't nice," he grumbled.

"Neither is drinking from my mug or eating from my spoon. Or walking around my kitchen scratching your testicles and sporting an erection."

"Will make sure to get rid of it before I join you for breakfast tomorrow."

She closed her eyes and bit back a groan. Now she pictured him lying in one of the spare beds upstairs, working on getting rid of his morning hard-on by himself.

"If you didn't notice..." Her words came out a little too breathless when she forced herself to return to the subject at hand. *Oh God*, she couldn't get that image of him touching himself out of her mind. She cleared her throat and continued. "There are brown eggs in the fridge. There's turkey bacon in the freezer, along with three pints of Ben & Jerry's. I'm pretty sure there's whiskey in my liquor cabinet if you look, but I prefer you keep your faculties about you while you're here since we don't know when Billy will show up. You're welcome to eat and drink what's already in the house since right now, I don't have time to go grocery shopping and, anyway, I'm hoping you won't be staying very long."

One side of his mouth pulled up. "Got it. Make myself at home, but don't get too comfy. My presence is only welcome 'cause it benefits you." Justice barreled through the partially open door, tail held high and wagging. He closed the door behind his dog.

"Well, of course. Why else would you be here?"

He moved closer to her and murmured, "I wouldn't. Unless you invited me for another reason." He let that hang for a moment, then his half-grin disintegrated. "We're helpin' each other out, Reese. You seem to forget that."

She hadn't.

She sighed. "I'll grab some things at the store if I get a chance, but I've got a full day ahead of me."

He gave her a smile. "Appreciate it."

That smile... *Holy shit*, it was too damn tempting. She needed to get the hell out of her house and to her office before she did something stupid.

We all do stupid shit, Reese. He's an expert at suckin' women in.

Billy Warren wasn't the only one who was an expert. The man in front of her might not steal a woman's money, but he probably stole other things. Like her sanity. Or her will to keep him at arm's length. Or her heart.

Reese mentally groaned.

"You okay?"

No. No, she was not okay with a practically naked Deacon Edwards in her kitchen and who planned on masturbating in one of her bedrooms.

She grabbed her bowl of now cold cereal, scraped it into the trash and as she turned to put it in the sink, she froze.

Again.

And took a better look at him digging through her freezer.

She automatically stepped forward and frowned as she slowly studied the ink on his broad back. It took a few seconds to put together what she originally thought were smaller tattoos were really one large one.

The "banner" at the top of his back said *BLOOD FURY*, the bottom banner, *PENNSYLVANIA*. There was a little box to one side that had the letters *MC* in it. It was all done, like the rest of his tattoos, in black and grey. Except for the center drawing, where the only color was red blood coming from the skull and crossbones.

"What is that?" she whispered, hoping she was wrong.

He turned with a frozen, grass-fed New York strip steak in his hand, instead of the suggested turkey bacon, and rubbed his unencumbered hand over his bare chest. "What?" He peered over his shoulder. "My great ass?"

She circled her hand in the air. "That tattoo... What does it mean?"

"Which one?"

"You know *exactly* which one I'm talking about."

"*If you didn't notice*, got a few. Need to be specific." He placed the butcher-paper wrapped steak on the counter and turned back to the fridge, grabbing the carton of free-range, local brown eggs. "You got tater tots hidin' in that freezer somewhere?" He put the eggs down next to the stove.

She wanted to talk about tattoos, not tater tots. More specifically the meaning of those tattoos that made up one large one. A tattoo that wasn't faded in any way, which meant it was inked into his skin not too long ago. So, it wasn't from a "past life." Oh no, that life, the reason he'd get a large tattoo like that, was current.

A burn began in her chest and worked its way up her throat. "Is my sister with a bunch of bikers?" Her stomach twisted and she dropped her bowl and spoon into the sink with a clatter. "Please tell me she's not staying with a bunch of bikers."

He crossed his arms over his chest and lifted his chin. He reminded her of an obstinate child.

So, she treated him like one. "Answer me."

"If I fuckin' answer you, you ain't gonna like my answer."

She pressed a hand to her forehead and groaned. "You

took my sister, who has a habit of making bad decisions, to stay with a bunch of bikers. I need you to tell me I'm wrong and she's staying with your family instead. Your cousin, even."

"My cousin is one of those bikers."

"Fuck!" exploded from her, making Justice whine and nudge her hand. She strode to the other side of the kitchen, then spun on the dog's owner. "You said she'd be safe."

"Nowhere safer."

She doubted that. She might be safe from Billy there, but...

Reilly didn't have the self-control that Reese did when it came to men like him.

And now she was surrounded by men who acted like Deacon, rode motorcycles like Deacon, had tattoos like Deacon, and if they looked anything like...

"Deacon," she groaned.

"Reese, she'll be okay. Promise."

She hated the fact she had to rely on his word. "I only ever wanted what was best for her."

"Yeah, and hookin' up with a biker would be the fuckin' worst."

Her hands clenched into fists and she pinned them to her thighs. "She doesn't need to be hooking up with anyone right now. That's my point. She needs to recover from the mistake she already made recently and get her life back on track." She ground the heels of her palms into her eyes, not worried if she smeared her mascara, she was more worried about having a meltdown right in the middle of her kitchen.

Right now she felt helpless, that the control she normally held onto was just out of her reach, and she hated every second of it.

Fingers wrapped around her wrists and pulled her hands away from her face. She took a deep breath to slow her spinning world and stared into his brown eyes. Concern. Confusion. That was what she saw in them.

His fingers remained circling her wrists when he said, "Look, I'll get the word out no one's to fuck with her. That she's untouchable."

"You probably think I'm overreacting. And maybe I am. But... She's the only person I have left. She's it. She's everything. I've helped her her whole life, since the day she was born, and now... Now I feel like I've failed." She didn't even like admitting that out loud.

"You didn't fuckin' fail. Failin' woulda been not doin' shit and hopin' that fucker didn't show up. You're doin' the only thing you can do right now. Helpin' me set a trap for that asshole."

His words should make her feel better, but they didn't. The only thing that would, was to get Billy Warren out of their life for good. Put him in the past and move forward. Then get her sister set up again so she could continue building on the foundation Reese provided for her.

Then Reese would have to, once again, let her go. But this time, she only hoped whoever Reilly hooked up with in the future wouldn't knock her back down again. Physically, mentally or financially.

But Reilly might not have a future if Billy got to her. That bastard needed to be dealt with first.

She stared at the man whose goal was to do just that.

She needed to let him do what needed to be done. She needed to let him take control of the situation.

She also needed to fight the temptation of the almost naked man in her kitchen.

"I have to get to the office." She grabbed her leather tote, which was sitting by the side door, and paused. "And don't you dare ruin that steak by defrosting it in the microwave. Seal it in a Ziploc bag and put it in a bowl of water."

She rarely ate red meat, but when she did, she paid a premium for a good cut from a local farm. The cost of that steak—one he would probably slather in ketchup and cook until the center was gray instead of a perfect red—was nothing compared to what Reilly's life and happiness was worth.

So, if he wanted to eat that steak, he could eat that damn steak. It was a small price to pay.

Before walking out the door, she let herself take one last glance at the man who was searching the drawers and cabinets to do what Reese suggested.

Now, what would letting a man she wanted, but shouldn't, into her home cost her?

She was afraid to find out.

———

DEACON HAD SET up a spot at the built-in bar in her lower level as his temporary office space. He had his laptop, a comfy chair and his cell phone. It would keep him from getting too bored, plus it would keep Judge off his ass. Especially since he didn't know how long he'd be holed up in this house.

Reese was right. She had plenty of booze behind the home bar, most of it unopened. She also had a small wine cooler which was half full. No beer, though.

But he wasn't downstairs to drink, he was there to get the plan rolling and hope it worked to draw out Warren.

Judge had sent him Reilly's username and password for her Instagram account. Along with a photo of the two sisters standing on the deck of Reese's house with their arms around each other's shoulders and huge smiles on their faces.

They looked a lot alike. And Deke had stared at that

photo for way too long. Reese looked happy and stress-free in that picture.

Judge said it wasn't recent but since it was taken at a distance, it was hard to judge how old either of them were in the photo. Even so, it would work. It would be the perfect bait for Warren.

Especially when he posted, "Staying with my sis at her awesome house! Those who know me know why. Watch out, women! Don't fall for con artists and violent criminals like my ex," to go with the picture.

Being blatantly called out would infuriate Warren. And if, on the slim chance, he hadn't been looking for Reilly before, he probably would be now.

He scrolled through his phone to find the contact he needed and pushed Send.

Judge answered on the second ring. "Justice Bail Bonds."

"Trap's set."

"Want me to send someone else up there to sit on the house with you?"

"No." He didn't want anyone else crashing in Reese's house. She didn't even like him being there. It would create more problems than they were worth.

"Gonna tell you again, she shouldn't be there at the house."

"No shit. She's stubborn."

Deacon heard a snort through the phone. "Her sister's just like her. Fuckin' stubborn as all fuck. Can tell why Warren did a number on her."

"Why? What happened?"

"She's bored. She's twenty-somethin' and doesn't know how to just chill. Wants to keep busy. Can't bring her here to the office. Ain't smart to send her to Crazy Pete's with Stella. Ozzy don't want her at the motel 'cause that means he'd have to watch her ass. And Ozzy's Ozzy. Everybody's got shit to do and no one wants to be a babysitter to a woman we said was off-limits. 'Specially a hot blonde."

"Don't give a fuck what she wants, she needs to stay safe and out of sight 'til this is over."

"No shit, asshole. And her bein' on club property right now means I'm the fuckin' one responsible to keep her ass safe. Problem is, everybody's got a job to do and we got no one to spare. 'Specially since we're not sure how long this is gonna take."

"We'll keep postin' online 'til he bites."

"What if he don't bite? What if he went underground and couldn't give a flyin' fuck about Reilly Porter? We need a time limit on this job. Once his bond expires and he ain't caught, then what?"

"Then it's over. We're out. We'll wash our hands of it and let the women deal with their own fuckin' mess."

Another snort came through the phone and Deacon could picture his cousin shaking his head. "Right."

Right. "Bianchi said the court date's not 'til the end of the month. We got 'til then."

"You ain't stayin' there 'til the end of the month, cuz. We got other shit to do."

"Will do what I can from here."

"While that's somethin', it ain't everythin', Deke," Judge grumbled. "Hard to leave the office to do shit when you're gone." He grunted. "Got an idea. Gonna run it by Dutch and some of the guys and let you know if it works out."

"Dutch?"

"Yeah. Thinkin' my idea might make everyone happy and ease the pain of not havin' enough brothers to watch the girl." The phone went dead.

No *bye*, no *see ya*. Nothing.

Judge just hung up. Deacon grinned.

His cousin was an asshole. But he was a big, lovable asshole.

Chapter Eight

"Gotta tell you somethin'."

Reese sighed before taking another sip of her large glass of white wine.

She had come home late and found him planted, once again, on the deck in the dark, with his laptop and phone nearby. Also with his four-legged best friend by his side, curled up and taking a snooze, since Justice had a rough day of eating, sleeping and licking his junk.

Deacon kept checking Reilly's Instagram account about every half hour, just in case Warren left a comment on the picture he posted this morning. So far, nothing.

He didn't believe Warren was stupid enough to out himself on social media, but fugitives have done some pretty fucking stupid shit before. Which sometimes made his job a little easier.

If Warren didn't show up in the next couple of days, Deacon would make another post on Reilly's account. Until then, he just had to have patience.

So did Reese.

But he also didn't want to lie to her about her sister if he could avoid it. And while he wouldn't give her Reilly's exact location, he also wanted to keep Reese somewhat in the loop.

It might help her feel a little more in control of the situation. Which might ease her stress a little.

Might.

The way she was sucking down the wine, he wasn't so sure.

When she had joined him a half hour ago, she came outside wearing a loose, wide-necked sweatshirt that hung off one slender bare shoulder. Which confirmed the fact she had gotten rid of her bra at the same time as the rest of her dress clothes. She had pulled on some sort of loose cotton pants, maybe pajama bottoms, but he couldn't tell with the lack of light. She had folded her long legs and tucked her bare feet beneath her when she curled up on the lounge chair next to his.

She hadn't said a word. Not a damn one. She simply came out and settled in with her big-assed wine glass.

He assumed she hadn't had a good day, so he had said nothing for a while to let her unwind, but he wanted to give her an update before she went inside and shut him out.

"What is it?" She sounded drained. Like she didn't have much energy left to deal with anything besides closing her eyes and going to sleep.

He glanced at his phone. It was only eight. "Your sister voiced her opinion about just hidin' away in my place and havin' nothin' to do."

"Sounds like her."

"'Cause of that, we found her somethin' to do." Or at least Judge had and reported back to Deacon with the details.

She didn't say anything for a few seconds. Maybe she was just waiting for him to explain. So, he did.

"My cousin, Judge, is our club's Sergeant at Arms—"

"What's that?"

"He enforces the club rules and by-laws. Also is in charge of makin' sure we all don't get our throats sliced in the middle of the night."

"What?"

"Kiddin'." But not really. He couldn't tell her that and have her worry about her sister more than she already was. "Anyway, he wants one or two of my brothers—"

"You have brothers?"

"Yeah. A bunch. Not blood, but family just the same."

"They belong to your club."

"Yeah. *Anyway*, he wants one or two of our brothers with Reilly twenty-four seven."

"I'm willing to pay them for their time, if necessary."

"That ain't what this is about, Reese. Let me get this shit out and then you can say whatever you gotta say."

She stared at him. He stared back and tilted his head.

She blew out a loud breath and gave him a nod. He continued, "Got a brother who owns a garage. Got four other brothers, besides him, who work there, too. Judge gave Reilly the option to spend her days there helpin' out. Believe me, the office needs a woman's touch bad and hasn't been organized since Dutch's ol' lady left him a couple decades ago. It's a win-win situation. Reilly makes a little scratch helpin' out and will have five of my brothers watchin' her durin' the day. One or two others will watch her at night at my place."

"Are you sure she'll be safe working there?"

"Nobody knows her in—" he caught himself before he mentioned Manning Grove, "the town we live in. Judge asked her to make sure she had no connections there. Not only that, she's gonna use a fake name when she's dealin' with any customers. Ain't gonna be a lot of money, but it'll put somethin' in her pocket. And somethin's better than nothin'," he quoted Trip's favorite saying. "Somebody will be with her at all times, which is the most important part."

He shut up and waited for her reaction.

She lifted and drained her wine glass. When she was done, she put it down on the table to her left and turned her head to where he sat at her right.

His eyebrows shot up when she pointed at the makeshift ashtray he'd formed out of a piece of used aluminum foil he found in the trash.

"Are you going to light that?"

He lifted his gaze from the fatty that balanced on the edge of the foil to her. "I can wait 'til you go inside, if it's gonna bother you."

She shook her head. "Light it."

He normally didn't take orders from a woman. But that was one he'd willingly follow.

She must've had a really fucked up day.

He slipped his Zippo from the front pocket of his jeans, snagged the joint, tucked it between his lips and lit it.

Before he was even done taking his first full inhale, she leaned over, yanked it from his lips and did several little delicate puffs on the end of it.

He grinned. "You ever smoke before?"

"A long time ago," she got out between a few coughs. Before she was even done choking, she was sucking on the end so hard, his dick began to pay attention. She fought the cough this time while holding it deep within her lungs before blowing it out so fast it was like she was trying to blow out birthday candles. She dropped her head and hacked a couple more times.

He did his best not to chuckle.

She pressed a hand to her chest, emphasizing the fact she wore no bra. "That stuff burns."

"That shit's smooth. High grade Kush. You're just not used to smokin'. Smoke a bowl of stems and seeds, then tell me what fuckin' burns."

She took one more hit, managed not to cough at all, and

handed it back to him before stretching out on the lounger. Looking a little more relaxed.

"Feel better?" he asked, releasing the smoke from his own lungs.

"Not yet." She held out her hand.

"How long's it been?"

"I don't know. Since I was fifteen or sixteen, maybe? So, almost twenty years?" She was almost thirty-five, which was about three years older than him. If he hadn't looked it up himself, he never would've guessed it.

"Before you hit the bud again, why don't you wait to see how hard the bud hits you first."

"Then save some for me."

"Got plenty," he said, amused, but pinched the end out and placed the joint back on his homemade ashtray.

She smacked her lips. "Now I need something to drink."

"Maybe you shouldn't have downed that wine so fast."

She cocked an eyebrow at him. "Are you judging me?"

He lifted up a palm in surrender and shook his head. "Nope. You wanna get plastered, get plastered. I'll make sure you get inside and to bed if you do."

"That's nice of you," she mumbled.

He snorted. "Yeah, I'm a complete fuckin' gentleman."

"I should've brought the bottle out with me," she muttered, picking up her empty wine glass, sticking out her tongue and turning it upside down to catch the last couple of drips.

Jesus fuck.

She smacked her lips again and he groaned, imagining her making those sounds as she sucked his dick.

He surged from his seat, making Justice jump up in surprise and look around for a threat. "Gonna grab it for you." He rushed toward the door, ordering Justice to stay outside with Reese, and went inside.

He located the half empty bottle on the counter,

snagged it and before he went back out on the deck, he adjusted himself. He stepped outside and, as she held out her glass, he dumped the remaining wine into it, causing a little to splash on her hand.

She licked it off and he smothered his groan.

If a bottle of wine and a couple of hits off a joint didn't disintegrate the stick up her ass, nothing would.

"Good?" he asked, because he was not good with wanting a woman who didn't want him.

"Perfect," she murmured, taking a sip, then leaning back in her chair and releasing a long, loud sigh.

He went back to his, settled in it and Justice came over for ear scratches. He obliged because he never denied his dog. His fingers rubbed his soft ears and Jussie let out a groan and his eyes became narrow slits.

"I never had a dog."

"Yeah? Best thing I ever did. Had a Doberman who died of old age. My life felt empty without one, so spotted an ad about a litter of American Bulldogs. Did a bit of research on the breed, decided they were for me. I didn't pick Jussie, he picked me. And Jury wouldn't leave Judge alone, so he got suckered into takin' her home, too."

"You said Judge is your cousin."

"Yeah, but more like a brother. Not only 'cause we belong to the same brotherhood and are partners in business, but 'cause he and his sister moved in with my family when they were younger."

He could feel her eyes on him, even though he was staring straight out into the dark woods in front of the deck.

"Did their parents die?"

"Their pop did, yeah. In prison. Long story short, they both got busted. Ox was killed in the joint while doin' life."

"Life?"

"Yeah. For murder."

"Damn," she whispered. "What about their mother?"

"She got out a while ago. They want nothin' to do with her."

"Really?"

"Trixie encouraged Ox to use Jemma as a shield when the pigs stormed the house. She was only five at the time."

Reese sucked in a sharp breath.

"Judge never forgave her. He heard she went back to prison, but he didn't care enough to find out why or where."

"Sounds like great parents."

"Yeah, well..." He avoided mentioning the part where Ox had been the Sergeant at Arms for the Blood Fury MC at the time and was violent as fuck. She already wasn't thrilled about Reilly being with his brothers. He didn't want her thinking his club was the same as it was back in the day before the Fury imploded.

She took another sip of wine. "Judge runs the business with you. What does Jemma do?"

"She's an RN."

"Good for her. Just because we start out from shitty beginnings doesn't mean we need to stay there. I tried to instill that into Reilly."

Wait. What?

He guessed the wine and pot was loosening up more than the stick up her ass.

She had said she put her sister through college. She put herself through school, too. She drove a newer BMW and had a house worth a nice chunk of change. He'd been nosy and found what it was worth online. She also had her own law firm, even if it was only her and two employees. Something else he had looked up online.

In fact, he'd scoured the internet for everything he could find on Reese Porter Ackerson.

It hadn't been much. Almost as if the internet had been scrubbed of any info on her besides her firm's public website and some info on her being a graduate and alumni of Villanova University's Charles Widger School of Law.

The woman was doing well in life. Usually it was easier to do when coming from a background where opportunities were plentiful and within reach. It was much fucking harder when starting with nothing and having to scratch and crawl up the ladder to success.

For fuck's sake, while she had judged him by the way he looked, he was guilty of doing the same shit. Because of her current status, he had assumed she had come from a well-off family. But her little admission proved she hadn't.

Even though he didn't know the details yet, he understood her need for control and even her need to control Reilly's life. She most likely had protected and taken care of her younger sister, just like Judge had done with Jemma.

He now got it.

But he wanted to know more about the woman who came from "shitty beginnings" and what drove her to scrape that shit off.

He waited to see if she'd spill any details but she didn't. Instead, she nursed the wine she had a tight grip on.

By now, between the Kush and the fermented grapes, she should be mellow as fuck. Most likely ready to crash in that big bed of hers.

She sat up and moved to the edge of the lounger, facing him. Just studying him. Her mouth opened and he waited...

"I want..." She released a breath and her mouth slowly closed again.

What? What the fuck did she want? More wine? Another hit on the joint? His beard between her thighs?

He had this strange need to give her whatever she wanted, whatever she asked for. He glanced down at the blunt. Had it been tainted or something?

Since when did he want to cater to a woman?

Since never. That was when.

Maybe this woman was more intoxicating than any premium Kush.

Fuck. She was staring at his lips. Like she had the munchies and she wanted to snack on them.

Was she drunk? Did she even realize what she was doing? Because his dick sure did.

"You have really nice lips."

He grinned, though he was unsure where she was going with this.

"A nice smile, too."

His grin widened.

"It's sort of sexy."

Sort of? He'd have to disagree with that.

"Bet women just fall into bed with you when you direct it their way."

It was one of a few weapons in his arsenal, but... "You didn't."

"You swear you didn't know who I was that first night?" Her words weren't slurred, so that was a good sign she wasn't trashed. Yet.

"Had no idea. Just spotted a beautiful, confident woman struttin' across the bar. Now that's fuckin' sexy." His way with words was another weapon to charm the ladies.

"And you were confident enough to approach."

"Can't get a yes, if you ain't willin' to risk a no."

"Did you really think I'd say yes to a one-night-stand with you?"

He never said anything about a one-night-stand. Though, he had to start somewhere. And, usually, one night was enough.

When she stood, disappointment pulled at him. He wasn't ready to end the night. He'd liked the easy conversation they'd been having. He had taken it as a good sign when she had willingly joined him without a stun gun in her hand.

His eyes went wide when she didn't head toward the door but toward him instead. She didn't pause next to his chair.

Fuck. No. She. Didn't.

She fucking climbed onto it instead and straddled his lap.

Straddled his fucking lap.

Even through his jeans, he could feel her heat against his dick, which twitched in response. Deacon was pretty sure that response was a resounding, "Fuck yeah!"

As she wrapped one arm around his neck, he began to ask what the fuck she was doing, but she sealed her mouth over his, muffling his question and capturing his moan. Her fingers dug into the top of his braid, not only pulling his scalp but keeping him right where she wanted him.

Not that he was resisting.

Hell no, his momma *didn't raise no fool.*

She tasted like white wine and quality weed as he snaked one arm around her waist, pulling her into him. Her tits brushed against his chest as her tongue swept through his mouth and then disappeared. He chased it, exploring hers instead.

The grip on his hair got tighter and more painful, but she wasn't pulling him away. The fingernails from her other hand scored the back of his neck, making his balls tighten and his dick even harder.

She ground against his lap, riding his erection, her hips rocking faster and faster.

Fuck, if she didn't stop, he was going to blow his load right in his jeans. He cupped her tit over the soft material of her sweatshirt, thumbing one hard tip.

He deepened the kiss and their tongues clashed.

He was glad he was wearing his boxer briefs, otherwise with the intensity she was moving, he'd have brush burn on his dick from the denim being driven against it.

He wanted her naked, but while he knew *what* she was doing, he wasn't sure *why* she was doing it.

Her arm tightened around his neck and she arched her back as she ground against him even harder, a whimper climbing up her throat and then sliding down his.

Or that might have been him whimpering. He wasn't sure.

Nor did he care.

What he cared about was he was on that very edge of exploding after she clearly just worked herself into an orgasm by using him as a tool. A very stiff one.

When her muscles finally loosened, she pulled away and her warm breath swept over his lips in a contented sigh.

At least somebody was fucking satisfied.

However, his current dilemma was, one wrong move and he'd need to borrow her washer and dryer.

She loosened her fingers from his braid and leaned back slightly. "Just as I thought. You know how to kiss."

Uh. That wasn't just a kiss. His dick was crying for relief right now as she wore a lazy fucking smile from using him to get off.

Like a piece of meat.

Huh.

She rubbed at her cheek. "Your lips are soft, but your beard is really scratchy."

"You don't fuckin' say," he forced between gritted teeth as he willed the pressure in his groin to lessen.

She planted a bare foot onto the deck like she was about to dismount.

Oh fuck no. "That's it? You're just gonna use me like that?"

She paused. "It was just a kiss."

Tell that to his dick. "That was it, huh? Just a kiss?"

She shrugged, the sweatshirt sliding down even lower on

her shoulder, exposing the upper curve of one tit. She continued to climb off of him.

He had two options.

Fuck. He had one option. Let her go. He wasn't going to force himself on someone who didn't want him. Who only wanted to dry hump his damn dick.

That was all he was good for.

Surging from his seat, he lunged for her, snagging her arm and stopping her.

Okay, he was back to two options. He was liking the second one better than the first. Even though he wasn't so sure she'd like it. But if she didn't, she wasn't the kind of woman who wouldn't be vocal about it.

But the fuck if he was just going to be used, then tossed aside.

"No," he growled. "That ain't fuckin' it."

With a jerk to her arm, he pulled her into him, their bodies slamming together. He released her arm, but before he gave her a chance to escape, he captured her face within his hands and took her mouth.

Her hand found his chest and he expected her to shove him away, but she didn't. She fisted his T-shirt instead, firmly enough he thought she might tear it.

But it would be worth it, because she had every opportunity to shove him away, to bite his lip or tongue, instead of returning the kiss. Or voice her objection.

She didn't.

Chapter Nine

HE GROWLED into her mouth as she crushed her tits into his chest. The hand she had pinned between them, fisted in his shirt, flattened out and pressed.

She pressed harder, then began to shove.

Fuck.

He broke off the kiss and realized all the blood left in his brain had gone south and all the air had fled his lungs.

But, of fucking course, she wanted him to stop.

Fuck.

She planted both hands on his chest and shoved him backwards with such force he stumbled over the leg of the lounge and somehow managed to stick the landing with his ass on the cushioned chair instead of the hard deck.

His mouth gaped open as she yanked her sweatshirt over her head and flung it, then bent over and shoved her loose pants down to her ankles. Either she had worn no panties or she just shucked them along with her pants with impressive efficiency.

Fuck!

"Reese..."

"Shut up and get naked."

This had to be the first time in his life where he actually hesitated. Where he actually questioned whether he should or shouldn't get naked.

Seriously, someone must have slipped something into his joint besides weed.

"You have thirty seconds or I'm going inside and taking care of myself with my vibrator... Thirty... Twenty-nine... Twenty-eight..."

"That's not a whole second. You're countin' too fast!" he shouted as he scrambled back onto his feet. Then he groaned and sat back down to work on taking off his boots first.

"Move faster, then."

Of course, his boot lace would fucking get knotted at a time like this.

He tried to slow his breathing and his spinning brain so he could work methodically at loosening the knot.

"Twenty-four."

"What happened to twenty-seven?" he yelled in a panic.

"Twenty!"

"What the fuck!" The knot finally unraveled. *Thank fuck.* He shot to his feet, unbuckling his belt with shaky fingers and thumbing open the button on his jeans. He ripped the wallet out of his back pocket and tossed it at her. "Wrap!"

"Ten."

This woman did not know the length of a fucking second.

He didn't even waste another one to see if she understood his order about grabbing a wrap from his wallet. Instead, he unzipped and peeled off his jeans, fighting with his boxer briefs as his hard as fuck dick got caught in that stupid opening. He winced as he jerked it free, from not only the cotton but almost from his body, too.

That crisis was luckily averted. He settled on the lounger and extended his hand to her.

"Five."

Five? "I'm naked! Gimme the wrap."

"You aren't naked. You still have your shirt on."

Christ! He ripped his tee over his head and threw it at her, then stuck out his hand again. "Wrap."

The gorgeous woman, who looked a million times better naked than he could've ever imagined, stared at him blankly, then blinked.

He sighed. "Wallet."

She glanced at the closed wallet in her hand like she was only now noticing it. She tossed it at him.

He caught it and dug out the one and only wrap tucked inside, relieved he had a box in his duffel bag... Just in case this night ended up being one long fuckfest where they christened every surface of her house.

Twice.

He tore it open with his teeth, dropped the empty wrapper to the deck, then rolled the condom down his throbbing dick.

He sat back and waited.

She still stood there.

"Thirty seconds to get on my dick or I'm goin' inside and takin' care of this myself," he threatened.

What was good for the fucking goose—

His thought disintegrated as she climbed onto the lounger just like she had his chair a little bit ago. But this time would be more memorable since they were both naked.

And, bonus, he'd get to come, too.

"What if he's out there watching?" she whispered.

"*Now* you're worried about that? You were just standin' on your deck totally fuckin' naked."

"I know, but..." She chewed on her bottom lip.

Oh no. Fuck no. She was not leaving him hanging just

because she suddenly became aware of where they were. "If he's out there, he'll probably be fuckin' jealous."

She slapped his chest lightly. "That's not funny."

No, what wasn't funny was his dick throbbing, wrapped and ready for action.

"Jussie will keep watch. Right, boy?"

Justice whined in agreement and wagged his tail.

"See? Nobody's gettin' past him."

"Apparently, pot makes me horny," she whispered, but still not making a move to climb onto his dick.

His lips quirked. "Noted. But I got a good solution to help with that."

She smiled. "What?"

Was she playing coy? "Could tell you, but would rather show you."

"Show me," she whispered.

"Just wanna make you aware of what's gonna happen." Especially since she basically drank a whole bottle of wine. By herself.

"I'm almost thirty-five years old. I think I know what's going to happen. I'm going to fuck you."

He lifted one eyebrow. *Okay, then.* The answer was supposed to be that he was going to fuck her. But he liked that little change in play. He could get on board with it if she ever got on board him.

"I want to touch your nipples."

He wanted that, too. He grabbed her hands and slapped one over each nipple. "There you go. You don't need to ask, just take the initiative."

Her fingertips brushed over his barbells, and even though it wasn't much, it was enough for him to bite back a groan.

"Why did you get them pierced?"

"So women like you would ask to touch them."

"Really?"

That wasn't quite the reason but it would work for the moment.

"Did it hurt?"

"Reese..." *Christ*, she was going to kill him before he even got a chance to fuck her.

She twisted one and his whole body instantly went electric.

"Fuck," he breathed.

"That's what I'm supposed to do with them, right? I've never been with anyone with pierced... anything."

"You do whatever you wanna do with them. Ain't gonna stop you." Hell no, he wasn't.

"I want to lick them."

Before he could respond, she dove for him, knocked him back into the lounger and planted her lips around one of his nipples. She sucked it as deep as she could get it into her mouth, then flicked the tip with her tongue.

As much as he wanted that, he was already ready to blow and if he filled that fucking wrap up before he got to fuck her, he would be pissed.

"You're supposed to be on my dick when you do that," he ground out, the muscles in his jaw popping.

She didn't let up on the torture of his nipple. She forced her hand between them, grabbed his dick, held it and lifted herself up.

Oh fuck.

"Oh fuck," he grunted as she tucked him between her warm, wet, plump lips and shimmied her way down his length. "*Ooooh fuuuuck.*"

She released his nipple and he dug his fingers into her long hair, wanting to pull her face to his so he could take her mouth, but she went for his other nipple. He kept his hand wrapped in her hair as she planted one palm solidly on his chest and used it for leverage, along with her feet planted on the deck, to rise and fall on his dick.

She wasn't kidding when she said she was going to fuck him.

He only wished they were somewhere where there was more light so he could see her clearly. He wanted to see every inch of her.

Next time.

He would explore every fucking crack and crevice. He'd taste, lick, suck, bite every bit of her. He'd make her toes curl, make her beg. Give her the best orgasm she ever had.

But for now, they were cramped on a deck lounge chair. He was just relieved it hadn't given out yet with their combined weight as her slick heat squeezed him tight. She wasn't riding him like a bucking bronco, but more like a pleasure horse out for a trail ride. Her pace smooth and steady.

But it was her mouth that kept pulling his attention away from that warm pussy engulfing his dick.

Because what she was doing with her mouth was going to be his downfall. It didn't help that, while she sucked, licked and nibbled on one nipple, she twisted the other one with her fingers.

Fuck yeah. This was why he'd pierced his fucking nipples. This right here.

"Reese," he groaned, keeping one hand firmly in her hair and, with the other, finding one of her rock-hard nipples, thumbing the tip before pinching it firmly. That got her increasing her pace, so he twisted it to the point where he knew it had to be uncomfortable.

And that had her slamming down on him and grinding.

Well, that fucking backfired.

"You close?" he forced up his tight throat. Because, *fuck,* he was close. He was closer than close. He was teetering...

Dangerously.

She began to rock back and forth, grinding her clit

against him. She groaned against his nipple, making the metal barbell vibrate.

Holy fuck.

She released his nipple, lifted her head and shouted, "I'm going to come," so loudly it made Justice tear across the deck, barking. She grabbed his face and took his mouth, smothering his own grunt as she drove down on him harder and faster, making the chair creak scarily.

If the chair collapsed...

Fuck the chair. The thick cushion would soften the fall.

"Oh, yes. I'm coming," she groaned, making him groan as she circled her hips and drove her clit harder into him.

She whimpered. He whimpered. And the pressure in his lower body built to the point of no return.

He swore he saw stars, other than the ones in the sky above them, when he exploded at the same time she did. With a grunt, he finally released all the cum he'd been desperate to hold back, relieving that pressure.

She collapsed onto his chest, her pussy still squeezing him tightly as his dick pulsed, emptying his balls until there was nothing left.

He gripped her hips, holding her there, keeping her connected, and dropped his head back to the cushion to stare up at the night sky, trying to catch his breath and slow his racing heart.

This was not how he pictured having sex with her for the first time.

Not like this.

He figured she'd want it to be more dignified.

He smiled.

She shifted her hips until he slipped from her. Way too soon. With a sigh, she swiped her hair out of her face and sat up.

She stared down at him for a couple heartbeats, then moved to get off him.

"Hey—" He wasn't ready for this to be over yet.

"Thank you."

Thank you? Was she shitting him?

"I have to go now."

"You live here," he reminded her.

"To bed," she mumbled, standing naked next to the lounge chair, staring at the French doors that led into the house.

"Reese—"

"Thank you," she repeated.

What the fuck?

"Reese..." He carefully removed the wrap and when he looked up, she was already heading inside.

The door softly clicked closed. And he hoped to fuck she didn't lock it on him.

He turned, still holding the full wrap. Through the window, he watched her walk naked across her great room, go into her room and close the door.

What the fuck just happened?

Justice came trotting up, his tail straight up and a fucking grin on his face.

"It's just me and you, dude. Guess she don't wanna cuddle."

———

SHE HADN'T SLEPT that good in...

Ages. She wasn't even sure when she'd last slept like she was buried six feet under.

She also didn't remember setting her alarm for four a.m. But, surprisingly, she had set her alarm for that insanely early hour. And now, dressed and ready for the day, it was five.

Apparently, her buzzed-self decided it was a good idea to sneak out of the house early and avoid a discussion of what happened on the deck with the person it happened with.

Completely sober-self agreed that was a great idea. It was one way to avoid any awkwardness.

She hesitated in the kitchen, desperately wanting a strong dose of coffee, but afraid the smell of fresh brewed caffeinated bliss might drift upstairs and wake Deacon. Then her plans of escaping early would all be for nothing. She'd stop at the local donut shop on her way into the office for a caffeine fix and maybe a breakfast sandwich.

She chewed on her bottom lip when she spotted the empty wine bottle on the counter. A reminder of what happened.

Well, one besides the vivid memory she'd replayed in her mind as she showered.

She spotted the clothes she'd abandoned on the deck last night draped over the arm of her leather sectional sofa. His black leather boots were lined up on the floor next to her clothes.

She closed her eyes and sharply inhaled to fight another replay of what they did in the lounge chair last night. That inhale reminded her of how she had smoked pot last night. Crazy.

But even crazier, she had actually stripped naked on her deck and told him to do the same.

Weirdly enough, it was the first time she'd actually relaxed since before the whole mess began with Reilly and Billy.

She now knew it took more than a glass of wine—or two *extra*-large glasses—to unwind.

It also took the company of a sexy biker/bounty hunter, who was also probably a player, along with a few hits off his joint.

Afterward, she had done the walk of shame across her great room and into her bedroom, flopped face first on her bed and couldn't remember anything after that. But apparently sometime in the night, she'd gotten up to use the master bathroom, cleaned up, and set the alarm for that ungodly hour.

Normally, she'd be dragging at four in the morning. But this morning? She was, for the most part, bright-eyed and bushy-tailed.

Hmm.

She eyed up his truck key fob, which was on the counter near the door where she left it last night. She needed to grab it and get out while the getting was good.

Yes, that's what she needed to do. Escape before being caught.

Yesterday morning was awkward as it was, this morning would be worse.

Way worse.

But instead of moving toward the door and snagging her key to freedom, she turned and headed toward the stairs leading up to the loft and spare bedrooms. She didn't tell her feet to move in that direction, they just did.

With every step up those stairs, she heard *stop, turn around, leave,* on repeat in her head.

Don't do this, Reese. It's stupid.

Just like last night.

Last night was a mistake only made once. It could easily be forgotten. She could chalk it up to the wine she drank and the unknown effect the weed would have on her. She could apologize to him and ask he forget everything that happened.

She rolled her eyes at her own pipe dream.

He wasn't going to forget. Hell no. He would hold it over her.

He thought he was irresistible.

Unfortunately, she'd proved him right.

And look at her now, creeping up the steps like Creepy McCreeper.

For what?

Simply to check to make sure he was okay since he was a guest in her house.

That was all.

Like a good host should.

She hit the loft at the top of the staircase and told herself it wasn't too late to turn around. And when her hand was on the doorknob, she told herself this was wrong.

Wrong.

She turned the knob quietly and pushed the door open just enough to peek in.

So wrong...

Sooooo so...

Oh.

Damn, whispered through her mind.

Deacon Edwards, skip tracer, bail bondsman, bounty hunter and creator of orgasms, was sprawled out over the bed on his belly.

The comforter was in a pile on the floor in the corner of the room. The top sheet was pushed down to the bottom of the bed in a rumpled mess. And he had one arm curled over a sleeping white and brindle American Bulldog.

Had she secretly been hoping he'd slept naked?

No.

Noooo.

Even so, her disappointment was short-lived as the man only wore a pair of boxer briefs that hugged his ass perfectly. An ass that was pure perfection encased in black cotton.

His lightly furred thighs...

Heat swirled through her and she groaned...

About her behavior the night before. Not because of the sexy man practically naked in her bed.

His bed.

345

The spare bed.

Justice lifted his head and whined softly.

Shit!

She made a *let's-keep-this-between-us* face at the dog and pressed a finger to her lips.

It was a dog! Would he understand that expression and hand signal?

Justice flopped his head back down with a groan.

Wait. Maybe he could.

She went back to her inspection.

Deacon's dark blond hair was unbraided, and the loose, wavy mess covered his face. She had an urge to wake him up, if only to see what he looked like with it down.

Would he look better? Worse?

She did dig the Viking look. It fit him.

She grimaced at her own thought while studying the club's colors inked into his back.

She didn't know much about MCs. Only what she'd seen in the news, or on TV shows and movies. She knew they could be a rough bunch who caused trouble. And the ones she'd seen in photos of Sturgis, or Myrtle Beach Bike Week, or in articles about the Hells Angels, Pagans or Mongols, didn't look anything like Deacon.

Maybe he was just an oddity amongst a bunch of beer-bellied, bushy-bearded bikers. He did have a business with a reputation to maintain, after all.

And she hadn't seen him wear one of those leather jackets or denim vests she'd seen the bikers, who belonged to clubs, wear before. Maybe his club was more of a gentlemen's club.

Not the stripper kind, but the sitting around playing poker, shooting the shit and smoking a stogie kind. Just substitute a joint for the cigar.

Okay, now she was living in some sort of fantasyland.

Had one quickie on the deck knocked the bottom out of her common sense?

I'm never doing that again.

She bit back another groan.

Who the hell was she kidding?

She was doing that—*him*—again.

She carefully closed the door before she decided to join him in that bed.

Chapter Ten

AFTER THE SECOND morning of her sneaking out early and coming home late...

Of her walking through the door, pouring herself a normal-sized glass of wine, then taking a couple tokes off his joint...

Of him scrambling to remove his boots and clothes when she stripped naked right on the deck, before riding his dick to orgasm and then heading inside right afterward to her room and shutting him out...

After all that, on Friday morning he made a plan.

On Friday night he left a glass of wine waiting for her by the front door.

Left his boots in the house.

Sat in the dark on the lounger, instead of the chair where he normally sat.

Wore only his boxer briefs.

On the table next to him was a wrap on standby.

Because, *fuck yeah*, his momma *didn't raise no fool*.

His dick already had a half chub because it was anticipating the same pattern as the previous nights.

No deep conversation. *Hell*, no conversation at all.

They'd sit in companionable silence, staring out into the dark while she finished her glass of wine, and took a few tokes off his joint. Then she drove him out of his mind as she emptied his balls before going inside to bed. Alone.

Wine. Pot. Dick. Desertion.

In that exact order.

Normally, he wouldn't complain about the easy lay. Until he realized the easy lay was him.

She was using him to fall asleep. Like he was a human form of Ambien.

But since it was Friday night, he assumed she didn't have to get up early the next morning. He wanted to be more than a dick she rode off into sweet dreams.

He actually wanted to have more than sex with her.

He wanted...

Conversation.

Holy fuck.

That can't be right.

He glanced at the freshly rolled, unlit joint in the makeshift ashtray. He needed to get a new stash of Kush. Or stop smoking dope all together.

Because that had to be the reason for that disturbing realization.

His half chub went to a full-blown erection in the blink of an eye, or more like the growl of his Ford's engine, as she smashed the accelerator to power it up the mountain. The high beams cut through the woods and slivers of light bounced off him and the windows behind him as his truck climbed its way to the top.

He strained his ears to listen for the slam of the driver's side door and, in the quiet of the night, the jingle of keys as she made it through the side door into the kitchen.

His blood began to surge, but he refused to turn around and watch her through the window. Instead, he imagined in his mind what she was doing.

Which was, taking way too long for his liking. She needed to hurry the fuck up.

Didn't she know how long he'd been waiting?

What if she just went to her room and went to sleep? Left him out there waiting with an erection and a plan?

Fuck no.

He smothered his grin when—*finally*—one of the French doors opened and she stepped out onto the deck, the red wine he'd poured for her in her hand and her gaze landing on him.

Her hair was down around her shoulders and her feet bare, but she still wore her dress pants. Her top wasn't like the blouses she normally wore when coming out to join him.

It was something a woman would wear underneath. With lace along the upper curves of her tits, where it would hide her cleavage. It was white and hugged those assets perfectly. She must have shucked whatever she had worn over it since he couldn't imagine her doing her "lawyering" wearing something like that.

Plus, even though she wore a bra under it, like his truck, her high beams were on.

He licked his lips, hoping tonight he'd get to wrap them around her nipples instead of the opposite. While he liked when she gave his nipples attention, it was time to turn the tables.

His preference would be to do it inside. In his bed. Or hers. He didn't care. Or, *hell*, on the plush carpet in front of the fireplace. Somewhere he wouldn't worry about the deck chair giving out on them and causing injury. Like him breaking his dick when they landed hard. He'd seen pictures on the internet of dicks after being broken and it caused nightmares.

He grimaced.

"Are you okay?"

He would be if his dick stayed in one piece and he got

to be on top tonight. "Yeah. You?" She hadn't sat down yet. So now he was starting to worry his plan might be screwed.

She raised the glass. "Thanks for the wine."

"That wasn't an answer to my question."

"Why are you sitting out here in your underwear?"

He brushed his palm over his erection. "Just tryin' to save time. But that still wasn't an answer to my question. You tryin' to avoid it?"

"I heard from the body shop today. My car won't be done for another three or four weeks. I can get a rental."

Once again, not an answer to his question. The woman was normally direct, so it made the little hairs on the back of his neck stand. "You got my truck."

"You won't be here for that long."

"I'll drop you off at a rental place when I leave." Once he caught that Warren bastard.

She nodded and went to the deck railing, perching her glass on the flat top. She stared out into the dark.

He was beginning to unfold himself from the lounge chair, to go to her, when she spun and faced him.

"Deke..."

Oh Christ, here it comes.

He plopped back down as if she'd shoved him. The way she said his name made him think he wasn't getting ridden tonight.

"Listen," she started.

He mentally groaned.

"I need to make a couple things clear first..."

First? That gave him some hope.

"I don't have time for anything more than sex right now. And sometimes not even that. Sex can get complicated and my life is complicated enough without some man trying to be my... hero."

Hero? Who the fuck was she talking about?

"I don't need a hero," she continued. "I can take care of problems myself."

"What problems? Warren?" No, she couldn't. Where was this coming from?

But if he wanted to get laid tonight, he couldn't argue that point with her. He'd end up the loser. She'd end up in her room with her vibrator and he with his fist.

"What you did was sweet..."

It wasn't meant to be sweet, just a time saver. But okay...

"And I appreciate it. But..."

That fucking *but*. Time to butt in. "But nothin', was just tryin' to save time and let you know I was out here willin' and able. That's it." That wasn't it, but it would have to be it.

Goddamn it.

"Listen," he started, because he couldn't just leave it alone. Fuck no, he had to risk the chance of getting her naked, like a dumb fuck. "When's the last time you let a man in?"

Even in the dark, he could see her brow drop low. "What do you mean? Like in my vagina?"

Fuck yeah, he wanted to know that, too, but... "I mean let a man *in*. Where you dropped your goddamn walls and just enjoy spendin' time with a fuckin' man. Naked or not."

Her mouth opened for a few seconds, then she lifted her glass and took a long sip of wine.

Well, there was his answer.

He got to his feet, grabbed the wine glass she was guzzling from and set it on the nearby deck rail. "When's the last time you let *anyone* in?"

"How about you? Do you normally talk about your feelings with your 'brothers?'"

"Ain't talkin' about me. Talkin' about you."

"So, it's okay for a man to keep shit buried, but not a woman."

"Women normally let their shit be known and do it loudly."

"Not all," she whispered.

"What's more perfect than to free yourself of any clingin' shit than to share it with someone who won't fuckin' judge you and you'll never see again?"

"What? You're volunteering?"

"Well, yeah." Of course, he wanted to know more about her than what he could find out online. In truth, he wanted to know everything about her.

But then, that didn't fall under the category of "just sex." Which was where she wanted to stay and where he normally did, too.

"Who are you? Oprah?"

"Do I look like fuckin' Oprah?"

At least that made her lips curl slightly at the corners before she flattened them out.

"When's the last time you let a man in?" he asked again.

It took her a few heartbeats, but she finally admitted, "My ex-husband long before he was an ex."

"You haven't had sex since your ex?"

Her chin jerked back. "I didn't say that. Sex isn't the same as sharing... *stuff* with someone. Sharing is more intimate than sex."

He recycled her words in his head as he stared at the woman in front of him. Was she secretly a man? No, he'd done a complete inspection, she was definitely not hiding anything. She was a woman and what woman didn't overshare? He wasn't sure he'd met one yet.

Until Reese.

"Some men don't want a strong, independent woman. They feel threatened."

"And some men do," he countered. "For some, it's a fuckin' turn on."

"Yes, well. Maybe a turn on for one night, but they don't want to deal with someone like that long term."

"What the fuck are you talkin' about?" He couldn't imagine being with someone long term who was a doormat, who didn't have a fire inside and a spine of steel. Who gave as good as she got. Who wouldn't fall to pieces at a little heated argument.

"I'm talking about people with penises. Like you."

"You don't think a man wants a woman who's scraped herself from the bottom of a shit pile, clawed her way up to be a strong, independent woman—a fuckin' lawyer, no less —and owns her own fuckin' home and law firm? Not sure where you're meetin' these fuckin' men."

"I was married to one."

His jaw shifted.

She sighed. "Let's have sex."

What?

His brain almost exploded when he answered, "No."

"You don't want to have sex? You're wearing only your underwear and when I came out, it was hard to miss the steel pipe inside them. Plus, you have a condom sitting on the table. Did I read the room wrong?"

He grabbed her arm and tugged her over to the seat next to the lounge chair. "Sit."

She pursed her lips, stared at him for a second, then sat with another drawn-out sigh.

"And no, you didn't read anythin' fuckin' wrong. I wanna fuck you. That was the plan. Did you hear how I said that? *I* wanna fuck *you* tonight. Been lookin' forward to it all goddamn day."

"You have?"

"Don't fuckin' act surprised. You ain't foolin' anyone."

She covered her mouth with her hand, probably hiding some semblance of a smile. He wanted to cover her mouth with his instead. But first, they needed to have a little discussion.

Why he should care about a woman he was boning being so closed off, he had no fucking clue. But it was bugging the shit out of him.

She seemed to loosen up more after taking a couple hits off his nightly joint, so he grabbed it off the table, balanced the aluminum foil ashtray on the lounge chair's armrest, tucked the fatty between his lips and lit it.

He took two good puffs from it to make sure it was burning evenly, then offered it to her. For a second, he thought she would turn it down, but then her hand shot out and snagged it. Unlike the first night, she didn't cough when she sucked the smoke deep within her lungs.

"You know," she said as the smoke rolled from between those lips he wished were around a fatty of a different kind. "Edibles won't screw up your lungs like smoke."

"No shit. But right now, in Pennsylvania, you need a medical reason to buy that shit."

She took another long drag and handed it back to him. "You don't smoke it for a medical reason?"

"Got a low tolerance for assholes and bullshit, that's my medical reason. So, don't bullshit me," he warned. "However, that excuse won't get me a card."

"Then I expect the same courtesy from you. My tolerance for assholes and bullshit is at a zero level."

"Probably deal with a lot of them with what you do."

She sat back and accepted the joint again. "Yes, I do. That's why I don't need it in my personal life."

"And your sister drug it right back into your life," he concluded.

"With a vengeance."

"So, your ex was an asshole," he also determined.

"Billy Warren might be the king of assholes, but Allen ended up with his very own crown."

He wanted to lean his chin on interlaced fingers and encourage her with a "go on." But instead he took another toke after she passed the joint back to him, then asked, "Had enough?"

"You have no idea."

"The joint," he clarified.

She waved a hand. "Yes. Thank you."

"Tell me about him." He pinched out the end, and put it and the ashtray aside on the table. He wanted a semi-clear head when she began to spill all her secrets.

Okay, maybe not all would be revealed tonight. He hoped she'd start with the ex first. He'd work on the rest, like her "shitty beginnings," at another time.

He had to draw the info he was curious about from her carefully or she might just shut down and shut him out. And though they hadn't spoken much in the last few days, she had gotten more comfortable with him in the time they spent together before they'd have sex and she'd disappear.

He really liked the fact she didn't run her mouth for no good reason. Some women just liked to fill the silence or hear themselves speak. When she had something to say, she said it and then shut up.

Unless he disagreed with what she said, *then* she had a lot more to say.

"I met Allen during college. We both attended Villanova. You know why I went, but he wanted to teach at the college level in environmental science. Once he finished his masters, he got an offer from Mansfield University to teach while he worked on his PhD."

Christ. Deacon barely graduated high school. Not because he was stupid but because he just didn't give a shit about school.

Or college. Or working a nine-to-five desk job.

He probably would've ended up working some minimum wage job if Judge hadn't decided to open his own bail bonds business a few years after working for one in Williamsport. His cousin learned the business inside and out, then, with the scratch Deacon's father left them in a life insurance policy, they started Justice Bail Bonds.

His father didn't leave them a lot of dough but it was enough for them to get their licenses, pay for a couple months' rent on their office lease and get a few other necessary things squared away so they could start out strong.

They hit the ground running and never looked back. Best decision ever. Besides getting Jury and Justice.

"So that's how you ended up in Mansfield."

"Yes. He began teaching while I opened my office, hoping I could attract clients. Luckily, this area isn't saturated with civil law attorneys, so it wasn't hard to grow my clientele."

"And you got hitched."

"Yes, even though I wasn't in any rush to get married. I wanted to concentrate on my career, building my business, and putting away cash once I paid off my school loans. He kept bugging and eventually I relented since I figured we were already headed on the path to marriage. So, he was right, why wait? Anyway, my business exploded."

"'Cause you kick ass in the courtroom, right?"

She shot him a grin. "I do, but like I told you previously, I'm even better at arbitration. And settling before having to go to trial saves my clients money. It's a win-win for both of us."

"You're probably like a pit bull when you fight for your clients."

"I can be, if necessary."

He liked the idea of her being ferocious and not some spineless woman. It turned him the fuck on.

"Okay, so, he's teachin', you're arguin'. Then what?" He wanted her to keep going and could see the pot and wine combo was doing their job of loosening her up.

"Let's just say I began to make a lot more money than him rather quickly. Working at a college, he gets a set salary. Me? The more I work, the more I make."

"The reason you come home late."

"I've been trying to come home at a more reasonable hour, so I could enjoy the house I worked hard for and do something other than work all the time. At least until this bullshit went down with Billy."

"Fucker fucked it up for you. You buy this house with hubby?" He wanted to hear more about the ex and not Warren.

"Hell no. We were living in an apartment right off campus and I hated it. I also hated throwing money away in rent every month, which he was fine with it. One of my clients is a real estate broker and happened to mention an open house she was holding. She gushed about the home and location, and what a good deal it was. So, I went and, of course, fell in love with this place immediately. When I told Allen about it, he said it was too much and we needed to wait."

"And, unlike your marriage, you didn't want to wait."

She gave him a look which clearly said *hell no.*

The more he heard the more he liked. This woman was the fucking bomb. "So, you bought it." Of course she did. Because she went after what she wanted. Like she had with him. She wanted his dick, she took it. She wasn't playing.

No games, no bullshit.

"Yes. That bothered him. I made the down payment, paid the closing costs and all the mortgage payments. All he had to do was show up to the damn closing and sign his damn name."

"Because you were married by then and a wife can't do shit without her husband." That had to piss her off and really make her regret saying *I do.*

"Yes. I should've drawn up a prenup. I didn't. It didn't

even cross my mind before we got married. We didn't own shit at the time. We were renting and we both had school loans..."

"And by the time you got this house, you were makin' more than him." He kept talking to keep her talking. It was like dangling the apple in front of the donkey... Wait. The carrot in front of the turtle...

Whatever.

"Yes."

"Your career was blowin' up." *Fuck yeah*, because she was a badass. This woman could probably do anything she put her mind to. And, while it was kind of weird, it made him hard as fuck.

"Yes, in a good way. I thought we wanted the same things. We talked about it long before we were married. And not just in passing, but in deep conversations about what we wanted out of life and what we saw for our future. Our careers would come first before beginning a family."

"Turned out he wanted kids and you didn't." That didn't surprise him with her. She seemed driven to be successful. Conquer the world first, then think about settling down later.

"I wanted kids but not right away. He was on board with waiting. Or so I thought. I guess he lied."

Fuck. "Jealous of your success."

"Intimidated, more like it. For whatever reason. His mother had always been a housewife and his father," she deepened her voice to sound like a man's, *"brought home the bacon.* That old misogynistic bullshit. So, maybe what thought he wanted, once he had it, he didn't. He realized he was wrong. He actually wanted what he grew up with. He wanted to be *the man* of the house. The provider. He wanted for me to rely on him. It's all bullshit. I never wanted that and was clear about it from the very beginning."

Okay, he was beginning to worry that this discussion was

getting her tense again. Maybe he should bail on this whole line of conversation.

He jumped up, grabbed her abandoned wine glass and gave it to her. She took a couple sips, then blew out a long breath.

"So, the asshole realized he couldn't handle bein' with a woman who kicked ass and he left." Before Deacon bailed from this story and worked on getting her loosened up again —preferably, with his dick inside her—he was curious about who left who.

"No."

"You kicked his ass out." He fought his grin at her doing so.

"Of course."

He shook his head. *Of course?* Would he have to draw the reason out of her? *For fuck's sake.*

"Because I came home to find him fucking one of his students in *my* bed, in *my* house. I got the perfect view of her on her hands and knees as he was pumping into her. I surprised him mid-stroke."

Oh fuck! "Don't they frown upon a teacher doin' one of his students?"

"You'd think so. But wait! There's more!"

Did he fall into some infomercial?

"Guess what?"

Apparently, he wasn't supposed to guess when she yelled, "He was breeding her like the dog he is because I found out afterward she was pregnant! PREG-NANT!"

Justice jumped up from where he had been crashed on the deck and ran to the railing, with his ears perked, his tail up and his head on a swivel, searching for a threat. Jussie yawned after a few seconds when he realized it was a false alarm.

"And you know what?" she shouted, now all worked up. "That motherfucker wanted *my* house for his side piece to play housewife in and raise his fucking child! My fucking house!" The last part came out in a snarl.

Deacon was beginning to believe maybe having this type of conversation after a long day at work wasn't the best idea for Reese. Even with wine and weed.

But he needed the rest of the story. "Is he still in Mansfield?"

"Of course. His sweet young thing dropped out of college to avoid any issues with him being a member of the faculty and impregnating a not even twenty-one-year-old student."

Damn. He could practically hear her teeth snapping like a pissed-off honey badger.

"You see him?"

"Him. Her. Their spawn. This town isn't big enough to avoid them."

"And you haven't stun gunned his ass?"

"What's the point? His current situation isn't as happy as he'd like me to believe. He stepped in shit and now realizes it was cement. He's unable to scrape it off easily, to fix his mistake. I take satisfaction with how miserable he looks."

She smiled. It wasn't a nice, sweet smile. It was one that, if directed at him, would make his balls retreat into his body.

"He's now supporting two children. His child bride and his spawn. On his income." She laughed. "I shouldn't laugh, but for me? It's karma."

"You still love him?"

Once that question escaped, he wasn't so sure he wanted the answer.

Chapter Eleven

Do you still love him?

Why would Deacon ask that? Why would he even care? Unless he was wondering if she was foolish enough to still love a man who screwed her over and then tried to steal her house from under her in the divorce. Not only that, he was having unprotected sex with someone else while he was having unprotected sex with Reese.

She downed the remaining wine and stared at the glass with a little bit of regret.

No, she didn't love him anymore, but like her empty wine glass, she regretted falling for someone who wasn't who she thought. Who lied to her about what he wanted for his future. Who lied to her about loving her. Because if he had, why would he go elsewhere? And, worse, try to steal what was hers?

Yes, maybe she'd been foolish enough to believe his lies, but not enough to still love him. She didn't even like him anymore.

"Reese."

Deacon saying her name softly pulled her out of her thoughts.

"I did until the very moment I walked in on him with her. Then everything inside me died, including my love for him. I've experienced betrayal before but not like that. He had told me he loved me before walking out the door to go to work. After having sex that morning, mind you. That same damn morning."

Deacon shifted in the lounge chair and rose to his feet, only wearing those damn boxer briefs. She had come home tonight to find a glass of wine, him and a condom waiting.

It was more romantic than anything Allen had done in those last couple of years. She should've known he was cheating. She should've picked up on the signs. But she'd been so focused on her career, instead.

Maybe it was her fault he cheated. Maybe she hadn't given him what he needed, which was her time and attention.

Something unfamiliar burned her eyes.

Tears? Couldn't be.

She hadn't even cried when she caught her husband in bed with another woman.

Not when she realized he no longer wanted the same things as her.

Not when she found out another woman was carrying her husband's baby.

Not even when he tried to take half of her house.

Hell no. She had gotten angry.

She wasn't going to wallow in self-pity. She had regrouped, spanked him in the divorce and got right back on her life's path before the ink was even dry on the divorce papers.

But in all that time, she never considered her failed marriage might have been because of her. Not once. Until now.

She stared up at Deacon as he came to stand in front of her. "Maybe it was my fault. Maybe I drove him away."

"He tell you that?"

"After I caught him, he said he didn't want to wait to start a family. And he decided he wanted something different for his life than what he originally wanted."

"Then it wasn't your fault."

"But I didn't even try to compromise. The person who gets paid to mediate didn't even try."

"Would you've changed your path for him?"

She tilted her head and thought about it. "I had a goal and I was working toward that. So, no, I wouldn't have, even before finding out he was cheating."

"He changed. You didn't. You knew what you wanted. He didn't. He just decided he wasn't gonna tell you things changed. That's a dick move." Deacon held out his hand to her.

She stared at it for a couple seconds, then put hers in his. He engulfed his large hand around hers and pulled her to her feet until they were eye to eye. Almost. He was taller than her without her heels on.

"Know what I say?" he murmured, dragging his thumb over her bottom lip.

"What?" she asked softly.

"Fuck that asshole. He fucked up a good thing. Know what else?" He dropped his head a little lower so the warmth of his breath kissed her lips when he talked.

"What?"

"If I ever see him, I'm gonna thank him."

"For what?"

"For being a stupid ass and lettin' you go. 'Cause if he hadn't, I wouldn't be gettin' ready to fuck you on your livin' room floor."

"On the floor? Why on the floor?" What was wrong with the lounge chair? Having sex with him in the house would feel like they were taking a step toward...

Toward she didn't know what and wasn't sure she wanted to find out.

"Gonna show you why," he growled, which made her nipples instantly harden and her pussy pulse.

"I'm not sure—"

He swallowed her complaint when he crushed his mouth to hers, shoving his fingers into her hair and tilting her face up even higher. The seal tightened between their lips and he swept his tongue along hers.

How did he get to be such a great kisser? Since when did merely a kiss make everything in and on her quiver?

Since when did the rough scrape of wiry facial hair turn her on?

Since when did tattoos stop making her think twice about a man?

She groaned.

He probably thought she was groaning from the kiss, while, in actuality, it was from her own thoughts. From the idea of getting involved with a man who wasn't on the same path as her. Not even close.

She couldn't afford to do that again.

No. They were just having sex. That was all.

A little detour in the bumpy road of life.

She reminded herself she should be allowed to have moments which didn't involve growing her business or being successful. She should be allowed to have moments where she could just let her hair down and forget about being a responsible adult.

And that was what these moments with Deacon were. Nothing more.

Right?

They were sexually attracted to each other and the only reason this was even happening. A sort of friends with bene-fits type of thing, except without the friends part. Forced roommates, more like it.

Deacon wasn't the kind of man who would push for more, anyway. He was a player who bounced from woman to woman. Because of that, she wouldn't have to worry about him wanting more.

So, yes, she could allow herself what they had without feeling guilty or feeling pressured for anything more.

As their tongues tangled, her nipples began to ache for his attention and a warmth spread through her belly. A trickle of arousal slipped from her and dampened her panties.

Yes, that was how turned on he made her with simply a kiss.

Okay, maybe it wasn't a simple kiss, they were sort of eating each other's faces. She grinned against his mouth, but that grin slipped away as he kissed her harder and deeper, at the same time walking her backwards. Slowly. Carefully.

To the French doors behind her.

To the floor where he stated he'd fuck her. *He'd* fuck *her*.

The last few nights she'd been on top, been in the driver's seat. Tonight, he hinted he wanted to switch that around.

She didn't have a problem with it. In fact, tonight she could use that. Simply letting the control slip from her hands, letting her enjoy those moments she should allow herself.

Of simply letting go.

Two adults, with no agenda, getting naked and sharing an orgasm or two.

His hand slipped from her hair at the same time her back pressed against the door. When it opened, he used his chest to nudge her inside. With impressive skill, he managed to get them both, along with Justice, through the door and secure it behind them without breaking the kiss.

With a hand on her hip and the other still weaved into her hair, he turned and pulled her with him as he walked backward toward the plush throw rug that sat in front of the fireplace. It was too warm for a fire tonight, so the only light in the room came from the kitchen.

When they stood at the edge, he released her lips, pressed his forehead against hers and panted for a few heartbeats. Her breathing was just as ragged and every part of her begged for his touch.

He pulled his head away. "Am I gettin' you naked or are you?"

"You, but slowly," she whispered. Him undressing her would be foreplay. It might even take her right to that edge where it wouldn't take much for her to have her first orgasm.

With a nod, he backed up, but only to give himself enough space to yank her lacy camisole out of her slacks and over her head. She didn't see where he tossed it because, for some reason, she had a hard time breaking their connected gaze.

When he reached for her slim leather belt, she shuddered as his fingers worked to unbuckle it. Once loose, he didn't pull it free, but instead went directly to the button and zipper to unfasten them.

Then he was shoving her pants down until they were free enough to fall to her ankles on their own. She stepped out of them and stood in only her matching black panties and bra.

Now they were both in their underwear, but they still wore too much.

As he reached for the waistband of his boxer briefs, she stepped forward and stopped him. "Let me."

He said nothing, only gave a slight nod. With his back to the sole source of light, she couldn't see his eyes clearly.

She took another step closer and cupped his face, leaning in to brush her lips over his, but as he opened his mouth to deepen the kiss, she moved downward. Her tongue followed her hands as she traced them over his throat, his bouncing Adam's apple, the tight corded muscles in his neck.

Her lips brushed, her tongue skimmed, her kisses peppered his heated skin from the hollow of his neck through the valley between his pecs, down the thin line of dark hair over his belly. As she slowly went to her knees, her fingers hooked the waistband of his snug boxer briefs along the way, dragging them down his thighs and letting them drop to the floor at his feet.

"Reese," came out strained. His muscles were tight, his fingers curling and uncurling against his outer thighs. Even so, he didn't touch her and he didn't say anything other than her name.

Her name had been enough for her to know the effect she was having on him.

He wanted to fuck her tonight and she wanted that, too, but she decided to start somewhere else first.

Her hands skimmed from his knees up his solid thighs, the light hair tickling her palms. Cupping his balls in one hand, she circled his length with the other. His hips twitched at the contact but he didn't move otherwise. His feet remained where he had planted them apart.

From on her knees, she peered up his body and met his gaze. His head had dropped forward and his skilled lips were slightly parted.

She could hear every shallow inhale and exhale he took. And when her lips surrounded his length, she synchronized the rhythm of her mouth to the rhythm of his breath.

"Reese," escaped him again, but this time on a groan, when she drew on his shaft as deeply as she could. His salty precum coated her tongue when she swirled it around the crown. She dragged it over the tip and slid it down the underside, along the thick pulsing ridge, and back up before swallowing his length again.

"Fuck," he breathed, his hands no longer pinned to his

sides, but holding on to the top of her head. Every time she swallowed him deep, his hips shifted forward just the tiniest bit and his fingertips twitched in her hair.

Her mouth began to water as he thrust a little harder. Not enough to make her gag, but close. She kept a fist around the root to keep him from driving too deeply, but let him set the pace.

With one hand, he fisted her hair into a ponytail, tugging it away from her face hard enough to pull at her scalp. "Fuck... Not comin' like this... Not this time." His breath was broken, and his words sounded like he had difficulty forming them.

He also didn't stop her. However, she didn't want him to come this way, either.

She enjoyed being on top the last few nights, but now, she was ready for him to take over. Her panties were soaked, and her nipples peaked to painful points.

She was ready.

He jerked his cock out of her mouth with a hiss and when she glanced up, he was grimacing as he stared at the ceiling, a muscle twitching in his cheek. He was fighting his orgasm. She released him to give him a minute or two to gather himself, even though she was impatient to have him inside her.

After a few moments, he blew out a loud breath and dropped his head to stare at her, still on her knees. "Fuck, babe, nothin' I want more than to come down your fuckin' throat right now. And it came close to happenin' but I'm thinkin' you're only givin' me one shot tonight and that's not the way I wanna end the night."

True. She was giving him one shot. Because anything more could be risky. Any kind of lingering could lead to something other than what this was. Something she wasn't looking for and neither was he, she reminded herself. Being sexually attracted to each other while living in close quarters was just a convenient situation they both were taking advantage of.

He offered his hand and she grabbed it, his long fingers gripping hers firmly as he helped her to her feet.

"Turn around," he murmured, using their clasped hands to guide her until she was facing away from him.

She could feel the heat radiating off him when he stepped closer, his fingers working the clasp of her bra. Within a second it was loose, and she let it fall down her arms and to the floor. His hands spread along the sides of her ribs and he skimmed them around to her front until he cupped her breasts while thumbing her aching nipples.

His broad chest pressed to her and his erection was a hot steel rod against her lower back. He squeezed her breasts, kneading them with his fingers, and she leaned back into him, resting the back of her head on his shoulder.

Her hands covered his and he drew them from the upper curves of her breasts, over her peaked nipples, around the undersides and down her belly.

Her fingers fell between his longer ones as he dove down the front of her panties and found how wet she actually was. How sensitive her clit was.

When he pressed it, she jerked against him and gasped.

"Fuck, babe, you're so wet," he growled directly into her ear, sliding one of his fingers along with hers through her slickness. Testing, teasing, playing.

Still connected, both of their middle fingers slid inside her and he worked her a few seconds before pulling them away.

She wanted more of that.

But then, she wanted more of him and didn't want to wait.

"Wanna do so many things to you, but..."

But he probably wouldn't have the chance, she finished for him in her head.

They had tonight. It was foolish to think beyond that. As soon as Billy showed up, Deacon would be gone.

Another reason why this should only remain a convenient opportunity.

"Condom?" she asked, her question catching at the back of her throat. He hadn't grabbed the one sitting on the deck table.

"On the table there. Was hopin' we'd get this far."

He'd thought ahead. Like the wine. Like waiting for her in only his underwear. He'd put a condom on the deck and another in her great room. He probably had one on her nightstand. Maybe his, too.

Just in case.

He was a regular Boy Scout.

"Grab it," she told him.

"Need to take your panties off first."

"Yes, you do." She almost didn't recognize her own voice, it sounded so husky.

He grinned and stroked his cock once. "Then I'm gonna eat you 'til you come."

She had wondered what his beard would feel like between her thighs. She was about to find out.

He jerked his chin toward the leather couch that sat perpendicular to the fireplace and faced the windows. "Sit on the edge."

Holy shit, the rough timbre to his order made her pussy clench. But she didn't argue, she moved to the couch and sat on the edge of the cushion. He moved between her knees and dropped to his own, leaving enough space between them to wiggle her panties off when she lifted her ass to assist. He took his time sliding them in a sensual way down her thighs, over her knees to her ankles. She lifted one foot, then the other as he removed them. Once her panties were gone, he placed both of her feet wide on the coffee table behind him so her knees were bent and her thighs open.

She was glad her couch was a cleanable leather because the anticipation of what he was about to do made her so slick, she could feel a trickle of wet sliding from her. His thumbs dug into her thighs as he spread her open even further.

When he reached up and dipped his right thumb between her lips, she swirled her tongue around it before he pulled it back out and over her bottom lip, dragging it down her body, following a similar path as she had done to him. Between her breasts, over her belly and then he planted it on her clit, pressing and circling.

Her hips lifted slightly and she dropped her knees open as far as she could, giving him the space he needed.

In a split second, his face was buried between her thighs and he sucked her pussy lips, one at a time, into his mouth, dragged the tip of his tongue between them, taking over where his thumb had been.

He was good at kissing.

He was better at eating pussy.

So. Much. Better.

It was sensation overload, the combination of his tongue, lips and fingers along with the scrape of his beard against her delicate skin.

Like a plundering Viking, he was taking no prisoners and wasn't being gentle or delicate with her sensitive flesh. *Oh, hell no.* He was eating her like he was starving and someone was about to steal his plate of food.

He'd probably snap like a dog if someone else's fingers got close. While she found that amusing, what he was doing was not. Because she was about to come.

No, not about to, she was.

Her toes curled, her heart thundered and her breath stopped as her hips shot up when an intense orgasm ripped through her. He continued to lick and suck her until the last ripple ebbed away.

A few moments later, she collapsed back onto the couch, almost falling off the edge and to the floor. He caught her, held her there and grinned.

Oh yeah, he knew what he had done. What he had accomplished.

He was proud of himself.

His mouth and bearded chin were shiny from her arousal. He licked his lips and wiped a hand down both. "Fuck yeah," he breathed.

That was his response to him making her come like that, a simple *fuck yeah.* She echoed the same response in her own head.

He cocked an eyebrow. "You gonna say anything?"

She shook her head. "I'm pretty damn speechless." She wouldn't lie.

"Didn't think that ever happened to lawyers," he teased.

"It usually doesn't."

"Guess I did all right, then."

Oh, now he was being a cocky shit. "I guess it was okay."

He snorted, grabbed his cock and stroked it once. "I'm hard as fuck."

"I can see that."

"Hard to miss, right?" The corners of his eyes crinkled when he grinned.

"Deke..."

"Done talkin'. Need to fuck you."

She needed him to fuck her, too. She slipped from the couch and onto the rug, offering her hand to him. "Then why aren't you suited up yet?"

He leaned over and snagged the condom off the nearby table, ripped it open, and rolled it on. Her eyes following the movement of his hands. When he was done, she lifted her gaze to the man who stood over her. He was too far away.

"Are you just going to stand there?"

"No." He tilted his head. "You're so fuckin' gorgeous. Not only sexy as fuck, but you taste like heaven."

"You know what heaven tastes like?"

"I do now."

"Deke..." She could not fall for this man. She could not. No.

Convenient sex. That was all it was.

He did not fit into her life and she didn't fit into his. And even if he did, she was too busy to even think about any kind of relationship. Even a casual one.

Concentrate on the sex, Reese, that's it.

Concentrate on only the man who was joining her on the rug. He had said she was gorgeous. But it was he who was gorgeous.

She never appreciated tattoos, piercings or beards until Deacon. But right now, she was appreciating that and so much more.

Like his cock.

And his tongue.

And those lips. Which curled up in a cocky grin when he noticed her checking him out.

He settled between her thighs, keeping his weight off her by planting his palms on the floor. The latex-covered tip of his cock slid along her inner thigh and he nudged her thighs wider with his knees. But he didn't move to fuck her.

Not yet.

Instead he went face to face with her, and she stared up at his shadowed features, for the first time regretting they never had sex in the light. Where she could see the minute details of this man, like the colors of his eyes, the ripple of every muscle, the slightest change in his expression.

Good God, was it the pot making her think like this? If so, she needed to stop. Her thoughts were teetering on a dangerous edge. An edge which could crumble easily, causing her to fall.

Maybe she needed to stop what was happening right now. Stop having sex with him and keep focused on why he was in her house in the first place.

Not for this.

But she didn't stop him when he dropped his head, whispered her name in a way that scared the hell out of her, and then pressed the crown between her slick folds.

With their lips just a hairsbreadth apart, they both sighed when he finally slid inside her, filling her slowly, completely. This was not fast and furious like out on the deck the last few nights. She had set the pace and got off as fast as she could, then got off him and went inside.

She hadn't lingered. She had no reason to.

This felt different. Not because the pace was slower, but because he was trying to connect with her. And not just physically.

A ball of anxiety ping-ponged through her.

What was he doing? And why was he doing it? Couldn't he see that they couldn't be more different? That it would go nowhere?

"Deke... what are you doing?" she whispered.

"Fuckin' you."

Maybe she was just imagining it. Maybe it was just his pace that was making it seem like something more. Because there was no way he wanted anything more than sex. They've only known each other for a few days and most of that time, they'd hardly spoken.

Yes, that was it. She was imagining it and tended to overanalyze everything. Now, she simply needed to lie back and enjoy what he was doing.

She pushed the worry out of her mind and cupped his face, her thumb lightly touching his nose ring, then brushing over his lips. He captured it between his teeth and bit down, not hard enough to hurt but enough to send a shock of lightning through her all the way down to where they were connected. Physically. The only type of connection she could deal with right now.

His hips flexed loosely as he took his merry ol' time sliding in and out of her. Not quickly driving her to the brink, which was what she expected, but stoking the fire slowly. The embers were smoldering, the flames beginning to lick deep inside her.

This man was not only good with his mouth, he was an expert with his hip action. If she would've known this days ago, she would have flipped things around sooner.

Much, much sooner.

She tilted her own hips when he powered deep and stayed there, circling his hips and grinding into her until she was no longer whole and there was nothing left of her but scattered particles...

He took her mouth, sliding his tongue across hers. Nothing forceful but in more of a coaxing manner. Not that she needed any persuading. With their mouths sealed together, she accepted his breath, and he accepted hers and a shiver shot down her spine.

She turned her head just enough to break that intimate connection. "Deke..."

"Yeah, babe."

"Fuck me." She couldn't be clearer on what she wanted with that demand.

"Fuckin' you."

"Without the extra stuff."

"What extra stuff? Like this?" He sucked one of her nipples into his mouth and flicked the tight tip with his tongue.

"No," she groaned. "That's... fine. Fuck me harder. Not so... sweet."

He released her nipple. "How 'bout this?" he whispered in her ear. "You think I'm fuckin' you sweet? This ain't sweet. This is me makin' it last because your pussy not only tastes like heaven, it feels like it."

Ugh, if he sucked at sex, at least she could keep this all business in her brain. But he didn't. He was so damn good at it. And the truth was, she wanted it to last longer this time than the previous nights, too.

Damn it.

"Deke..."

"Quiet, babe, just enjoy it. Lemme do the work this time."

Babe.

How many other women had he called that? Why should she even care?

She kept quiet. Which was not natural for a lawyer like her.

He was right. She needed to shut off her mind and just enjoy it. It didn't matter he wasn't her type. It didn't matter that he didn't fit neatly into her life. It didn't matter that it felt as though he was turning this into something more. None of that mattered.

What mattered was what she thought. What she believed it to be. How she saw it.

Which was only casual sex between the two of them.

Why was she working so hard to convince herself of that? "Deacon."

"Reese, shut up. You're thinkin' so fuckin' hard I can hear it."

Again, he was right.

She closed her eyes and inhaled deeply, picking up the now familiar scent of his sandalwood-scented body wash combined with a little bit of weed.

Finally, she let herself enjoy the moment. The way Deacon moved, the soft grunts he released with each thrust, the way the muscles in his back flexed under her fingers. The way he filled her so fully, so perfectly.

The way he used his barbell piercings to stimulate her nipples.

The way he grabbed her hair, pulled her head back and buried his face against her arched neck.

The way his teeth scraped along her throat.

A soft gasp escaped her.

His other hand wedged between their bodies and found her clit. Teasing her into a frenzy.

A low groan escaped her strained throat. "Deke..."

He powered up and into her. Over and over. Sucking her skin, circling her hard, sensitive nub.

Just when she thought she couldn't take any more of his slow pace, his body hitched and he groaned against her skin.

Did he come? Before she did?

Oh no. He better not have—

Oh, thank fuck, he didn't. He was digging his knees more firmly into the rug. And began to thrust so hard, her whole body jolted.

"Fuck, babe," he moaned.

He released her hair, planted his palm on the floor and raised his torso. His eyes caught hers and held. His jaw was tight, the muscles in his arm bulging.

She reached up and twisted both of his barbells. He dropped his head and grimaced.

"Gonna come," he grunted.

She twisted them again.

"Gonna come," he warned roughly.

She didn't care. She didn't...

Because so was she.

She threw her head back, breaking their locked gaze, opened her mouth and a wail escaped her that made Justice run over and check to make sure she was okay.

With a low grunt, Deacon thrusted one more time and stilled deep inside her, dropping his head, his ragged breath beating against her heated skin.

A few seconds later, when his muscles loosened, he lifted his head and pushed a concerned Justice out of the way. "Get, Jussie!"

The dog moved away, jumped on her sofa and with a groan curled up against the couch arm. Then he hiked up his back leg and began to lick his balls.

Great.

Deke dropped to his forearms and kissed her slowly and gently for a few seconds, then with his own groan, slipped from her and to her side.

She didn't watch him remove the condom, but she could figure out what he was doing just by the movements. And when he was done doing whatever he did with it, his arm snaked around her shoulders and he pulled her more tightly into his side.

What was this? "Deke."

"Hmm?" He yawned and wound a strand of her hair around his finger, then released it.

Her mouth opened as he did it again. "Deke..."

He turned to his side and propped his head in hand. "Yeah, babe?"

"I..." She closed her eyes and pinched the bridge of her nose. "I'm tired. It... It was a long day." When he curled another lock of her hair around his finger, she opened her eyes again. "I'm going to bed."

He stared at her with an unreadable expression. After a few moments, he nodded and released her hair. "'Kay."

He didn't move. He seemed to be waiting for her. An invitation for him to join her?

When she didn't say anything for a few heartbeats, he nodded again. She rolled up to a seat, then to her feet, grabbing only her bra and panties which were close by.

Without another look at the man who remained lounging on the floor, she headed to her room. Once the door was closed, she leaned back against it and pressed a hand to her face and just breathed until her closed throat began to loosen once more.

She threw her bra and panties, not caring where they landed and scrubbed both palms down her face. Forcing the air in and out of her lungs at a steady pace, she tried not to think about what occurred out in her great room.

Not the sex, but the subtle shift to something beyond that. The connection she was trying to avoid.

If she listened hard enough, she could hear him and Justice trodding up the steps to the spare bedroom.

She dropped her hands and stared at her empty bed.

At least he had Justice to keep him company.

She should've invited him in.

But if she had, that would mean she had lied to herself about not wanting more.

And she wasn't ready to admit it.

Chapter Twelve

DEACON WASN'T GOING to deny something had changed last night.

Nothing drastic, but something all the same.

And that something scared off Reese.

She couldn't hide it in her face. Or the way her body tensed against his when he wrapped an arm around her shoulders and played with her hair.

In truth, he was as surprised as she was he'd done it.

He hadn't meant to, it just happened. Like it was natural.

That never happened before with any woman. He wasn't the touchy-feely or clingy type. He usually got what he wanted, gave the woman what she needed and then split.

But Reese's strength and stubbornness drew him. He'd grown up around two women who had been the same. Jemma, Judge's sister, and his mother, Lottie.

He didn't realize how strong his mother was until his father had gotten really sick. She struggled to keep working and to take care of him at the same time. Jemma, still really young, helped out as best as she could. By the time Walter was bed-ridden, Judge had already been out on his own for a while. He had offered to move back in, but Deacon's mother wasn't having any of it. She wanted Judge to live his own life and not be saddled taking care of his uncle.

Deacon thought his mother would shatter into pieces when the cancer finally took his father. But she didn't, she managed to keep their patchwork family together.

They all helped where they could. Even if it was just around the house.

But his mother never gave up after losing the only man she'd ever loved. She kept putting one foot in front of the other, day after day.

Whether she broke down where Deacon and Jemma couldn't see or hear her, he didn't know. But he wouldn't blame her one bit if she had.

So, yeah, Reese reminded him of the two strongest women in his life. The only two women he'd ever loved.

With a loud sigh, he slid a hand down his chest and into his boxer briefs. He was hard as fuck this morning and it would have been nice to turn over to find a warm, willing woman next to him.

Not just any woman. Reese.

But she had gone into her room and shut him out last night. Just like she had the previous nights.

She got what she wanted from him and then split.

Wasn't karma a fucking bitch?

At least it being a Saturday, they'd finally get to spend some time together when she wasn't exhausted and had nowhere to go.

"Christ, I'm turnin' into a goddamn girl, Jussie. Gotta be that fuckin' pot. It's gotta be tainted."

Justice turned his head toward Deke and whined, his tail thumping on the mattress.

"Gotta pee as bad as me?"

Justice whined again and scrambled from the bed.

"Guess you ain't gonna give me time to work out the big

336

muscle cramp I got." He stroked his hard-on twice, then, with another sigh, threw off the covers and rolled out of bed.

He stopped in the upstairs bathroom and by the time he brushed his teeth and braided his hair, he was able to piss.

He did so and then followed an excited Justice down the steps. The house was eerily quiet and the kitchen empty when they walked through. He opened the door and his dog rushed past him onto the side deck, down the three steps and across the paved driveway into the woods to do his normal morning business by marking a few trees.

Deacon didn't watch him, instead he stared at the spot where his truck was usually parked.

The empty spot.

"Son of a bitch," he grumbled. She had snuck out again this morning, trying to avoid him.

That was starting to hurt his damn feelings.

"You didn't even give me a fuckin' heads up, Jussie," he yelled out into the woods, where his dog was now taking a dump.

He should've left his bedroom door open, so when she tried to sneak out, Justice would've heard her and woken him up.

He shook his head. Had she actually gone to the office today? On a Saturday? Was she that behind on her work?

Or maybe she was out getting him breakfast so she could surprise him.

Deacon snorted and shook his head. Right.

Justice tore across the driveway, up the steps and into the house, acting five pounds lighter.

"Feel better?"

With his tongue hanging out, Jussie gave him his doggy grin.

"Gimme a sec and I'll feed your ass."

He snagged his cell phone off the counter where he'd

placed it before letting the dog out and typed out a text.

UR gone.

He leaned back against the counter and stared at his phone, waiting for her response.

Nothing.

That wasn't acceptable.

U OK? he typed out.

He put the phone down and went over to Justice's container of dog food, throwing a scoopful into his bowl. Within seconds his dog had scarfed it down and snuffled all around the bowl, looking for any wayward kibble that escaped his massacre.

Deacon went back to his phone, not surprised to see a lack of response.

This was fucking bullshit.

He tapped the screen a little harder than necessary. *Where R U?*

He was going to call her in a second if she didn't respond. And keep calling until she answered.

She had his fucking truck, she could check in at least.

Finally, his phone binged. Her answer made him clench his jaws.

The office. Swamped. See you tonight.

Deacon knew what a blow-off looked like. He'd done it plenty of times himself.

She was working on a goddamn Saturday. Probably at the office by herself, too. His finger hovered over his phone's keyboard. He wanted to make sure she kept her office door locked. Even though she probably wouldn't like that he was worried about her.

She was used to being independent.

He thought back on what she had said. *"I don't have time for anything more than sex right now. And sometimes not even that. Sex can get complicated and my life is complicated enough without some man trying to be my... hero."*

"Goddamn it," he muttered.

His fingers itched to type everything that was screaming in his head right now. Demand answers, order her to talk to him. But he fought it, knowing it would do no good. Knew that she would just shut him out even more than she already was.

He had to be smart on how he handled this. Her. Not just be an *in-your-face* asshole.

So, instead, while grinding his teeth, he typed: *Red or white?*

Deke...

He quickly typed his next message before she could finish her response. *NM. Gonna surprise U. What time?*

For fuck's sake, he sounded like a teenage boy begging a bitch to pop his fucking cherry.

See you tonight was her last response.

It took everything he had not to throw his phone against the nearby wall.

———

THE COMPUTER SCREEN WENT BLURRY. Reese rubbed her eyes, pinched the bridge of her nose and glanced at the time.

Holy shit, it was ten o'clock already. She had made great headway with chipping at the mountain of work she had. Now it was just a small hill. She had delegated some of the work to her paralegal and also her assistant for Monday morning.

Sometimes she had a hard time giving up work but she needed to trust her employees more. They were capable and did a good job. She just needed to learn to let go and let someone else help.

She saved the document she was working on, turned off

her screen and slipped her feet into her shoes, which were under her desk.

She sighed as she spotted the half-eaten salad she had picked up at Mill Creek two doors down and brought back to eat while working. She hadn't planned on staying this late, especially on a Saturday, but time had slipped away.

She grabbed the container and headed toward the kitchenette to dump it in the garbage. She thought about sneaking out the rear door into the parking lot since it was a faster way to get to Deacon's truck, but the alarm panel was only at the front door and she needed to set it. It would be stupid not to and she planned on taking Sunday off. For once.

She needed it. She wanted to sleep in and maybe even take a long soak in her tub with the jets on.

Yes, that sounded like a plan. It would be the first full day of spending it with Deacon in the house. It would be interesting to see what he did all day while she was at the office.

She was surprised when he had texted her this morning, asking where she was and if she was all right. He seemed concerned, maybe even worried about her. She hadn't had that in a long time. She'd forgotten what it was like to have someone else to check in with.

Normally, she and Reilly called each other once a week to catch up. It was weird not being able to pick up the phone and call her right now. She had to trust Deacon that she was okay.

Maybe tomorrow he could call her and put her on speaker phone. Reese just wanted to hear her sister's voice. Even if it was just for a few minutes. Just to calm her worries.

She dumped off the soggy salad and headed through the office, set the alarm and locked the front door. It was Saturday night in a college town but even ten was a little early. Mill Creek had been busy when she stopped in for her order. Bambi had been hustling and could only shoot her a quick smile as she worked hard for her tips.

While the sidewalk was empty, she could hear the deep bass of the band playing at the bar and see a couple people out front smoking. She hooked a left into the alley and headed back to her private lot behind her building.

The parking lot was empty save for Deacon's truck. It sat alone, reminding her that it was a Saturday night and her life was so lame right now because all she did was work instead of enjoy it.

Instead of hanging out with non-existent friends. Or relaxing at home on the deck with the glass of wine Deacon said he'd have waiting.

Instead of mindlessly petting Justice.

Maybe she needed a dog. A loyal companion. She could bring it to the office with her. It would be nice to have constant company.

Normally, she'd be going home to an empty house.

While she had bought that house for solace, lately it had become lonely.

She'd had no boyfriend since splitting with her ex-husband. No time for friends. Not even time for any hobbies. She had concentrated on her career and making the best life possible for her and her sister. Unfortunately, she'd done it all alone.

Having Deacon in the house, having sex with him, too, made her realize how lonely she had been. She simply hadn't wanted to admit it.

She sighed and made her way through the small, dark lot. A row of thick bushes lined the right side separating the rear parking lot of Mill Creek and hers. Because there was the possibility of rowdy drunks from the bar, she always secured her leather tote over her shoulder, kept her phone in one hand and her keys tucked between the fingers of her other. However, the Ford's "key" was just a fob on a keyring. It was useless to scratch anyone's eyes out.

Even so, she usually didn't have any problems. This wasn't a rough town. Sometimes the college kids got out of hand, but they normally weren't violent.

When she rounded the truck to dump her tote on the passenger seat, she jumped and a squeak escaped her.

The bulky, shadowy figure stepped away from the truck and toward her. It was a man but she wasn't sure who.

Until he started talking and the hair on the back of her neck stood.

"Know you got someone in your house waiting for me. Know your sister isn't there. Where is she?"

With her heart thumping in her throat, she took a step back, poised to turn and run, but he snagged the wrist of the hand which gripped her phone and held her in place.

She jerked her arm hard enough to cause pain in her shoulder, but the fingers circling her wrist didn't loosen, instead they tightened until they were crushing it. "Let me go, asshole." She turned her body away from him and slipped her hand into her tote bag, hoping he wouldn't notice.

"Where the fuck is she?" he roared in her face.

"I don't know." She tried to hide the shake in her voice, but failed. She took a deep breath and pulled her shoulders back as much as she could, trying to appear a lot stronger than she felt.

"Bullshit."

"They won't tell me." Her fingers located her stun gun and she wrapped her hand tightly around it, switching off the safety. "Let. Me. Go."

"Who the fuck are 'they?'"

"Her hired bodyguards. You'll never get near her." She jerked her arm again and winced at the sharp pain. "Just give it up, Billy."

"When she gives up the idea of testifying against me."

"That'll never happen," Reese sneered. "You're going down for what you did to her. I hope you go away for a very long time."

She gasped as he crushed her wrist almost to the point of breaking bones.

"Fuck you, bitch."

"It'll be you getting fucked in jail, Billy. Hopefully without a drop of lube."

He jerked her forward and as she tried to catch her balance, he backhanded her across the face. Her head whipped to the side with the power behind his strike and she couldn't see anything for a good second.

Like the next hit. Her phone tumbled from her fingers to the pavement and she tried to jerk her arm free again, but it was impossible.

Warm liquid trickled from her mouth.

Blood. He'd made her bleed.

She dropped the tote from her free arm but held onto the stun gun. She pressed the trigger and jabbed it toward him but before she could make contact, he slammed his other fist down on her extended forearm. Severe pain shot up her arm and then there was nothing but numbness. He ripped the weapon out of her hand and whipped it.

Panic bubbled up her throat as she heard it skitter along the pavement in the distance.

She felt a second of relief when he finally released her wrist, but that relief was short lived when she caught movement toward her face and everything went black.

———

SOMEONE WAS CALLING HER NAME. She could barely hear it over the ringing in her ears. She forced her eyes open and stared up at the night sky. She was on her back on the hard pavement. She had a throbbing headache and her face pounded with each beat of her heart.

At least she was alive.

"Don't move!" Bambi's voice cut into her dazed thoughts. Reese turned her head to see the bartender squatting next to her. "I called the cops. They're sending an ambulance, too."

"I don't need an ambulance."

"The fuck you don't."

Reese groaned and sat up, her head spinning a little when she did so.

"Reese, don't move. Let the EMTs check you out first."

"I'm fine."

"No, you're not!" She sounded way too panicked for Reese's liking.

"Where is he?"

"He ran when I screamed at him that I had called 911."

"Where did he go?"

"He pushed me down and ran out of the alley. That's all I know."

"Where's my phone?" Her one eye was swollen almost shut but she used her good one to search the area where she sat.

"He smashed it into pieces."

"Fuck," Reese whispered. She couldn't even text Deacon to tell him Billy was in town. Not that he had any way to get around. Reese had his truck. "I have to go."

"No... Cops are here."

The flashing lights bounced off the office building and her, making her wince with pain. A cruiser pulled up and a few seconds later an ambulance.

Her stun gun couldn't be found, her phone was destroyed, nothing on her was broken and she didn't have a concussion. So, after the cops took her statement and the EMTs cleared her, they reluctantly let her drive home.

She owed Bambi a huge tip and free legal services for life. If it wasn't for her taking out the trash and somehow hearing the struggle, Reese might have ended up more seriously injured, or even dead.

She couldn't wait to go home and soak in her tub, but now for another reason. Her body ached, her face hurt, and she wasn't looking forward to having Deacon see her like this.

Even knowing him for only a week, she already knew what his reaction would be.

Not good.

———

DEACON RELEASED a little growl as he heard his truck pull up the driveway. It was almost midnight.

He'd been calling her non-stop for the past hour. She had not answered once.

Not fucking once. Not even a text to tell him she was all right. Nothing.

At least she wasn't fucking dead. Or in some ditch somewhere.

Fuck no.

He realized she was independent and didn't have to answer to anyone, but, *for fuck's sake*, a little common courtesy would have eased his fucking frustration.

He should've gone to bed an hour ago and just said *fuck it* and *fuck her*. She didn't deserve his concern.

It pissed him the fuck off that he couldn't. He wouldn't be able to sleep until she was home and he knew she was okay.

Facing the door, he waited in the middle of the kitchen, his arms crossed over his chest, every muscle tense, his jaw popping. As the door opened, his mouth also did the same to give her the shit she deserved. But as she stepped over the threshold and into the light, nothing but air escaped when an invisible foot kicked him directly in the solar plexus.

Then everything inside him exploded. "What the fuck happened?"

She jerked at his shout and once she closed the door, slowly turned to face him, an ice pack pressed to her eye.

He rushed over, grabbed her oversized tote off her shoulder and put it aside. "What the fuck happened?" he demanded again, tucking a thumb under her chin and tilting her face toward the light so he could see it better. The hand holding the ice pack had a circle of bruises around the wrist.

She had two butterfly bandages over one eye. He pulled her hand with the ice pack away to see her left eye bruised and almost swollen shut. Her mouth had dried blood at one corner, her right cheek had another bruise that was quickly turning an ugly color.

What. The. Fuck.

"Who did this?" he growled, his blood rushing, wanting to kill whoever touched her.

No, it was more than a want. It was a deep-seated need to make whoever did this pay. Because someone was going to pay a huge fucking price for this.

"You need to start talkin' right fuckin' now."

Her good eye met his. And his blood went cold when she said, "Billy."

"What!" She winced at his shout and he tried to tamp down the fury that engulfed him, but it was impossible. "You shoulda fuckin' called me!"

She pulled away from him and walked deeper into the kitchen, putting the ice pack on the counter. "I couldn't. He smashed my phone. I have your truck, anyway. What would you have done? Jogged to town?"

"Fuck!" he roared.

She went to the freezer and dug around, finding a bag

of frozen peas and holding that to her face with a hiss. "He knows you're here."

"What?"

"He knows you're fucking here!" she screamed and winced again. "He's never coming to the house. This was all for nothing." A tear slipped down her cheek from her good eye. And then another. She swiped at them.

She probably hated the thought of showing any weakness.

"Well, not nothing." Maybe it was nothing to her, but it wasn't for him. "Did you see what he was driving?"

"No. He ambushed me in the parking lot. Your truck was the only vehicle there."

"What did he say?" When she didn't answer quickly enough, he yelled, "Reese!" Because he was about to lose his fucking shit.

He was about to jump in his truck and hunt that fucker down, slice his goddamn throat and bury him in the woods. Then he'd piss on the grave.

But he knew better to leave Reese alone. Warren knew where she lived, he could be out there watching and waiting.

Like he had done in the parking lot behind her office.

"He said he knew you were here and demanded I tell him where Reilly was and when I wouldn't—couldn't—he began hitting me. He smashed my phone and when I tried to stun gun him, he knocked it from my hand." She sucked in a shaky breath. "Bambi saved me. She heard the commotion and rushed over, calling the cops."

Thank fuck for Bambi.

But Reese was right, that fucker was never going to approach the house now while Deacon was there waiting for him. Warren had to have spied on the house somehow to know that. He hadn't left this fucking house since he arrived.

But Warren still knew.

Deacon strode out of the kitchen and across the dark

great room, to stare out into the dark woods. He could be out there right now.

For fuck's sake, he bungled this shit up and Reese paid the price.

He spun on his heel and strode back to the kitchen, to where Reese stood leaning against the center island, her head hanging down and the bag of peas held to her face.

He'd hurt her.

Warren fucking hurt her.

This was no longer a skip.

This had become personal.

He needed to get Reese to a safe location Warren wouldn't know about.

Then he was doing what needed to be done.

Fuck Bianchi and fuck the bail.

"Pack some shit, I'm gettin' you the fuck outta town."

Her head lifted and her one eye went wide. "I can't leave! I have court coming up. I have cases to work on. I can't—"

"The fuck you can't. This ain't one of your legal arguments, Reese. I'm gettin' you the fuck out of here, whether you like it or not."

"Deke, no. Billy won't come to the house. He knows Reilly isn't here now."

"I. Don't. Give. A. Fuck."

"I can't leave."

"Where I'm takin' you is only about twenty minutes away from your office. We'll figure it out. But for now, you ain't stayin' here alone."

"Deke..."

"Reese, this ain't up for fuckin' debate." He squeezed his eyes shut, tamped down his rage and then softened his tone as much as he could. Which wasn't much. "Just 'til he's caught. But I'm takin' you somewhere safe and don't give a fuck if you don't like it."

She stared at him for the longest fucking minute of his life. Because he expected her to continue to fight. And he was ready to go as many rounds as necessary with her until he had her packed in his truck and on their way to Manning Grove.

This was a fight he wouldn't lose.

Maybe she saw that in his face.

He loosened a little when she sighed and said, "I need to shower, at least. I need to wash off the blood, change my clothes. I'm... a mess..." The last came out broken.

Her whole body lurched as a loud sob escaped her and she began to crumble in front of his eyes. He rushed over and caught her before she hit the floor. The bag of peas fell from her fingers and landed at their feet when she pressed her forehead lightly to his chest and fisted his shirt.

Jesus fuck.

He wrapped his arms around her, giving her the support she needed to remain on her feet while she cried.

Justice circled around them, whining, not understanding what was wrong with Reese. Her muffled crying had his head tilting and him getting more frantic.

"Jussie, it's okay," he said softly, in an attempt to soothe them both. "It's okay. She's okay."

Thank fuck she was okay. Just a bit battered and she'd be sore and bruised for a little bit, but nothing that wouldn't heal.

He moved her hair off her forehead and after staring once more at the cut above her left eye held together by the butterfly bandages, he pressed his mouth to her right temple which wasn't bruised or broken.

He held her and simply breathed.

He waited for her to finish crying. Because she needed that.

And, if he admitted it to himself, he wanted her to need him.

"It's okay, babe. That motherfucker will get what's comin' to him. Promise. Just need you somewhere safe 'til that happens. We'll make it work."

Her sobs slowed, but she continued to hang on to him. And he continued to hold on to her.

He didn't want to let go.

Not yet.

When she was ready, he would. Until then, he gave her what she needed.

After a few more minutes, she lifted her head and sniffled.

He was tempted to pick her up and carry her, but she might fight him on that, causing herself more injury. Instead, he escorted her across the house to her room. Helped her out of her ripped and dirty clothes, and went into her bathroom to turn on the faucet in her tub. As the water filled, he helped her pack a bag.

When hot water filled the tub, he helped her into it and while she soaked, he ran upstairs to pack his shit. He piled everything by the side door, along with Justice's stuff.

And when he was done, her fingertips had pruned, so he helped her out of the tub, dried her off and then curled up on the bed with her, holding her tight.

She hardly said a word, but then, nothing else needed to be said.

She was allowing him to make the decisions right now, but when the sun rose and she was no longer in shock at what happened, he knew that would change.

He decided they'd spend the night in her house and then leave first thing in the morning. He knew by delaying their departure, he risked her arguing with him about leaving in the morning, but he'd deal with that then.

It was only a few hours before dawn, but he laid awake for every minute of those hours, plotting his revenge.

Chapter Thirteen

CAGE WHACKED him on the back, leaned in and wasn't as quiet as he probably thought he was when he stage-whispered, "Fuck, brother, this is every man's fantasy. Two hot fuckin' blondes. Goddamn sisters, too!"

Heh.

Deacon quickly smoothed out his grin in case either of the women had heard Cage.

Fuck.

No. Staying in his apartment above the club's bunkhouse with both Reese and Reilly wasn't going to work. Not only was it way too small, but two women, only one bed and one small bathroom was a no fucking go.

Well, it might not be if the women weren't related. Maybe some men were into having two sisters at once but if Deacon had two women in his bed, he'd prefer they both be able to get in on the action. Not only with him but with each other.

But the two blondes were related and one of them was Reese, who'd probably rip out one of his nipple rings if she knew his thoughts.

Luckily, she didn't, and he wanted to keep it that way.

She was already cranky enough about leaving Mansfield, her house and her practice to come to Manning Grove.

However, it was Sunday morning and they had all day to figure out how she'd run her law practice from a town only twenty minutes away, since he was not letting her go back unless he was with her.

And since he was back in Manning Grove, he was planning to head back into his own office on Monday to appease Judge.

Well, there was his fucking answer. She could go with him and use his office to do her lawyer shit. She could use his office phone, her laptop and, if she needed to go to court, she'd just have to take Deacon along with her. Tomorrow he planned on picking up a new cell phone for her in the same strip mall as Justice Bail Bonds.

Problem solved.

But the problem about where Reese and Reilly were bunking was not settled. If it was only Reese, they'd share his apartment. But the fuck if Deacon was sleeping on the couch and having the two women share his fucking bed without him.

"This ain't gonna work," he muttered.

"You're right," Stella agreed. "Ladies, we can put you two up at the main house. We have plenty of room."

Trip and his ol' lady crowded into his small apartment along with Red, Cage and Sig.

What? No. Reese was staying with him. Reilly could go up to the main house with Trip and Stella, if needed.

"We don't want to put you out," Reese said. The discoloration of the bruises on her face had gotten worse over the past few hours. But it was nothing like what Warren did to Reilly.

Thank fuck.

The pictures the pigs took of Reilly in the hospital had made him cringe.

"You won't," Stella continued. "We've got a big farmhouse and it's just the two of us."

Trip cleared his throat. He probably didn't like the idea of one woman he hardly knew, and one he didn't know at all, staying in their house. "Or the ladies could stay in the apartment and Deke can take one of the empty rooms in the bunkhouse."

Fuck. He had just moved out of his room downstairs not too long ago. The rooms weren't bad, but they weren't great, either. And at least his apartment had windows and more space.

Even so, it was a damn good suggestion. The bunkhouse was full at night with his brothers and Sig was right next door to Deacon's apartment. It was much safer for the women to remain in his place. It had a solid lock on the door, and he'd be right downstairs. He could also let Justice stay with them at night as an added precaution.

But he still didn't like it. Last night was the only night in the past few days where they hadn't had sex. But last night they'd finally shared a bed. He'd held Reese all night while she slept restlessly.

He'd been too pissed at Warren to sleep, plus he'd wanted to keep an ear out. Just in case Warren decided to pay them a visit anyway.

He normally didn't carry a gun while he worked a skip, but Judge had brought one for him when he came to Reese's house to pick up Reilly, knowing how violent Warren was.

If Deke needed to plug a hole in Warren's noggin, his excuse could be self-defense. But the actual reason would be the fucker simply needed to die. Though, shooting Warren would be too easy. That woman beater needed to suffer as much as he'd made his victims. Maybe even more.

"You good with stayin' here, just the two of you?" he asked Reese, who was scanning his place from where she stood.

She nodded as she continued to visually inspect his apartment. She hadn't wrinkled her nose in disgust, so he took that as a good sign.

"We got a run later," Trip reminded him. "You gonna go? We can leave Tater and Possum with the ladies."

"Tater and Possum?" Reese asked, her brow dipping low.

"Two of our new prospects," Trip explained. "Tater Tot and Possum."

"How'd they get those names?" Reese asked with a straight face, but Reilly rolled her lips under. She most likely knew what the BFMC's newest prospects looked like already.

He wouldn't be surprised if those two, or any of his other brothers, had hit on Reilly. Hopefully Judge had put the word out, like Deacon asked, about Reese's baby sister being off-limits. Not only to prospects, but to anyone with two eyeballs and a functioning dick.

"When you see them, you'll know why," Cage answered. "It's why I gave them those stupid fuckin' names. One's the shape of a tater tot and the other's got a face only a possum's momma would love."

"Oh." Reese glanced toward Deacon, pinning her lips together. He shrugged. "So, what's this 'run?'" she asked, staring directly at him.

"When the whole club rides together," he explained. "When the weather's good, we try to do one at least once a month. If you want, you can ride with me."

All eyes sliced toward him. He ignored the surprised looks. That was because his brothers rarely had a backpack other than their ol' ladies. Bringing a woman along wasn't a normal thing to do on an official club run.

You trying to impress pussy? Take her on a solo ride. But don't bring her along on a club run until you bagged her. That spot on the back of their sleds wasn't for just anyone.

And once a bitch was in that spot, it was hard to get her out without causing a whole bunch of headaches.

"I wouldn't want to leave Reilly by herself," Reese murmured with a frown.

"She can come along," he quickly offered.

Trip choked. Stella smothered a laugh. Cage only shot him a toothy grin.

Autumn, aka Red, said with a hint of amusement in her voice, "That's really nice of you, Deacon."

Yeah, wasn't it? *Fuck.*

"We can't both ride on your motorcycle. Plus, I've never even been on one."

"It's easy," Cage told Reese. "You just hang the fuck on. Me and Rook's been takin' your sis back and forth to the garage on the back of our sleds. She got the hang of hangin' on really quick."

Reese's head spun toward her sister, not looking happy with hearing that. Though, it was hard to look happy when your face was all busted up, even when you were. "You've been riding on their motorcycles?"

Reilly sighed and rolled her eyes. "I don't have a car, Reese. And they live downstairs. It's just another form of carpooling."

"Yeah, carpoolin'." Cage's grin grew even wider. "Tell you what, big sis, you wanna ride with Deke, sissy can ride with one of us."

"Oh. I would love that," Reilly breathed. "Come on, Reese. It'll be fun and after the night you had with that asshole, you need to clear your mind. And, anyway, you're way too serious all the time."

That was for damn sure.

"It's also relaxing," Autumn added. "It's beautiful out today, too."

"Couldn't be a better day for a run. Not too hot, not too cold," Stella said.

Now that the women were encouraging Reese, Deacon was beginning to regret his invitation. "Hey, if you don't wanna go—"

"No. Reilly's right. I... It might be good." She turned toward Cage. "You don't mind taking Reilly on the back of your motorcycle?"

"Fuck no. Who'd fuckin' mind a hot, young blonde smashin' her titties—"

Deacon clapped his hands really loud and shouted, "Alrighty then! Guess that's settled." He gave Cage a look he hoped to fuck the man picked up on. Though, sometimes he wondered about Cage's thought process. Or lack of it.

The club's Road Captain glanced at Reese and back at him, giving him the slightest chin lift.

"Right. That's settled. Thank fuck," Trip muttered as he grabbed Stella's arm and pulled her from the apartment. "We got things to do before the run."

Sig dropped an arm around his ol' lady's shoulders and also steered her toward the door.

Autumn called out, "If you ladies need anything, we're right next door."

"Yeah, but give us at least twenty before you need anything. We gotta get a couple things done before the run, too." He shot Deacon a smart-assed grin before disappearing out the door.

"Yeah, me, too," Cage said. "But I need more than twenty."

Deacon shook his head as the man walked out and shut the door behind him.

Then it was only the three of them. Reese, Reilly and Deacon.

Reilly's head swiveled between him and Reese. Wearing a sly expression, she said, "I'll go shower and get ready," before heading down the short hallway.

"Is that," Reese raised her eyebrows, "normal before your ride?"

"Before, after, sometimes even durin'."

Those eyebrows shot up to her hairline. One a little crooked due to the butterfly bandages. "During?"

"Let's just say if someone cuts off from the formation, they ain't stoppin' to smell the flowers."

"Deke..."

"Don't worry, your sister will be fine. Cage is our Road Captain, which means he's in charge of the run. If he veers off, we all do." He laughed. "That'd be pretty damn awkward. Maybe not for him, but for the rest of us."

Reese lowered her voice. "You know, I was worried about her being here before. But now I've seen some of you? I was kind of hoping you were all fat, sloppy and stunk, so Reilly wouldn't be tempted."

Most of his brothers took pride in their bodies, a habit they got into while in prison. One, so they were strong to protect themselves while in the joint, and two, to fight off the boredom and depression. But even the ones who hadn't done time weren't fat and sloppy.

Well, except for Tater Tot.

"They were all given the order to keep their hands to themselves."

Reese grimaced, then winced, putting her fingers to her busted lip. Once again, reminding Deacon that Warren fucker had to die. They also needed a plan. Which meant the prez needed to call a meeting tomorrow night to get that in place. Especially since the plan would most likely involve more than just him and Judge. And if the brothers got involved, then a vote was needed.

He'd talk to Trip before the run about setting that up.

"Listen, we'll get a plan together so you and Reilly can go back to livin' your life soon. Know you're bent about bein' here. I get it. But we'll figure it the fuck out." He stepped toe to toe with her and tucked a thumb under her chin. He didn't want to touch her bruises, since he knew that would be painful, instead he let his gaze touch every damn one, letting her know silently Warren would pay for what he'd done. Not only to Reilly but to her. But touching Reese had been done on his watch. And that had put the last nail in Warren's coffin. "In the meantime, it'll be good to let your hair down. But you gotta do somethin' before you get your ass on my sled."

"What's that?"

"Get that fuckin' stick out of it first. You'll enjoy the ride more if you do."

"There wasn't a stick up my ass when I rode you."

He had not expected that comeback, especially when she said it with a straight face. "Fuck, woman. If you weren't so sore from that motherfucker, I'd drag you somewhere where we could do what everyone else is doin' or about to do."

A small puff of breath escaped her parted lips. The eye that wasn't still swollen and various shades of purple, became heated.

Heh. She liked that idea. So did his dick.

"You would have to take me from behind, so you don't see my messed up face."

"Babe, I got no problem seein' past those war wounds."

"Deke," she whispered.

"Can't wait to feel your tits pressed to my back, your arms wrapped around me and your hot pussy against my ass. Gonna warn you now," he whispered, "probably gonna be hard the whole fuckin' run 'cause I'll be thinkin' of you ridin' me on that deck chair or me slidin' inside you on that rug. I'll be rememberin' how hot and wet you were." He tucked a strand of her long hair behind one ear and put his mouth to it. "You were wet for *me*, Reese."

Her breath hissed from her. He grabbed her unbruised

wrist and slid her hand along his hard-on. He held it there for a second and her palm curved around him, making him want to thrust. He gritted his teeth instead.

"Is that what Cage will feel against him, too?"

"Damn right. And he'll enjoy every fuckin' second of it, like I'm gonna."

"Maybe we shouldn't go, then."

"It'll be fun. Promise."

"He'll be a gentleman with her?"

Deacon bit back his snort. "Fuck no. But I promise he won't step over the line. Look, they've been workin' together for the past week. If somethin' was gonna happen, it woulda happened by now, right? And believe me, Cage ain't doin' nothin' with your sister that'll have Judge whuppin' his ass."

She shook her head. "I can't believe I'm going on my first motorcycle ride."

"Every time you call it a motorcycle, I see that stick slidin' up your ass a little higher."

She laughed, then hissed with discomfort. "What am I supposed to call it, then?"

"Bike. Or sled, if you wanna sound like a real biker bitch." He grinned.

"Sled," she repeated, like she was tasting the word. "I guess I'll be straddling your sled."

He groaned. This might end up being a rough ride for him. "Fuck yeah. And if you relax enough and let it, the vibrations might give you an orgasm."

"What?"

"That's what I'm told. Maybe today you can test that theory and let me know."

"I'll be sure to give you a full report."

She dropped her hand from his dick and stepped back when they heard the bathroom door open. "I need to unpack my things and hang up the couple of suits I brought so they don't wrinkle."

He pressed a kiss to her forehead. "You do that. We'll be ridin' out soon. I'll stop back and grab my shit later. Wear jeans, layers, closed-toed shoes. I'll find a brain bucket—a helmet—if you want it, otherwise I got a face coverin' you can wear with your sunglasses. Up to you."

She nodded and, as he turned to leave, she called out, "Deke..."

He paused and glanced over his shoulder at the woman he never expected to walk into his life.

Funny how fucked up life could be. Didn't take much to stumble on the road called life.

"Thanks. I thought I could do this on my own..."

She probably would've died trying, too, that was how stubborn she was.

"Now you don't have to," he murmured and walked out the door.

REESE SQUEEZED her arms around him a little tighter, causing him to grin. She had left the stick she had a close relationship with behind at the farm.

Hell, she'd left it back in Mansfield.

Deacon didn't care where she'd left it, he was only glad it was gone for now.

He glanced into his Low Rider's mirror and saw how carefree she looked with her chin on his shoulder and long blonde strands of escapees from her tight bun whipping around her face. She decided not to wear a helmet since she didn't want it pressing on her injuries, but instead tied one of his bandanas loosely around her nose and mouth to keep from swallowing bugs.

He could only imagine she was smiling under it. Even with the face covering and the sunglasses, it was obvious the weight of the world had been lifted from her shoulders.

Even though, in reality, it still existed. But right now, on his sled, that burden had become weightless. At least for a few hours.

The heaviest burden being Warren, of course, who was still out there. Deacon wouldn't rest until he got the bastard.

They were in the second row behind Cage and Reilly because Reese insisted they stick close so she could keep an eye on her sister.

Reilly seemed to be enjoying the run, sometimes sticking her arms out like an airplane and throwing her head back so the April sun would light up her face. Deacon had no doubt she'd caught every man's attention on that run, even the ones who had ol' ladies clinging to them. Seeing Reilly's blonde hair flowing freely behind her in the wind and hearing her carefree laughter was hard to ignore.

Cage led the pack in the opposite direction from Mansfield since their ride would be a few hours long and Deacon didn't want to risk being seen by Warren if he was still lurking around town. Two blonde sisters riding with a bunch of bikers was hard to miss.

His preferred method to catching Warren would be to ambush the motherfucker, so he didn't want to give Warren a head's up as to where Reilly was. Since they were all wearing their club colors, it wouldn't be hard to figure that out.

The man might be a piece of shit, but he wasn't dumb.

The ride did more than help Reese relax. Seeing Reilly on the back of Cage's sled gave Deacon an idea of how to set that trap for Warren. He'd run it by Judge first, then the exec committee Monday night when they met to discuss the situation.

Come Tuesday, he hoped to have the trap baited and set. Then they'd just have to wait to see if Warren took the bait. If they did it right, Deacon hoped the fucker wouldn't be able to resist tracking Reilly down.

If Reilly would've taken the beating and let it go, Warren would've just moved on. But Reilly had the same blood running through her veins as Reese. And Deacon now saw why Reilly had fought back. Plus, she wanted her hard-earned money returned. She wasn't going to get it by staying quiet.

Today's club run took a route that would last about four hours total and when they finished, they'd end up back in Manning Grove and at Dino's Diner.

Sometimes they ended up there. Sometimes back at the farm, depending if someone had thought to get the sweet butts organized to set out a spread for them.

And the sweet butts could not be called dependable. Motivating them wasn't an easy task. Sig had joked that they needed a head sweet butt who'd be responsible for not only keeping their asses organized and in line but be able to vet them.

It wasn't enough that they'd put out whenever and wherever, they had shit to do to be able to get and keep the privilege of hanging around the club. In exchange, they got free booze, free food and plenty of free dick.

Ozzy had mentioned that back in the day, the Originals had one of the ol' ladies in charge of the sweet butts. Problem was, as of now, the MC only had three ol' ladies. He couldn't see Red or Cassie dealing with managing the club girls.

And Stella had her hands full with Crazy Pete's since the bar was busier than ever. In fact, as soon as Tater and Possum became prospects, she claimed them as free labor for the bar.

The Fury still needed more prospects to do their dirty work. Some shit the sweet butts would never do. And a lot of shit they shouldn't even know about.

A husky, "You were right," filled his ear, drawing him out of his thoughts.

Of course he was. He was rarely wrong. She just didn't realize it yet.

As they headed toward Manning Grove on a back road that wound through the valley, he squeezed one of her hands planted on his gut.

"You hungry?" he yelled over the wind.

"Not yet."

"Good." He motioned to the pack behind him, signaling that he was cutting out of line. And he did so at the next crossroad.

He'd find a quiet little spot to relieve the hard-on he'd been sporting long before she'd whispered in his ear. Him being right about her *getting off* on his bike meant her pussy and panties were wet and that thought made him hungry. But not for food.

They'd catch up with the rest of his brothers at Dino's because they needed to make a quick pit stop first.

And it wasn't to smell flowers.

Chapter Fourteen

REESE STARED up at the dark ceiling. She was lying in Deacon's bed, but instead of Deacon, her sister slept next to her.

It had been a long day and as exhausted as she was, she still couldn't sleep.

Less than two weeks ago, her life consisted of going into the office, dealing with clients and then home to sleep, only to turn around and do it again the next day.

Now she was on a farm, sleeping in a biker's bed in a building full of bikers, and she had not only gone on a club run but had a quickie on a bike.

Sex *on* a bike.

She never thought that was possible. Deacon proved her wrong.

Again.

It was crazy and spontaneous, and the fear of getting caught made it even more exciting.

She couldn't believe she was thinking it, but...

It had been a great fucking day.

Watching Reilly around the club members proved her sister could fit in with anyone and anywhere. Her sister had never been as rigid about life or goals as Reese. She'd always been more of a free spirit.

Sometimes Reese caught herself being envious of her sister.

Today showed her what being a free spirit would feel like. Reese liked it, but knew it wasn't practical. Today was just a momentary "vacation" from her real life and responsibilities.

That was all it was.

While the guys could be crude, rude and loud, Reese had still enjoyed spending time with the club. And she loved Autumn, Stella and Cassie. The three women, while all so different, meshed perfectly.

No jealousy, no cattiness, and they respected and supported each other.

Plus, they loved their big badass men and it showed.

Even better, their big badass men loved them back. They weren't embarrassed about it, nor did they hide it.

Reese noticed it was rare the men were far from their "ol' ladies." They were always touching them in some way. A hand wrapped around the back of the neck. An arm casually thrown over the woman's shoulders. Fingers intertwined. Some sort of constant connection.

And when their women weren't within reach, they kept one eye on them at all times.

Reese wondered if that kind of attention became smothering. She'd always been independent and couldn't imagine what it would be like where a man insisted on some sort of constant "attachment."

Reese and Reilly had been the only two other women on the ride and once she and Deacon had caught up with everyone at Dino's, she had watched Reilly interact with them all.

In about a week, Reilly had become a part of the club.

Reese thought it would bother her more than it did. But

she still worried. Her sister needed to find her way and being a part of an MC—however she'd fit in—was not one of Reese's dreams for her.

After returning from the diner, everyone had gathered downstairs in what Deacon had called The Barn, which, she was told, was the Fury's clubhouse.

The club's "home" was not dirty. It wasn't disgusting. Admittedly, it was pretty cool. Planted in the center of the floor was a see-through fireplace that wasn't currently burning. Two large side doors and another door at the front were open to let in the breeze of the comfortable spring night. Fifty-five-gallon drums sat scattered outside in a courtyard burning bright. The place reminded her of a rustic ski or Midwest hunting lodge complete with a bar, pool tables, dart boards, and old green bus benches lining the walls.

Seeing those had brought back some memories of making sure Reilly was dressed and fed before putting her on the bus. If Reese hadn't gotten Reilly going every morning, her sister never would have gone to school. Most of the time their mother was gone before they woke up or she hadn't even bothered to come home.

Or she was home and unable to function.

Reese pushed the distant past out of her head and went back to just a little while ago, when she and Reilly had taken quick showers before heading down to the barn together.

Reilly had thrown on a long, flowy skirt with a wide belt, cowboy boots, and a Harley Davidson tank top Reese didn't even know her sister owned. Or maybe she borrowed it from one of the other ladies, since Reilly didn't have a lot of clothes with her due to leaving the Philly area so quickly.

But once again her sister looked carefree and happy, and Reilly was practically skipping alongside Reese as they made their way around the backside of the building and through the big, open double barn doors along the side.

When they stepped inside, the deep bass of the loud

rock music had hit Reese right in the chest. Since there wasn't a live band, the club had to have some insanely large speakers.

"Hey, there's Deacon," Reilly announced close to Reese's ear.

The man, wearing Levi's that fit his ass like a glove and a snug T-shirt that hugged his shoulders and biceps and showed off his arm tattoos, sat in front of what looked like a long, handcrafted wood bar. The shelves behind it were packed with all sorts of liquor bottles, mugs and everything else a typical neighborhood bar would need.

Though, this bar wasn't in any kind of neighborhood, or open to the public. Reilly had mentioned that hanging out in The Barn was by invitation only.

Since Deacon's back was turned toward Reese, her gaze landed on the black leather vest he'd worn on the run and still wore. What he called his "cut" which displayed his club's "colors." What identified him as a "brother," or member, of the Blood Fury MC.

His cut was the same as all the other "brothers" who had been along on the run, and the patches also matched the large tattoo inked into his back.

She'd heard of college fraternity and sorority members getting matching tattoos, and sometimes even being branded, but she wasn't aware of any type of "member-ships" requiring them.

She wondered if it was a requirement of this MC.

Her sister leaned into her. "Isn't Ozzy really cute? He's about your age."

Reese turned her head toward the biker, who sported a short salt and pepper beard, and did *not* look her age. He wasn't much older, but still...

"Why are you telling me this?"

Reilly shrugged. "Just in case it doesn't work out between you and Deacon."

Reese frowned. "What doesn't work out?"

"Whatever you two have going on."

"There's nothing going on."

"Well, good. Because it looks like one of the piranhas is ready to nibble on him."

Piranha? "What are you talking about?"

"One of the sweet butts."

Reese stared at her sister like she was an alien. "Will you speak English?"

"A sweet butt. That's what Brandy is." Reilly tilted her head toward the bar and Reese glanced that way again.

It was kind of bothersome that her sister was already speaking their language. That did not give Reese the warm fuzzies.

Reilly nudged her forward gently. "Better go claim your man before one of the piranhas do."

"Reilly, what the hell—"

Reilly jerked her head toward the bar and bugged out her eyes. "Go! Don't dawdle, or he'll be diddling someone else."

"I—"

"Go!"

Reese snapped her mouth shut and glanced at the girl approaching Deacon. Looking like a...

Hungry piranha.

Damn it.

"Why is she called a sweet butt?"

"If you keep standing there like a dumbass, you'll find out firsthand."

Reese pressed her lips together and checked out this Brandy, who was unashamedly topless and wore a very short, pleated schoolgirl skirt with thigh high socks. Her brandy-colored hair was pulled into two long pigtails coming out of the sides of her head. She was also cracking her gum with an open mouth.

Apparently, she couldn't afford panties—or at least had forgotten that part of her outfit—since every time she flounced another step toward Deacon, Reese could see the bottom curves of her bare ass cheeks.

Had Reese stepped into some sort of cheesy porn?

Was the girl even of legal age?

God, she had really nice, young perky breasts. Even if her age was legal, her breasts shouldn't be.

How could Reese compete with that?

She closed her eyes and shook her head. What was she thinking? She wasn't in competition with anyone. She was here on this farm, with these bikers, only to stay safe from a violent psycho. Never in her life had she tried to "get her claws into a man" and she certainly wasn't planning on doing that now.

She was turning thirty-five next month, not fifteen.

She sighed and opened her eyes. Setting her sore jaw, she strode across the barn and stopped just a couple feet behind Deacon. Close enough to see Brandy press her perky breasts into Deacon's arm and purr, "Hey, baby, where've you been?"

Deacon turned on the stool to face his visitor, breaking the nipple to bicep contact. "Not tonight, Brandy."

Lithe, young Brandy did a sexy little pout. "You already have plans? I bet mine would be better, handsome."

She reached up to touch his braid and he jerked his head back. "No plan yet. Just chillin'."

Reese did not miss the moment Brandy noticed her standing just outside of Deacon's radar but watching the exchange.

The younger woman's eyes slid from Reese back to Deacon and her smile got even bigger. "Have a question for you, handsome."

"What's that?"

She plucked at both of her perky, tight nipples and said,

huskily, "I'm thinking about getting my nipples pierced, too. D'you think that would look good?"

"If that's what you want, Brandy."

She reached into Deacon's open cut and planted her hands on his chest. Right over his nipples. "Does it hurt?"

"What d'you think it feels like when you jab a big needle through a sensitive part of your body?" Deacon asked her.

Brandy cringed and dropped her hands.

"It also hurts when you hit them with a stun gun," Reese announced as she took the final two steps up to the bar to stand at Deacon's back.

His head twisted toward her, but his face remained unreadable. "My plan's arrived."

Brandy stared at Reese but directed her question at Deacon. "Is that your mom? What happened to her face? Your daddy beat her?"

Deacon's face was no longer unreadable.

Reese smiled despite the sharp pull of her injured lip. "He does call me Mommy sometimes when I twist those barbells."

Deacon surged to his booted feet, almost knocking Reese backwards. "Stay here," he ordered her. He turned back toward Brandy, who looked like she was about to jump Reese with her claws out.

Reese already had a bunch of bruises, what would be a few more?

But Deacon grabbed Brandy's arm, growled, "You. Come with me," and dragged her down to the other end of the bar. When they got there, Reese watched Deacon say something to the young woman she did not like because, once again, she pouted and even stomped her foot slightly while she did it.

Deacon said one more thing to her and finally Brandy nodded, glanced around The Barn and zeroed in on her next victim.

Deacon remained where he stood, his beefy arms crossed over his chest as he watched her. After a few seconds, he turned and came back to Reese who had taken his spot on the stool.

When he stopped in front of her, she said, "She's cute. She has a really perky... personality. Did I screw up your plans?"

"Nope," he grunted.

"Just curious on how she knows your nipples are pierced."

Deacon stared at her for a few long seconds, then grinned. "Yeah, she's cute and perky as fuck and she gives great head. She also loves anal. Not gonna lie. Anything else you wanna know?"

Actually, that had been too much. "Is she legal?"

"Everybody currently standin' on this property is legal, Reese. Trip don't tolerate jailbait slippin' through the cracks. He's real particular about not lettin' this club crash and burn a second time. And underaged girls will do that."

Reese rolled her eyes. "Well, it's good you guys have some morals, then."

"Yeah, *Mommy*, we do got a few."

The little bit of annoyance about Brandy quickly disappeared. "You like that, do you?"

"Never was my thing, but if it's yours, might be willin' to play along."

"Just so you know, Reilly offered up Ozzy to me, said he was closer to my age."

"She did what?"

"Yes, apparently, you all are like a biker buffet, and if I get tired of one dish, I can try another."

Deacon scratched at his eyebrow with the tip of his thumb, then dragged his fingers down his bearded jaw.

"I didn't think you could be speechless," she teased him.

"Now I know. Also... just so you know, I won't be thirty-five until next month. I'm not old enough to be your mother."

"Thank fuck for that. But even if you were, I'd still do ya. You'd be like a sexy MILF."

"Not if I'm your own mother."

"Fuck no... Fuck. Never mind." He shook his head. "Let's stop talkin' about mothers, for fuck's sake."

"That's a good idea." She turned toward the bar which didn't have anyone standing behind it like at the Mill Creek. "There's no bartender."

"Nope. It's help yourself."

"Apparently," she murmured as she watched another woman—this one totally naked with a set of red handprints on her ass—walk behind the bar and get on her very tiptoes to finagle a whiskey bottle off a shelf she could barely reach. When she finally got it without it crashing to the planked floor, she cracked open the full bottle and put it to her lips, taking a long swig like it was water.

Another man came up behind her, snaked an arm around her waist, jerked her against him, dry humped her a couple times as he shouted something Reese couldn't decipher, then he snagged the bottle from her and took a long swig himself. He kept the bottle but pushed the dark-haired, blue-eyed woman away and smacked her ass so hard that Reese could feel the sting. The woman squealed and giggled, pushing at—

"What's his name again?"

Deacon's lips twitched. "Whip."

—Whip's bare chest, since the man was only wearing a pair of jeans that weren't even fastened. They hung off his hips, showing off the top edge of black pubic hair and an actual V of muscle that disappeared into the denim.

Reese pursed her lips. She had to admit, they grew bikers hard and healthy in this club. She mentally tossed away all her previous misconceptions about bikers.

Or at least some of those mistaken theories.

When Deacon didn't answer, she pulled her attention away from the "couple" as Whip dragged a giggling—

"What's her name?"

"Angel," came out of him with a snort.

Angel. Right. She was really young and perky, too. A bit on the skinny side, though.

"Is she a sweet butt?"

"Reese."

She locked gazes with the man standing next to her. "It's a valid question."

"Who told you about sweet butts?"

"Who do you think? Certainly not you." Reese glanced over her shoulder to see where Whip and Angel went. Not far. The younger biker was now sitting on one of the bus benches, no longer wearing jeans, and Angel was riding his cock while drinking the whiskey straight from the bottle. Like a booze guzzling rodeo queen.

"Does she like anal, too?"

His muttered, "Reese," sounded like a warning. How about that?

"How would you rate her blowjob skills?"

"Jesus fuck," he muttered.

"A ten out of ten? Does she have the capability of sucking your balls totally dry like a Wet-Vac?"

Deacon sighed and shook his head. "She does all right."

"So, let me just say, I've never been to a party quite like this. Not even in college."

"This ain't a party."

"It's not? Then what is it?"

"A typical Sunday night after a club run."

She raised her eyebrows, which reminded her of how messed up her face was. "This makes me feel so much better about my sister being here for the past week."

"Trip hasn't approved her sweet butt status yet."

Reese whacked his upper arm. "That's not even funny."

"Neither is you askin' about anal and blowjobs."

"Well, don't you know? I'm sure you guys have some sort of rating system."

"Yeah, babe, I know. And I know how good Billie gives head and Lizzy and Crystal and all the rest of them. It's just the way it is."

It's just the way it is.

"What kind of woman would want this kind of life?"

He leaned in really close and growled, "One who doesn't have a stick up her ass. There isn't one fuckin' woman here tonight who don't wanna be here... Includin' you."

Reese sucked in a sharp breath. "I didn't have a choice." She rather had stayed in Mansfield.

Deacon cocked an eyebrow at her. "Didn't you?"

"You told me I didn't have a choice." Did that just come out of her mouth?

"Woman, when was the last time you did what a man told you to do?"

Reese pinned her lips together.

Deacon lifted a hand. "You don't need to answer that. Already know the fuckin' answer. Never. So, don't fuckin' tell me I gave you no choice. You're fuckin' smart and shrewd. You didn't wanna be here, you'd find a way to get gone."

"I did it for my sister."

"Don't treat me like I'm stupid, either." He jerked away from her and rounded the bar. He slapped two glasses onto the shellacked bar top and grabbed a bottle of tequila, pouring a couple of fingers worth in each glass.

"Got vodka but nothin' fancy like tonic water. Don't got wine, either. You want some, I'll make sure it's stocked for next time."

"For when?"

"Next time." He slid one of the glasses in front of her.

What next time? She and Reilly didn't belong there. This was not their life. They were just here lying low. That was all. As soon as it was safe to go home, she was dragging Reilly out of there as fast as possible.

She downed the tequila in one swallow, then coughed when she tried to breathe. It was almost as bad as the first time she had puffed on his joint back at her house.

Deacon downed his tequila, set his glass back on the bar and filled both of their glasses again. He placed hers back in front of her but kept his hand on it. "Now... you done bein' jealous?"

She lifted her gaze from his long fingers caging in her drink—the ones that made her come earlier on his bike— and met his deep brown eyes. "You're mistaken."

He tipped his head down, not breaking their locked gaze. "Sure I am." He blinked in slow motion and smiled a smile that instantly made Reese's panties damp. *Damn him.* His voice was low and gravelly when he said slowly, "Oh, yeah, I forgot. You don't need a fuckin' man... That is, unless he's fuckin' you so hard your pussy juice is runnin' down his fuckin' balls."

Suddenly, Reese couldn't catch her breath and her nipples pressed painfully against the soft cotton V-neck tee she had worn with her jeans.

She blinked slowly and remained focused on his face, unsure what else was going on around them. Not even caring.

All she knew was she had been in some sort of Twilight Zone. And now reality was clubbing her over the head. Just like when Warren had struck her.

She reminded herself of who she was, the reason she was there, how hard she had to work to get everything she had and how far she had come.

This man before her, this club, was reminding her of a life she had worked hard to escape. She had dragged her baby sister along with her out of the darkness and into the light where they could both have a future. Good ones.

She was not going back.

Not ever.

And neither was Reilly.

She'd make sure of it.

She slipped off the stool and glanced around until she found her sister. Ignoring Reilly's complaints, Reese grabbed her arm and dragged her out of The Barn and back up to the apartment.

She locked the door, even knowing full well that Deacon had a key.

No matter how much she wanted him, this lifestyle was just too far out of her comfort zone. And, right now, having the door separating her and her sister from what surrounded them helped her gather the control that had slipped from her fingers.

And that false sense helped her breathe a little easier.

Chapter Fifteen

REESE CHECKED to see if Reilly was sleeping. She was, if the soft, steady snores coming from her sister were any indication.

She carefully rolled out of bed and tagged the jeans she had shucked earlier. Once she hit the living room, she shimmied them up her legs and hips and under the peach satin mid-thigh chemise she had pulled on before bed. She found a pair of Reilly's flip-flops on the floor by the couch. She slid her feet into those and her body out the front door into the mid-April night. The temperature was comfortable, and she wouldn't need a jacket.

A creak had her head turning and she found a bare-chested Sig sprawled in a folding chair in front of his own apartment. His denim-clad legs were extended, his knees wide, his head back and he appeared completely chill. Probably because of what was in his hand.

"Hey." He put the bowl to his lips and lifted a Bic to light it. She was a little impressed with how long he could hold the smoke in his lungs, before letting it roll from his lips into the ink-black sky.

No lights lit up the second-floor landing. Only the moon and the stars.

"Hey," she returned the greeting, staring out into the darkness toward the open space she knew was just beyond. Stella told her the Amish farmed their fields and, in exchange, gave them an endless supply of fresh vegetables, meat, eggs and milk. "It's peaceful out here."

Sig snorted. "Not always. Parties can get a little wild. So can the sex. Nobody's shy 'round here, so expect to see some naked tits and ass, if you haven't already. You watch long enough, might learn a thing or two."

Reese's mouth opened, then snapped shut. Maybe he was only kidding, so she played along. "I don't think I need to learn a thing. Or even two." And she had already seen plenty of naked bodies, and more, in the short time she spent downstairs earlier.

"Yeah? Then Deacon's a lucky bastard."

"Why's that?"

Sig took another puff off the bowl before offering it to her, most likely just out of courtesy. But she moved closer and snagged it from his fingers. Since the contents were still lit, she took a long inhale, hearing the crackle of the pot burning.

"Damn, woman, didn't expect you to take it."

Suddenly, she felt fifteen again and hiding behind the B-wing of her high school with her classmates. She never had time to hang out with them after school or on weekends, so she took advantage of spending time with them between classes.

She blew the smoke out and away as she handed it back to him. She waved a hand. "Apparently, it helps me pull the stick out of my ass."

Sig barked out a laugh and it sounded deafening compared to the quiet night.

"Do you know where Deacon is?"

"Prolly down in the bunkhouse. In his old room."

"His old room," Reese repeated in a murmur.

"Yeah, he'd moved into Judge's old apartment when the Grumpy Green Giant moved out."

She'd only been here one day, and she already knew who Sig was talking about. "Where did Judge go?"

"Rented a place in town temporarily 'til his and his ol' lady's house is done bein' built."

She was still getting used to some of the terms these guys used. During the motorcycle ride earlier, she'd heard a few of them and asked what they meant. Apparently, Reilly had all the terms down pat already. She was fitting right in already. Which, again, worried Reese.

In just a week, her sister had become comfortable with the MC's way of life. Going from one bad boy like Billy to a whole club of them was not what Reese wanted for her sister's future.

"Oh, so they're building their own home?" That sounded promising *and* responsible.

"Yeah," he jerked his hand toward the left, "over yonder past the tree line. Cassie's got a kid. And Rev's baby sister just moved in with them to be their house mouse."

House mouse. That was one term she hadn't heard yet. She wasn't sure she wanted to know what that meant, but asked, anyway. "What's a house mouse?"

"Kinda like a housekeeper. Or a housewife. Takes care of a brother and his place but ain't an ol' lady."

Great. She would now need to have a little discussion with Reilly to make sure she didn't get the bright idea of becoming one.

"I guess that doesn't pay well."

"Don't fuckin' pay at all. She gets a roof over her head and other shit. Better deal than a sweet butt, but not the status of an ol' lady."

Great. Reese wondered what the "other shit" entailed.

And while Sig was a master conversationalist, she decided she'd learned enough about the club life for one night.

"Where's Autumn?" The redhead was young and she and Sig seemed mismatched. But she had appeared content, if not happy, while clinging to her *ol' man* on the earlier club run.

"In bed."

When she and Deacon finally caught up to the large group in town, the club had taken over Dino's Diner. Sig never let Autumn out of his sight once and most of the time held onto her hand as if he was afraid she'd float away.

Reese noticed a couple of times when the woman's hazel eyes would go completely empty. A moment later she'd snap out of it and be smiling and joining in on the rowdy conversation at the long, crowded table.

Judge's ol' lady, Cassie, didn't seem to fit in with this crowd, either. The only woman who did was Stella. She was exactly how Reese would picture a biker's woman. She looked and acted badass when she kept the guys in line, especially when they were in town, by reminding them to behave. Almost like a den mother. She seemed the perfect partner for the club president, Trip. Reese had been surprised to see Stella had almost the same amount of authority as Trip did. Almost.

Reese had expected a group of rough and tumble bikers to be nothing but misogynistic assholes. And while some acted like that, not all of them did. Especially the ones who had ol' ladies. Reese was pleased to see they might be complete jerks to each other by riding each other's asses, or even to outsiders, but they treated their women like queens.

"I was having a hard time sleeping. You can't sleep, either?"

Sig lifted the bowl. "This will help."

"Okay, well, I need to talk to Deacon."

"Talk, huh?"

It was a total lie and Sig could see right through it, but she was sticking to it. "Do you think he's still awake?"

"Could be." Sig smirked. "If he is, don't be surprised if he ain't alone. Sweet butts were on the prowl tonight."

Again, that term. She was smart enough to put two and two together after what she saw downstairs. But apparently not smart enough to abandon her restless need to find Deacon.

He was probably not happy she just up and deserted him earlier without a word. But he hadn't stopped her or chased her down, which meant he could very well be with someone else right now. And if he was... Well... They'd only known each other for a week and had no ties, so it shouldn't bother her.

"Head down the steps, hook a left and go through the back door into the bunkhouse. Doubt it's locked. Rarely is."

"Thanks." She paused at the top of the steps. "Hey, I'm curious. How did you and Autumn meet? She's an accountant, right?"

"Yeah. She's an accountant. For us, mostly." He pulled on his bearded chin. "We met by fate."

Reese frowned at his ambiguous answer.

Just when she figured that was all she would get from him, he continued. "Never had anythin' good happen in my fuckin' life 'til her. Fate musta decided I'd eaten enough shit sandwiches and gave me her as a reward for makin' it through the fuckin' meal without dyin'."

"I don't understand."

Sig unfolded himself from the chair and got to his feet. "Yeah. Me neither. Let's just say I'm a lucky motherfucker."

"She's very sweet... and really young." If Autumn was as old as Reilly, Reese would be surprised. "I'm sorry if that sounds like I'm insinuating anything inappropriate, I'm not. She just looks very innocent to be tied in with a bunch of bikers."

Sig stared at her with a tilt to his head for a long, uncomfortable moment. "Yeah, she's young. But like me, she's lived a lifetime already. Stella might look like the baddest bitch of the bunch, but scratch the surface and you'll find it's Red."

"She has a story."

"Yeah. She's got a story. One that ain't gonna be told tonight. Go find Deke. Heard he wasn't happy when you bolted earlier like your ass was on fire." With that he turned and went into his apartment, closing the door softly behind him.

She stared at it for a second, hoping she didn't insult one of Deacon's "brothers" when she hadn't meant to. In truth, they'd been nothing but accommodating since Reilly arrived last week.

She should be grateful.

She was grateful, but she still couldn't help but worry. She'd worried about Reilly for the past twenty-four years, even when it shouldn't have been her job to do so. When Reese should've been a child herself, she had to step up and be the adult. She thought back and wondered how she, at only ten, figured it all out.

Had she made mistakes raising Reilly? Too many to count. But she learned from them. And she wanted to protect her sister any way she could.

But even Reilly looked and acted more worldly than Autumn.

Reese had to remind herself that Sig's "Red" wasn't her problem. The *rough-around-the-edges* biker seemed to dote on her and she him.

She headed down the steps, made a left and found the back door to the bunkhouse unlocked, just like Sig said. With only one light midway down the corridor, the interior was bathed in shadows and she made her way inside, pausing long enough to let her vision adjust.

While it was dark, it wasn't quiet. The sounds of someone—or *someones* since they didn't sound alone—having sex echoed down the long hallway.

The shouted chant of "*Yes! Yes! Yes!*" was pretty high-pitched. Loud, deep grunts accompanied each one.

She peeked in at the first open door and saw it was a bathroom, which consisted of a couple stalls, showers and sinks. It reminded her of a shared bathroom in a college dorm.

Even though she couldn't afford to live on Villanova's campus, nor could she leave her sister alone at home, she had used a few while studying with classmates. The ones she'd had the pleasure of using made her appreciate not having to use it on a daily basis.

She was pretty sure if she turned on the light, she'd find this one much worse since a group of bachelor bikers used it. She wrinkled her nose and then gasped after doing so, forgetting how messed up her face was. She needed to perfect her "resting bitch face" so she wouldn't cause herself pain until she was healed up.

She wandered down the corridor, cursing silently when none of the rooms or doors were marked with whom they belonged to. And she wasn't about to start opening them to peek inside. Not unless she wanted to bleach her brain afterward.

The sounds of the enthusiastic coupling got louder as she made her way toward the front of the bunkhouse. She wasn't sure if it was Deacon doing all the grunting. Her stomach twisted.

She had no idea how to find him without yelling out his name.

A door to the right, near the end of the hallway, opened and a naked man stepped out with his head tipped down and he was running his fingers through his long, hair as he walked her way. Reese froze and made a small warning sound so she wouldn't spook him.

His head popped up and he only hesitated for a split second before continuing to saunter towards her, not bothering to cover any of his nakedness.

Reese was thankful because she kind of appreciated the view. The man's hair was now loose, unlike earlier when he had it pulled into a man-bun for their ride. Undoubtedly to keep his long hair from knotting in the wind. She noted he looked good either way.

Christ. Not counting the prospects, she hadn't met an ugly Fury member yet. No wonder those sweet butts liked to... *hang out.*

He gave her a crooked grin when he recognized her. "Lookin' for Deke?"

Did he just ask if she was looking for dick? No, that couldn't be right. Her tired brain just changed Deke to dick since it was hard to ignore what was hanging casually between his thighs.

She tried to remember his name while not staring at it. When he reached down, she figured he was going to finally cover himself. She was wrong.

He scratched his balls instead.

When her eyes rose again, he said with a low, rumbling chuckle, "Easy, remember?"

"I'm not easy," she whispered.

"Not you. Me."

Oh shit, that was right. His name was Easy. Seemed like his attitude was the same way. Easy.

He slowly and deliberately dragged a hand up his tattooed chest.

Gah. He needed to stop drawing her attention to everywhere but his face. He was baiting her on purpose.

His repeated, "You lookin' for Deke?" got her attention back on track. Barely.

"I... Yes, I... uh..." Since when was she at a loss for words? She shook herself mentally. "I have something I need to discuss with him."

Easy snorted just like Sig had.

Was she that transparent? "Do you know where he is?"

"Fuck no. Check The Barn. But if you can't find him, I'm available." He hooked a thumb over his bare shoulder. "My room's down there on your right. Door will be unlocked." He jerked his chin at her. "Easy. Don't forget."

It wouldn't be easy to forget his name again.

Reese mentally groaned.

Yes, this was the Twilight Zone. She was now sure of it.

"Which door leads to The Barn?"

"The one at the end of the corridor. Behind me."

She nodded and walked around him, giving him a wide berth.

"Hey, Reese!" Easy called out, halting her forward progress. "It's okay if you wanna check out my ass."

Without turning around, she lamely lifted a hand and let it drop in a silent acknowledgement, but kept her eyes focused on the closed door ahead.

If Deacon wasn't in The Barn, she would continue walking right out the front door and take the long way around back to his apartment. It was a mistake to come down here and search for him.

Any discussions she needed to have with him could wait until morning.

Yes, this was a mistake. She should just go back upstairs and watch TV until she fell asleep.

As she hit the end of the corridor and was ready to head into The Barn, a *woosh* came from her left and a hand came out of the dark, grabbing her and yanking her through a swinging door.

A squeak escaped her, and her heart jumped up her throat. She swung her fist to strike whoever it was, and it was caught in a bigger hand than hers. Now both her hands were restrained, and she couldn't see shit in whatever room she'd been pulled into.

"Let me go!" She jerked up her knee but missed her target.

"Yo! Need my fuckin' junk in one piece, woman."

Her breath rushed out of her and every muscle loosened as she recognized the voice. And then his scent.

Pot. Whiskey. Sandalwood. Deacon.

"Gonna let you go. Don't maim me."

"Is this your room?"

Suddenly, a bright overhead light turned on and blinded her. This was not a bedroom, but a large, commercial-looking kitchen. A chef's wonderland of stainless steel between the large appliances, the expansive counter space and variety of cooking implements. Everything looked restaurant quality. And not a dumpy diner type of restaurant, either. More like a four-star establishment.

It was unexpected. Just like the interior of The Barn. These men were not slumming it.

"Wow," she whispered, looking around. "Do you have a chef among you?"

"Nope. Though, that'd be a good fuckin' idea. With Trip rebuildin' this club from scratch, he decided to do it right from the start. But we're all responsible to make our own shit. Plus, the sweet butts use it to make food for our pig roasts and parties."

"They can cook, too?"

"Some. Not all. But this discussion ain't why you're here, Reese. So, why you here?"

Her wide eyes landed back on him. He wasn't naked like Easy, but he was pretty damn close. He only wore a pair of snug boxer briefs. She licked her lips and lifted her gaze slowly from his thick thighs, over what she knew was tucked in those navy briefs and up his tattooed and pierced torso.

When she reached his face, he had one eyebrow cocked which was barely noticeable under the dark blond waterfall of his long, loose hair.

She expected to see amusement in his expression, but it wasn't there. His lips were nothing but a thin, angry slash.

Had she interrupted something? He could be grabbing a late-night snack for whoever was spending time with him in his room.

"Why you here?" he grumbled again.

"I..." *Good God*, even angry, his voice caused a flutter in places it shouldn't. "I don't know."

"Yeah, you do. You walked the fuck away from me without a goddamn word. Left me standin' there cold, with just my dick in my hand. Bolted like a damn deer hearin' a gunshot durin' huntin' season. Didn't think you were afraid of anything 'til I saw it in your eyes."

"What did you see?" She knew what it was. Had it been that obvious?

"Somethin' spooked you." He pulled his chin back and stared down at her. "Was it 'cause you were jealous?"

Had she been jealous? No. Impossible. "It just hit me while standing there that I don't belong here."

He crossed his arms over his bare chest, causing the muscles to bunch. His eyes glittered like brown diamonds. And not in a good way. "Then, good thing it's only fuckin' temporary. You don't gotta like what goes on here. You don't gotta fuckin' fit in." One side of his lip pulled up in a sneer. "Sorry this is all fuckin' beneath you. Thought you lost your stick. Musta found it again. Hopefully you used lube to shove it back in place." A muscle popped in his cheek. He dropped his arms and headed toward the exit behind him. "Go to bed, Reese."

"Deacon..."

He stopped with his palm planted on the door, poised to push it open. He didn't look back, but he did wait.

She closed her eyes and inhaled deeply. When she opened them, she asked, "Did you fuck any of those sweet butts after I left?"

Every corded muscle in his back and extended arm went as hard as his eyes had been. "Would you be pissed if I did?"

Lord help her, yes, she would. And that thought *did* scare the bejeezus out of her.

Silence shrouded them. Reese could no longer hear whoever had been going at it down the hall.

Then she asked something stupid. A question which would intentionally cause a reaction. Anything to avoid admitting she would be jealous if he'd ended up with one of those women. "Would you be pissed if I accepted Easy's invite?" She knew it was petty the second it escaped.

He spun around and she automatically took a step back, her breath catching in her throat.

"What invite?" he growled. His nostrils flared as he raked his gaze down her. "What the fuck you wearin'?"

She glanced down as if she'd forgotten what she had on. "Jeans."

"No. On top." He took a step toward her, his hands now clenched into fists, and she took another one back. "That goddamn thin, silky thing with no bra. No fuckin' wonder he gave you a goddamn invite. Walkin' down here in the middle of the fuckin' night wearin' that shit. I can see every fuckin' detail of your nipples." The last came out in a barely-controlled roar.

Dumbstruck, she glanced down again and realized he was right.

"Why you here, Reese? Were you lookin' for me? Or any available dick?"

She picked her dropped jaw off the floor and knocked it back into place. "That's not fair."

"Yeah? Life ain't fair. You of all people know that. And I'm just callin' it as I see it."

He took another step forward and she held her ground this time, snapping her spine straight and lifting her head.

"Why you here, Reese? You here to ride my dick, then disappear as soon as you get off?" He reached out and pressed his thumb to her lips. He dropped his head and stared directly into her eyes. "You here to give me just enough of you to make me want more? That why you here? Let's talk about fuckin' unfair." He dragged his thumb roughly across her bottom lip and her breath swept over it. "Wanna know why there's no one waitin' in my bed right now?"

She didn't. But she was pretty damn sure she was going to find out.

"'Cause I didn't wanna use them like that. The way you've been usin' me. Know what the fuck it feels like now. To want more from someone who don't wanna give it. It sucks, Reese." He tucked his thumb under her chin and tipped her face up. Their lips were now so close she could feel his hot breath mingling with hers. "You... fuckin'... broke... me."

Her chest tightened to the point where she couldn't breathe.

He released her and jerked away, spinning on his bare heels and slamming the swinging door with both his palms.

Reese blinked, frozen in place.

She broke him? What did that mean?

It was her fault that he couldn't use a woman, like one of those sweet butts, and not feel guilty now?

Bullshit.

Oxygen flooded her lungs and she lunged forward, pushing through the still swinging door. She spotted him down the dark hallway, turning right and disappearing into the room at the very end. Down by the shared bathroom.

She kicked off Reilly's flip-flops, ran down the hallway and just as he was shutting his door, she shoved it open.

"Oh no. No, you don't. You don't blame me for not being able to treat women like nothing more than a piece of fucking meat."

"Keep your fuckin' voice down or we're gonna have an audience."

"I don't give a shit. Let them listen."

He yanked her into the room, far enough to be able to close the door. "I don't need my brothers ridin' my ass 'cause of some woman squawkin' at me."

"Some woman?"

"Yeah, Reese. Some woman."

"Am I just *some woman* to you?"

"Just like I'm only a dildo to you."

"Isn't that supposed to be how it works?"

"What the fuck you talkin' about?"

She waved a hand between them. "This thing between us."

"This thing..."

"Yes, this thing... Oh wait. *You're* supposed to be the one who usually disappears. Did I beat you to it? Did I damage your fragile ego when I walked away earlier?"

He huffed. "Don't got an ego."

"The hell you don't."

"You know who has a fuckin' ego? You. Think you're too good to have a man in your life. One man fucked you over and now they're all trash."

It wasn't only one. "Tell me something... When's the last time you've been in a long-term relationship?"

Deacon pursed his lips.

Reese's flattened out. "Thought so. You've probably been banging your way through all the available women in this town, right? And maybe even surrounding towns. Not to mention, all those sweet butts your club keeps around to use like whores or slaves, or whatever. Women you use when it's convenient. So, you have no room to talk, Deacon. None.

Why can't a woman do the same as a man? Why is it that when a man sleeps around and doesn't settle down, it's okay. When a woman does it, it's not. Tell me."

His brow was pulled so low, his brown eyes appeared almost black. "Tell me what made you."

"What made me," she repeated, once again dumbstruck. What did that have to do with anything?

"Yeah. Why you're so goddamned driven and have a hard time lettin' loose. Reilly ain't like that. If you didn't look so much alike, I'd doubt you were even related, forget bein' sisters. What the fuck made you the way you are? And I'm not talkin' about your lyin', cheatin' ex, either. You said you came from shit beginnings but never told me the details."

Suddenly, her mouth went dry and she needed to escape. Yes, it was a mistake coming down here.

"It's not something I want to share with anyone. Or even remember."

"Why? Whatever it was made you the way you are."

"Why are you turning this around?" She was getting loud again. She was sure if the rooms near Deacon's were occupied, they could hear their conversation.

"Ain't turnin' shit around, Reese. Wanna know why you are the way you are."

"Why do you care? And why would you even think you have the right to know?"

His head jerked back, and a couple veins protruded near his temples. He stared at her, unblinking, as he growled, "Get the fuck outta my room. Use your own fuckin' fingers if you need to get off."

"Deacon—"

"No. If your own hand ain't good enough," he jerked the door open, "then Easy's down the fuckin' hall. Hook a left, last door on the right. He'll be more than accommodatin'. Just make sure he wraps it tight first, since you probably ran into him while he was headin' to wash off the last snatch he fucked."

"I don't want Easy."

He leaned in real close and grumbled, "No? He ain't good enough, either? Then what the fuck do you want?" roughly enough it vibrated against her chest.

"I want you to close the door."

Chapter Sixteen

I want you to close the door.

If he wasn't so fucking stupid, he'd kick her ass out right now.

But that wasn't what he wanted. He wasn't telling her that, though. Fuck no.

He sighed, cursing himself out for being so fucking weak. Reese was so fucking wrong for him and he couldn't give a shit.

He still wanted her.

"I didn't come down here to ride you like a dildo," she said with a grimace, then her fingers went to the cut on her lip.

The reminder of what Warren did to her got his temper flaring again. "You didn't?"

"Well, that's... No... I mean... I need to talk to you about tomorrow."

"It's tomorrow already. Couldn't wait 'til the sun came up?"

"No."

"Is that the only reason?" Of course it wasn't, otherwise

335

she would've brought it up earlier or in the morning when most people normally discussed shit.

She blew out a telling breath.

"Didn't think so." He reached behind him and pushed the door shut, flipping the lock on the knob. He didn't bother to turn the deadbolt Trip had installed on the rooms since he wasn't sure how this conversation would go.

She was either going to end up in his bed down here with him or his bed upstairs without him. If she didn't want to give him the piece of her he needed, then it would be the latter.

Because of that, he laid it out. "Watched you totally melt down in front of me earlier. Never saw a woman lose her shit without sayin' a fuckin' word. Truth? Kinda made my asshole pucker. Most women just let their shit fly. But you? You pack that shit tight and deep. Figured it's as volatile as gunpowder. One mistake and it'll explode. I'm not gonna be one of your casualties when it does. So, here's the thing... You ain't gettin' what you want 'til I get what I want. You ain't gettin' the D 'til I know the shit you *don't share*."

She reached past him for the doorknob. "Last door on the right, you said?"

"Woman," he growled.

Grabbing her waist, he lifted her up and shuffled the few steps to his bed. He dropped her in the center, her arms snaking around his neck as he followed her down but not completely. Instead, he went to his hands and knees, caging her in.

He did his best not to touch her and also ignore her nipples pressing against that silky fucking material. They were so hard, every bump stood out even around the outer edge. If he touched them, it would be like reading Braille.

But he couldn't touch them. Not yet. "Let's get the talkin' outta the way, so we can get to the part where neither of us will be able to even form a valid thought."

He let his gaze slide over her face, which was fucked up. Her one green eye blinked up at him, the other was still so fucking purple and swollen. But none of her injuries took away how much he wanted her.

He'd been bothered by how spooked Reese looked in The Barn earlier. But, in truth, he was just as spooked. Never before had he experienced a pull toward a woman like he did with her. It didn't make any fucking sense.

"Business shit first."

"I have court tomorrow. Plus, I have things I need to get done at the office."

"What things?"

She sighed. "Stuff."

"What stuff?"

"Lawyer stuff."

He clenched his teeth, trying to keep his fucking patience. "Reese."

"I need to be in Judge Thomas's office by nine am. I'm meeting my client there."

"Judge Thomas." He frowned. "He's the local district justice. We deal with him on occasion. He's right in Manning Grove."

"Yes. But I have paperwork at the office I need for this case."

"Have one of your girls meet us at the DJ's office. Have her bring that and whatever other shit you'll need this week."

"Deacon..."

For fuck's sake, this wasn't one of her negotiations. "Listen, this is how it's gonna go..."

She arched her unbruised eyebrow. "Oh? Can't wait to hear this."

He put all his weight on one hand and slipped the other down to protect his junk before he spoke. He might do dumb shit sometimes, but he wasn't stupid. This woman did not like being told what to do and that was what he was about to do.

It was risky, but necessary.

"Gonna take you and Justice to the office in the mornin'. Leave him with Judge. Take you to the DJ's office. You do your thing by kickin' ass, makin' them sweat. Hell, even make them cry. Once you're done with that, headin' back to my office and settin' you up at my desk. While you're doin' more of your ass kickin' shit, I'm gonna go grab you a new cell phone. After you're done slayin' your enemies for the day, gonna bring you home. And by home, I mean here. But listen carefully..."

She lifted her other eyebrow to match the one glued to her forehead. That one was a bit crooked and she hissed softly with the pain, but she was determined to make it known how she felt about his orders. He ignored her searing look and continued, since, *fuck it*, he already stepped one foot in it, he might as well go all in.

"No late hours. When I'm done, you're done." He shut up and let what he just said simmer.

He was pretty fucking sure she'd never been told anything like that before when her brow dropped low as her eyes narrowed dangerously on him. Or at least one did. The other was no more than a slit in the first place.

Maybe her marriage wouldn't have gone sideways if her ex had the balls big enough to set down some rules. Though, he was keeping that possibility to himself.

"Got a meetin' tomorrow night to discuss this shit about Warren and what we're gonna do. Tuesday, if my idea gets the go-ahead, we're settin' the trap for that fucker."

She finally said something and, *thank fuck*, it wasn't a pissed off screech accompanied by clawing out his eyes. He'd done good by distracting her with that last part about Warren. Yeah, he wasn't always so dumb.

Just sometimes.

"What idea? What trap?"

Feeling safe enough to remove his hand from his now bulging boxer briefs, he gently brushed some blonde strands off her forehead. She had an ugly bruise at her hairline, too.

Fucking Warren. Did he want the man to die? Fuck yes. But only after he suffered first.

"Reese, I got this. Let me figure it out, yeah? Know it's hard for you to understand, but you don't need to be in control of everything."

"She's my sister, Deke."

There it was. Her getting bristly. Preparing to throw down. Not liking the fact that someone other than her could take control and get the job done. He did his best to keep his tone even as he said, "Yeah, she is. And I got this. Trust me."

She didn't take trust lightly. He got it. Not only was she a lawyer who dealt with a lot of people who lied, but something in her past, besides her ex-husband, made her stingy when it came to trusting people.

Did he want to fuck her? Hell yes. But, surprisingly, he wanted her to trust him even more. If she handed that over to him...

"Will you get tired of hovering over me like that?"

He blinked. It took a second for him to realize why she asked that. She was going to trust him with her story. *Thank fuck.*

"Is what I wanna know gonna take long?"

"It could."

He slid to her side. "You still hurtin'?"

"I took some Aleve. It's helping."

"You didn't complain when I had you bent over my sled on the run," he reminded her.

"It didn't hurt enough to complain."

"I'm takin' that as you sayin' gettin' my dick's worth any discomfort."

"That's not what I said. And you just told me you didn't have an ego."

"Look, a man likes to hear he gives good dick."

"Wouldn't not hearing it motivate you to do better?"

He dug his bent elbow into the mattress and propped his head on his palm. "My dick ain't good enough for you, either?"

"You're more than just a dick, Deacon."

Huh. "Yeah? What else am I?"

"Do you want to hear my story or not?"

Now he was debating whether to hear what she really thought about him first. Not about the sex, he knew she liked that part, but the rest about him. "Yeah, babe, wanna hear your story."

She turned her head slightly, enough to make eye contact and hold it. Was she thinking twice about telling him? Or was it just so bad, she had a hard time talking about it?

He knew one thing. The woman before him was not broken. Fuck no. She wasn't even cracked. She was as strong as a damn fifty-year-old oak tree. Her branches extended out with confidence and she wouldn't let a storm topple her. She'd probably laugh in the face of a hurricane.

He could see why her ex wussed out. He couldn't stand his wife being the stronger person. She had intimidated him. Strong women were a threat to some men's manhood.

Fuck that. That part about her turned him on.

If he wanted to wipe his feet on something, he'd buy a doormat. He wanted a woman who'd force him to leave his dirty boots outside. Or else.

He wanted a woman who he could have an argument with and wouldn't curl up into a ball and cry. No, she'd give as good as she got.

His dick jerked in his underwear.

"Okay, you're hearing this story once, then we're never

discussing it again. Not ever, Deacon. It's the past and that's where it belongs. It's never to be used against me, either. Promise me that."

"You mean like a lawyer would?" *Damn.* Once again, sometimes he said or did dumb things. "Promise."

With a deep inhale—probably so she wouldn't clobber him—she began. "My mother was an alcoholic. From what I know, she started drinking heavily after I was born. I'm not sure if it was post-partum depression which started her down that road or what." She paused and took another deep breath, this one sounding less irritated and more to help brace herself. "She didn't stop drinking, even when she was pregnant with Reilly. Though, somehow she hid it for most of her pregnancy from everyone else. I guess because, by then, she was a functioning drunk and my father worked a lot, which meant he was gone a lot. Even though my mother also worked, he was the main source of income in our family. The older I got, the more I had to do for myself because she was no longer capable of it and he wasn't around."

"Your pop didn't do nothin' about her drinkin'?"

"From what I remember, he tried in the beginning, but eventually gave up. Until the day he caught her drinking when she was... Oh, I don't know, six months pregnant? He hated her drinking as it was. Mostly because it cost a lot of his hard-earned money and she was pretty much useless as a mother when she hit the bottle hard. But that day was the final straw. He started coming home less and less which, of course, made her drink more. The irony was, the more she drank, the less he wanted to be with her. The less he wanted to be with her, the more she drank."

"Vicious fuckin' cycle." Her story wasn't a new one, unfortunately. He'd heard similar ones before. Most didn't have a good outcome, which he assumed was the direction her story was going.

"Him avoiding the house turned eventually into him never coming home. He went from being gone from one night to two nights. Then a week, a month. I heard her crying on the phone, promising she'd stop, begging him to come home. Not for me. For her. She didn't stop hitting the bottle, but she did slow down for a little while. Until Reilly was born. How my sister didn't have FAS was a miracle."

"FAS?"

"Fetal Alcohol Syndrome. I was ten when Reilly was born, so, at the time, I didn't know anything about it. But when I was older, I researched it to make sure she didn't have any of those lasting issues."

He had no idea what effect FAS would have on a baby, but if Reilly still had it, he couldn't tell. She looked and acted like any normal twenty-four-year-old.

"A typical day for my mom would be to come home from work and drink until she blacked out. Every damn night. I'd find her on the couch passed out. Sometimes on the floor. I once found her in the empty tub with a bottle still in her hand. She stopped caring about herself. Whether she lived or died."

"She stopped carin' about you and Reilly." Whether they lived or died.

"I'm not sure she ever cared about Reilly. I think she had this drunken misconception that it was Reilly who caused my father to leave. I believe she got pregnant on purpose to try to hold onto my father. But it was her own drinking that caused him to leave, not an unplanned pregnancy. I had heard the arguments about her alcoholism for years before he left."

"A real man woulda taken his kids with him. Or at least handed them off to relatives who could raise them." The same way his parents raised Judge and Jemma. No way would his mother allow her niece and nephew to make their way in the world on their own. And Judge had been older than Reese at the time. Ten wasn't old enough to raise a baby. Ten wasn't old enough to handle the responsibilities of a household. Ten wasn't old enough to take on the adult world.

"Well, he never even said goodbye, so I guess he didn't give a shit about what happened to us. I'm not sure if he sent my mother money every month. If he did, she probably drank every dime of it."

"You raised Reilly on your own."

"I did my best to raise her *as* my own. I never told anyone about my mother. Or the fact my father abandoned us. My biggest fear was that CPS would discover we didn't have a responsible parent in the house, and they'd split us up. I couldn't allow that to happen. I *would* not allow that to happen. My sister didn't ask to be born or ask for irresponsible parents—"

"Neither did you. Did she buy food and pay the bills, at least?"

"My mother went from job to job. While she managed to earn just enough money to keep us surviving, it was up to me to get everything from groceries and diapers to school supplies. If I didn't do it, it didn't get done and we went without. The only good thing was, where we lived, I could walk to stores. I learned to cook, learned to forge my mother's name on the checks to pay the rent, the utilities and everything else. Then when I was old enough to get a job, I did and squirreled away every cent so I could get us as far away from where we were. From the lifestyle we were living. I swore to Reilly we'd never live like that again. *Swore* it. I told her the only direction to go from where we started was up. I was determined to prove to her we would not end up a product of our environment. We would do better. Be better."

He could taste the drive and determination in her words.

He'd been allowed to be a kid. She never had that. All because of selfish motherfucking parents.

"Eventually, I felt nothing for her. I only saw her as a source of income for us to survive. I hated my father, too. For abandoning us. Because in truth, we were orphans. We were on our own."

"You did more than a lot of parents, Reese. You should be proud of that."

"I had no choice."

"Yeah, you did. But your other choices sucked. Is your mom still alive?"

She stared blankly at the ceiling for a long moment. "I don't know."

"Do you care?"

"I don't."

"Does Reilly?" he asked.

"I'm not sure."

"She never said?"

"If she did, I think she wouldn't tell me for fear of hurting me."

"'Cause you're more her mom than sister." And that was fucked up.

"She knows what I sacrificed to raise her."

She sacrificed her whole fucking childhood.

He reached out and snagged her hand, interlacing their fingers. She was tense and it wasn't surprising. He had even tensed up while listening to her. He'd wanted to reach into her past and punch her father the fuck out. He wished he could go back and be with her. To help her. To relieve some of that burden. "Never got the chance to be a kid." That explained why she had a hard time letting loose. Having fun. Just enjoying life. She didn't know what it was like. It didn't come naturally.

Her voice was thick when she said, "I swore we'd never live like that again. Never live day to day, wondering if we'd have enough money for our next meal. Wondering if the next day the electricity and water would be shut off. Wondering if my mother might not ever come home." Her fingers squeezed his tight. "But it drove me to make something of myself."

"It drove you to the point you don't know how to pick your foot up off the fuckin' gas pedal." She was driving herself into the ground, trying to get where she *thought* she needed to be. Where Reilly needed to be.

She had a goal, but Deacon could see she was the type of person who kept moving the goal posts. She couldn't stop until there was nothing left of her to give.

"She's not grown yet."

She sacrificed her childhood for her sister, and now, as an adult, she was doing the same even though Reilly was no longer a kid. "She's grown, Reese. You're just havin' a hard time seein' it. The rest of us can."

"But Billy—"

"Bullshit. Lots of Warrens in the world, babe. More than you know. You can't protect her from all of them. You can't stop her from makin' mistakes."

"I can try."

"Who protected you?"

"Nobody."

"Right. And look at you now."

"Lying in a biker's bed."

She was ignoring the success she worked hard to build by making light of where she currently was. With him. "Ain't so bad, is it?"

"Depends who you ask."

Yeah, he wasn't stupid. He knew full well he wasn't on the other side of the goalposts. He wasn't even on her playing field. "I'm askin' you."

"Earlier today on the run and again in The Barn... Being around your brothers. The sweet butts. The whole lifestyle. It reminded me of how far I've come and how I never want to go back."

"This life ain't bad, babe."

She was a woman afraid of losing everything she worked for. She'd clawed her way with broken and bloody nails to the top and didn't want anyone or anything dragging her back down to the bottom.

Apparently, she had it in her head being involved with him and his club would take her back. That his lifestyle would grip her by the ankles and drag her back to the bottom.

"But it's not my life."

He got that this life wasn't for everyone. Didn't mean it didn't bother him that Reese felt that way. Normally it wouldn't, but it did with her.

"I'm sorry but today caused a flashback. It made me panic and realize where we might have ended up if I hadn't worked so damn hard. That could've been me—or Reilly—walking topless around a bunch of men, doing whatever I could, just hoping one of them would shower me with a little attention. Even if I needed to suck them off or have sex with them."

"They know what they're walkin' into when they come here. And they can leave at any time. No one's forcin' them to stay. No one's forcin' them to suck or ride a cock. No one."

"What are they hoping to get out of it?"

"Like you said, the attention, I guess. Maybe they like the fact no one's gonna judge them for sleepin' with Easy one night and Whip the next. You said yourself that we judge women differently from men. You're doin' it, too. How d'you know they ain't here 'cause they can get all the dick they want? Maybe they love sex. They know it's an environment they ain't gonna get raped or beat the fuck up if they say no. Or even for talkin' back. When, if it comes down to it, they're under our protection 'cause they belong to us. They can drink all they want and not worry about wakin' up in some alley after being gang banged. Yeah, maybe their morals are a little loose but then, so are ours. They belong to us and we protect what's ours."

"Property."

"Yeah, Reese, property. They belong to the BFMC 'til they decide they don't. But that's their decision unless they do somethin' stupid."

"What about you? Your brothers? Is it just as easy for you to walk away?"

"No reason to walk away."

"What if there was?"

"There won't be."

"Humor me."

He normally didn't talk club business with the women he fucked. But Reese wasn't just a woman he was using, and she just unloaded a lot of shit because he asked, so he could give her an answer on this. "You buy out your membership. Cover your colors. Give up your cut. But the hardest part of all that is givin' up your brotherhood. Givin' up havin' your brothers at your back."

"That loyal, huh?"

"Yeah, that fuckin' loyal. Some clubs are fucked up. Lot of shit goin' down. Backstabbing. Drama. Fightin' within the ranks. Power struggles. Illegal businesses which could bring in the pigs, if not the feds. Trip's workin' hard to do it right and avoid all that. He and some others, like my cousin, witnessed the way the Fury burned to the ground over twenty years ago. They learned from the Originals' mistakes. Not sayin' we won't make any, but he and the others know what not to do. Gotta respect him for that. You had a goal to make somethin' from nothin', so did our prez." He grabbed her chin and forced her to meet his eyes. "Believe it or not, you two are a lot alike. But while he's super fuckin' focused, he also knows how to let loose. He knows how to forget the heavy shit for a while and enjoy everything he's built. You need to learn that. What's the point of buildin' a life like you got if you can't enjoy it? Or die tryin' 'cause you don't think it's enough?" Or will ever be enough. She could drive herself so hard she could destroy herself.

"Now you know why I am how I am. What's behind my motivation and my need to succeed."

"Yeah. Thanks for trustin' me enough to share it."

"Talking about it isn't quite like living it. Believe me, it was way worse at the time."

"I believe it. When I said life's unfair, you're proof that's true. A child shouldn't raise a child. A kid shouldn't ever be liftin' that heavy burden. So, I realize what you said ain't nothin' like what you lived. I get it. But, babe, here? You're surrounded by people who are survivors of their fucked-up family life. If anyone would understand, they would. Remember that when you look at them. Or if you get the urge to judge them. Look past their fuckin' cuts and sleds, their tattoos, drinkin' and cursin'. Instead, see how far they've come. Just like you. Your measure of success just might be a little different, that's all."

"How about your childhood?"

"Mine was fuckin' awesome. We might not have been rich, but I had great fuckin' parents. Maybe you'll get to meet my mom. She'd love you unless you got that stick jammed up your ass when you meet her."

His lips curled up slightly when hers did.

She ran her fingertips from the hollow of his neck to one of his nipples where she gently flicked his barbell with her fingernail. "What about your dad?"

"Cancer took him when I was a teen."

Her fingers stilled for a moment. "Sorry. That had to be difficult."

"It was. But thank fuck I had him for as long as I did. I was ten when Jemma and Judge came to live with us. Can't imagine raisin' a baby at that age. Hell, I was pissed I had to share my room and my fuckin' toys."

Her soft laugh had him grinning. It was a good sign that they were done talking about serious shit and could get down to serious naked business instead.

"Now you get the D you so desperately want."

She rolled her eyes. "You're just..." She sighed.

"Yeah, I know. I'm so fuckin' amazin' I make you speechless."

"That's not why."

"Anyway, got a coupla hours before you gotta sneak out. Trip don't want women stayin' overnight in the bunkhouse. Don't want it to turn into a whorehouse."

"Great. So, I'm a whore for sneaking down here?"

"Babe, whores don't have sticks up their asses. Just dicks."

"Are you saying if I like anal, I'm a whore?"

He rolled over her, caging her in again. His voice was gravelly when he asked, "You into anal?"

"It was a rhetorical question."

He narrowed his eyes, tilted his head and studied her face. "Sure it was. But we'll explore that deeper at another time. Got other plans for now."

"What kind of plans?" she whispered as he lowered his lips to hers.

"Shit that'll make you forget any man's name but mine."

"Wow," she mouthed.

"You think I'm kiddin'."

"Honestly? I hope you're not."

"Fuck yeah."

"Fuck yeah," she repeated as he took her mouth.

Chapter Seventeen

Reese quietly turned the key in the lock and opened the door.

She hadn't left Deacon's room as early as she should have. One reason was, every time she tried to leave, he pulled her back into bed.

She also knew she left too late because bikers in the form of zombies were wandering around the bunkhouse in various states of undress. Sig hadn't been lying when he said no one on that farm was shy. Not one of them cared that Reese had gotten an eyeful. Or more like many eyefuls. She tried not to ogle them too badly as she found Reilly's flip-flops she'd kicked off, then escaped using the back door.

She stepped into the apartment, turned after closing the door and... froze.

Her sister was awake already? Showered and dressed? Her hair was neatly pulled back into a cute ponytail and a Pop Tart was clenched between her teeth as she poured a glass of OJ.

"Morning." Reese cleared her throat since her greeting came out rough and scratchy from lack of sleep. *Aaand* maybe from calling out Deacon's name one too many times. In a very high pitch.

Reilly took a bite, then asked around a mouthful of the frosted toaster pastry, "Where've you been?"

Her baby sister seemed amused.

Justice loped up to her and Reese gave the bulldog his required ear ruffle and pat on the butt. "Walking. I couldn't sleep."

Reilly's gaze dropped to Reese's feet tucked into her flip-flops and her lips twisted. "Right. Walking. I think you mispronounced fucking."

She ignored that by asking, "Why are you up so early?"

"It's not so early, sis. I'm surprised you don't know that since you have every minute of your life scheduled."

"What time is it?" She wondered if Justice had been outside yet.

"Almost seven."

"That's early for you."

"I have a job, remember?"

One she was taking seriously? That was surprising. "Do you like it?"

"Yeah. It's great. Dutch is a bit gruff, as well as rough around the edges, but, hey, one of the benefits of the job is a great view."

"The garage has a great view?" Reese had assumed the shop was in town.

"Yeah. Can't get a better one than four hot guys who look great wearing jeans and grease."

Reese rolled her eyes. "Reilly..."

Her sister raised a palm. "Don't worry. My panties might get a bit damp, but they haven't fallen off yet."

"Yet," Reese murmured. "Well, the job's only temporary."

"Sure it is," Reilly answered, then downed half the juice.

They heard a horn beep.

"Fuck, that's my ride." Reilly downed the rest of the OJ and fed the last bite of the Pop Tart to Justice.

"I don't like you being on the back of a motorcycle so much. It's dangerous."

"I do," Reilly said as she passed Reese, then paused with one hand on the knob. "You seemed to enjoy the run yesterday. Especially when Deke took you on that little detour."

"He had something he wanted to show me."

"Sure he did. Same thing he showed you just a little while ago."

"Reilly..."

"Sis... It's okay to get laid. No one around here cares if you're boning Deke. Well, Deke probably does. He's not beating you off with a stick, right? You're not forcing that handsome Viking stud to do all kinds of naughty things to you against his will?"

"We're not discussing this."

"See? The only person it bothers is you."

Reese's mouth gaped as Reilly jerked open the door. Justice pushed past them, ran down the steps to do his business.

"Look at you, big sis, getting fucked by a bad boy." Reilly wiggled her eyebrows. "And it bothers you that you like it so much." She grinned and planted a peck on an unbruised spot on Reese's cheek.

Reese followed her sister outside and stood on the landing as Reilly jogged down the steps to the awaiting bike. A spring was noticeable in her sister's step that she did not have while at Reese's house in Mansfield.

"Sweetheart, your chariot awaits," the biker shouted over the loud, rumbling exhaust.

Reese tried to remember the name of the biker who Reilly settled behind and wrapped her arms tightly around. She was normally good with names, she had to be in her line of work. Nothing worse than forgetting a judge or client's name. Or getting it wrong.

His name was some sort of chess piece.

Rook. That was it.

If she remembered correctly, he was Dutch's oldest son. The one that had been in and out of jail in the past few years.

He was as tattooed up as the rest of them. This morning he wore jeans, a T-shirt and his Fury cut.

As she stared down at Rook, he stared back up at her. Even with the distance between them, she could feel his eyes inspect her bruised face and saw his jaw shift sharply.

After a moment, he glanced over his shoulder. "Ready?"

"Yep." Reilly called up to her on the landing. "I love you, sis. Don't worry."

Reese would always worry about her. That would never change.

And right now, seeing her sister slide so easily into the club life and onto an ex-con's bike worried the hell out of her.

Deacon could say there was more beneath the surface of his club and brothers than met the eye, but she wasn't sure if she believed that yet. She needed to see it for herself.

––––––––

REESE LIFTED the red Solo cup to her lips and let the red wine slide down her throat to join the rest of the wine already filling her gut. The evening was perfect. The breeze light. The sun still up but fading. And good company surrounded her.

The Blood Fury's executive committee was upstairs in the barn having their meeting about taking the next step in capturing Billy Warren.

She wasn't sure how this whole situation turned from

Deacon trying to capture a skip to suddenly a whole MC getting involved in finding the man.

It probably went back to the loyalty Deacon talked about. Having his brothers at his back. If he needed their help, they all stepped in.

Maybe with all of them involved the curtains would soon be closing on the Billy Warren Shit Show.

She could only hope.

But right now, she was drowning her worries in wine. Lots and lots of wine since Deacon insisted she stop working at five and forced her to leave his office.

She still had so much work to do and she'd spent three hours of her day in Judge Thomas's courtroom this morning. Three whole hours on a case that should've been settled weeks ago.

Some clients were just too stubborn for their own good.

Her snort of irony echoed inside her plastic cup as she tipped it once more to her lips.

"What do they do in these meetings?" Reese asked her dwindling cup of boxed wine.

"Measure their dicks, probably," Stella answered after taking a long swig off her beer bottle.

Reese glanced up. "Has anyone actually witnessed what they do?"

"None of us," Autumn answered. "Women aren't allowed."

Reese's mouth made an *O* shape as she stared at the redhead. "By the way, do you prefer Red or Autumn?"

Sig's ol' lady smiled. "Whatever you want to call me."

"You're really nice."

Autumn's smile grew even bigger. "So are you."

No, she didn't feel nice. Didn't nice people have friends? She didn't have friends. She had two employees and she sometimes talked to Bambi at the Mill Creek Bar & Grill.

That was it.

She hadn't even had time to make friends in school. She was too busy taking care of Reilly, working, or studying hard so she could earn college scholarships.

Even during college, it was the same. Working and studying hard to keep those scholarships. She hadn't lived on campus so she could keep Reilly with her. The few spare moments she had were taken up by making sure Reilly was doing her homework and assignments, so she, too, could get into college.

She had gone to one college party and that was when she met Allen. Instead of drinking, they ended up talking all night and sharing their dreams of success. She had thought he was as driven as her.

She was wrong.

Now, here she sat, under a pavilion on a farm owned by a biker club. This was *after* she crawled out of a biker's bed this morning.

She groaned.

"Are you okay?" Autumn asked softly, touching Reese's forearm lightly.

Honestly, she wasn't sure. Her life had spun out of control and until Billy was caught, she couldn't get it back to normal. And that thought caused a rock to sink to the very bottom of the red wine pond in her stomach.

"Have you ladies always been a part of this?" She swept a hand around the courtyard.

"I only met Judge a few months ago," Cassie answered.

"And you're already building a house together?" Reese raised a hand. "Sorry, did that sound judgy? I didn't mean it to be judgy. I meant, you knew he was the one right away?"

Cassie laughed. "Oh no. Not right away. I have a daughter—you haven't met Daisy yet—I had to look out for her. I was worried about bringing her into this life. She's not even six yet."

"But you're comfortable with doing so?"

Cassie hesitated for a moment. "Yes. You have to look past the surface to see the value of this club."

Interesting. "You don't mind her being around those sweet butts?"

"For the most part, we keep her away from The Barn and the parties. That's why we now have Saylor as a house mouse. Plus, my sister and her husband live in town. It's another reason why we're building our house on the other side of the trees. To keep a bit of a separation. However, this club is a family and I want her to be a part of that. We just control what activities she's involved in."

That sounded like a responsible plan. Reese turned to Autumn. "I asked Sig how you two met. He didn't go into details."

"Fate," the redhead said simply.

"That's what he said."

Autumn wore a small smile. "We saved each other."

"I was born into the original Blood Fury," Stella interrupted, pulling Reese's attention to her. She had a feeling that Stella was protecting Autumn, which made her even more curious about Sig and Autumn's story. "My father was Crazy Pete and was an Original. It's his cut hanging on the wall in The Barn. So, this lifestyle is nothing new to me, even though I left it for a long time. Though, in truth, I really didn't leave it because I married a musician and the life around a musician isn't much different. This life isn't for everyone." The last sounded like a warning.

Did they think she was considering it? "I'm more curious than anything."

Stella and Autumn exchanged looks and Cassie stared at her red plastic cup with a knowing smile on her face.

"I noticed on the run, you ladies wore vests, but yours claimed you were property of your men. You don't mind being considered property?"

"That's typical for an MC. To be an ol' lady your man

has to claim you at the table. Not all women wear the vests, it's not required." Stella shrugged. "And we only wear them on the runs. Like Cassie said, you have to look past the surface, Reese. Not everything is what it seems."

"You wear a vest that says Trip owns you. How is that not how it seems? It's a pretty clear statement."

Stella took another sip of her beer and, when she lowered the bottle, asked, "Do you think Trip owns me?"

"You seem pretty powerful in your own right." Stella didn't seem the type to be easily owned or manipulated. Neither did Cassie, who was also outspoken.

"Trip respects my opinion because we both witnessed the Blood Fury implode all those years ago. We were both victims when our lives fell apart due to how the club was run. Trip doesn't want to make the same mistakes his father, the president at the time, did and I want to help him avoid those same mistakes. He's invested in this club. We all are." Stella made a sweeping motion with her hand, encompassing the other two women. "One thing I need to clarify... The MC life isn't a life you choose, it chooses you. Then it's up to you to decide whether to accept it or not."

Reese was starting to see that this club was much more than simply a group of bikers. The inner workings were more complex than what was shown to the rest of the world.

However, it still had some crude practices most women in a serious relationship might not agree with. "The men seem loyal to each other but are your men loyal to you?"

Stella smiled at her beer. Autumn's expression turned soft. Cassie threw her head back and laughed openly.

How these women didn't start throwing things at her and chasing her away with a pitchfork, Reese would never know. They took her questions in stride. Luckily.

"We don't have to worry about them being loyal to us. They're too busy worrying about us being loyal to them. You've seen them all. Besides the newest prospects, have you seen one you wouldn't climb like a beanstalk?" This coming from Autumn surprised Reese. Maybe the woman wasn't as sweet and innocent as she looked.

Reilly muttered, "Dutch."

"Well, okay. But, whether you believe it or not, the old man has no problem getting women, either. I remember Dutch in his prime," Stella added. "He might've always been rough around the edges but he wasn't hard to look at. He also made two very good-looking sons."

Cassie glanced around quickly, then leaned forward and whispered, "Hey, I've seen Dutch naked. He has an impressive... *asset*."

Stella snorted. "We've all seen Dutch naked."

"I haven't," Reilly volunteered.

"Just give it time," Stella assured her.

Time. With what the guys were meeting about upstairs, whatever they decided would hopefully mean it wouldn't be much longer until Billy was captured and delivered to the bail bondsman in Philadelphia.

"You know," Cassie started with what sounded like a wine-induced giggle, "we should have them do a BFMC calendar. For charity, of course." She did an exaggerated wink. "All profits donated to the Kids Can Do Foundation. Wouldn't that be a good idea? I know we have the Poker Run planned in June, but I want to do more."

"The club does charity work?" Reese asked, surprised.

"We're just getting started," Autumn answered. "You ladies won't mind other women ogling your men?"

"I don't mind sharing if it's for a good cause." Stella laughed. "And there's a difference between looking and touching. We get to see plenty of eye candy ourselves. As long as we're not tasting that candy..." The black with blue stripes-haired, tattooed woman raised her bottle and both Cassie and Autumn clunked their plastic cups with it.

"I only peek. I try not to be *too* obvious about it," Cassie announced with a grin.

"The men would mind you looking?" Reilly asked, again surprised. Especially when they had naked sweet butts wandering amongst them.

"My man would," Cassie said. "Judge has this mistaken notion that he's the only man on Earth I should look at." She slapped her own knee and bent forward with uncontrollable laughter.

The other two ladies howled along with her.

"Well, the guys certainly don't hide anything, which makes it about impossible to avoid seeing their... *goods*," Reese mumbled.

"Yes, you got to experience an eyeful while you were in The Barn last night," Stella said, still laughing while tipping her almost empty bottle to her lips. "Before you rushed out." She finished the last swallow of her beer.

Reese didn't want to confess to the "eyeful" she got last night with Easy in the bunkhouse. Or the peeks she got this morning while sneaking out. She was getting to know these men better than she'd ever expect to in ways she never expected.

Her gaze sliced to Reilly, who sat at the next picnic table over, also drinking a beer and looking like she belonged.

Reese felt a flash of envy. Her sister could fit in anywhere, unlike Reese. She needed to work on that more. Maybe when she had more time she'd make more of an effort to find a hobby... And some friends. Like the women she was currently sitting with.

"Speaking of an eyeful," Stella said under her breath, just loud enough for them to hear. "Yours is coming our way."

Who was she talking to? Reese twisted her head in the direction Stella was staring. Her chest tightened when she realized Stella was talking to her.

Deacon was headed toward them with Justice meandering behind him at a distance, stopping to smell and mark things along their path.

"He'd look great on a calendar," Cassie said on a sigh before guzzling down more wine. "He reminds me of a Viking ready to conquer a village with his big sword." The blonde might need to be cut off from the box of wine. "Has he conquered your village yet, Reese?"

"You just made my sister blush!" Reilly crowed way too loudly. "I don't think I've *ever* seen her blush! And hell yes, that Viking's ship has been pounding the shores of her village."

The heat in her face turned another degree hotter. "Reilly! Stop before he hears you."

Her sister shot her a wicked grin.

Cassie was laughing so hard, she was wiping away tears. Autumn had her face covered with her hands as she shook. Stella had jumped to her feet, giving Reese a standing ovation.

"Stop it!" Reese hissed. "He's... here."

The women's laughter instantly sobered, even though they didn't wipe the smirks off their faces.

Deacon stopped in front of the picnic table where they were sitting and his gaze circled the group, his expression holding suspicion. "What's goin' on?"

"Nothing. We're just discussing history," Reilly said quickly.

His gaze landed on the box of wine sitting on the table, then the Solo cup in Reese's hand. "The wine makin' you red like that?"

Stella snorted and dropped her head.

Deacon frowned at her and looked to Reese again. "You done here?"

"She's ready for her village to be pillaged," Reilly

announced loudly, trying to keep a straight face. Cassie wasn't the only one who needed cut off.

Reese needed to get this conversation under control. "Yes, we need to discuss tomorrow's plan."

Cassie arched an eyebrow. "Plan. Uh huh."

"You can use the apartment for your *discussion*. I'm going to hang here for a bit, then go to Crazy Pete's with the boys from the garage. It's open mic night and I could use some fun to get my mind off that motherfucker." She leaned toward Reese. "That means I'm going to be late." She did an exaggerated wink. "Just change the sheets before I get back."

Reese gave her sister an eyeroll. "Thank you, ladies, for keeping me company and entertained."

"We'll do this again real soon," Autumn said.

"We should make it a regular thing," Cassie suggested.

"That sounds like a plan," Stella agreed. She threw both fists up into the air like a boxer who just won a match. "The official executive meeting of the ol' ladies. No men invited."

"Right. Just a box of fuckin' wine and a six-pack," Deacon muttered. "Not sure Trip's gonna like you women havin' your own executive meetin'."

"Well then, good thing it's not up to him," Stella stated.

"Woman power!" Cassie yelled.

"All right, let's go," Deacon ordered Reese, jerking his head toward the building.

She stared at him.

"We've got things to discuss," he tried again.

Muffled snickers surrounded them, making Deacon's frown deepen.

Reese slowly got to her feet and turned to face the women. "Again, thank you, ladies. This was... enlightening." She turned back to Deacon. "Is it safe for Reilly to go to Crazy Pete's tonight?"

"Besides them being assholes, yeah. With four Fury members there and Dodge? Ain't gonna be a problem."

"See?" Reilly called out as Deacon grabbed Reese's arm and dragged her away. "Don't forget to change the sheets. I'm not sleeping in the wet spot!"

"I'm not sure what pod she hatched from," Reese muttered as she was pulled toward the back of the bunkhouse.

"She just knows how to have fun. Somethin' you need to learn. Let her have tonight 'cause after tomorrow? She ain't gonna be happy when she's told she'll be stuck at Dutch's and here. That's it. She's goin' on lockdown 'til Warren pops up his weasel-ass head."

He released the tight grip on her arm and spread his hand along her lower back, instead, propelling her toward the bottom of the back stairway. Justice ran by them, racing up the steps.

"Sounds like you got the okay on your plan."

He scrubbed a hand down his beard. "Yeah. Let's hope it fuckin' works."

"And if it doesn't?"

"It's gotta. Now..." He paused and steered her around to face him. "We gonna go dirty the sheets?"

Reese shrugged one shoulder. "How can I resist that grin?"

"Told you I'm irresistible."

"I didn't say that."

"Didn't have to. Can see it in your one good eye."

She rolled that "one good eye" at him. "Do you have a spare set of sheets?"

"Fuck no. I just know I won't be sleepin' in the wet spot tonight."

"You think there will be one?"

He tipped his chin down, his smile now blinding. "Challenge accepted."

Chapter Eighteen

TEN DAYS.

Ten whole fucking days since they'd posted the first staged picture of Reilly in front of Dutch's Garage. They'd even made sure the business's sign was visible in the photo. They had her smile brightly with Rook's arm wrapped around her waist, squeezing her close. Deacon's club brother was also giving Reese's younger sister a hungry look that appeared way more authentic than it should.

The photo's caption on Instagram was: *New job! New HOT boyfriend! Life can't be better!* Along with five million hashtags and emojis. Some of those being flames, hearts and a dash of eggplants.

They figured if it seemed as though Reilly was enjoying stuffed eggplant by a new man, it might bring Warren out of the woodwork a little quicker.

They'd even tagged Manning Grove as the location to make it easier for the asshole to find her. Nothing like spoon-feeding the fucker to help him surface.

If Warren went back underground and said *fuck it* to cleaning up this loose end, then they were doing this all for nothing.

But Deacon had dealt with fugitives like Warren before. Abusers like him had a tough time letting things—or women like Reilly—go. Especially when Reilly was determined to send him to prison for what he did to her.

Men like Warren didn't appreciate a woman getting the best of him.

About five days ago, Reese had lost what was left of the little patience she'd been clinging to. Not being able to go home, to court, or her office without an escort—who usually was Deacon, sometimes Judge, and in a pinch, Shade—had her climbing the walls and snapping at the smallest thing.

Usually a couple hits off his joint and a glass of wine beat back the beast. But that dragon couldn't be slayed until after business hours.

Since setting her up at Justice Bail Bonds almost two weeks ago, she had completely taken over Deacon's office by claiming every inch of desk space, and even a corner on the floor was piled high with files. Worse, he was locked out of his own damn office when she held virtual meetings with her staff or her clients.

Though, he'd grin when he could hear her giving someone shit through the closed door. Sometimes it would even give him wood. Once she'd unlock the door, he'd go in, twist the lock and bend her over the desk, making her neat, organized piles of paperwork not so neat. Or organized.

All of this also pissed off Judge because, even though they tried to muffle their noises, his office was right across the narrow hall and the walls weren't thick. It didn't help his grumpiness that Deacon was sharing his office and claimed his couch as a temporary work space. Judge would glare at him when Deacon would return with beads of sweat on his forehead and a satisfied grin.

"You'd be doin' the same shit with Cassie if she was workin' here."

"It ain't Cassie and it ain't me. So, fuck you."

Comments like that would make Deacon howl which pissed off his cousin even more.

But Deacon agreed, sharing Judge's small office sucked. The only good thing about the situation was—besides getting an occasional bend-over action in the afternoon—Deacon was getting laid every night, too.

Sometimes in his room in the bunkhouse. Sometimes in his apartment. Once on blankets spread in the bed of his Ford truck in one of the distant fields under the moonlit night and surrounded by stars. That night, Reese's cries, sighs and whimpers joined the mating calls of the crickets. And Deacon's grunts might have drove the bucks into early rut.

Heh.

Reese tried to insist he stay at the garage all day with Reilly, but between Dutch and the old man's mechanics—Rook, Cage, Rev and Whip—her sister was more than covered.

When business at the Tioga Pet Crematorium was slow, Shade would grab Cassie's old Honda, park down the street from the garage and help keep an eye out.

While Judge would have felt better if they weren't using Reilly as live bait, they needed Warren to see normal activity at the garage—in case he was watching—and not suspect it was a set-up.

But here it was ten days later and Deacon was stuck in a cranky pants sandwich while at the office. He was ready to go hang out at the garage all day, like Reese wanted, just to escape being snapped and growled at from both sides.

They had posted two more photos on Reilly's IG page since the first one. One was of Reilly behind the desk in Dutch's now organized office, looking perky and giving a thumb's up. Another of her and Rook kissing. Yeah, kissing. With tongues and everything. Rook's hand was planted firmly on her ass with the other dangerously close to squeezing the young blonde's tit.

As soon as Reese saw it, Deacon knew he wouldn't be getting any lunchtime action and he'd have to work hard to get some after dinner. He did, but he almost died trying.

It was still fucking worth it. Angry sex with Reese was still damn good sex. And definitely better than no sex. Better yet, no stun gun was involved, both nipple piercings were intact, and his nuts remained tucked safely in his sac.

Thank fuck.

Just the other day, Reese finally put her high heel down and gave them a time limit. If Warren didn't show up by April thirtieth, she was going home and back to her office. She didn't care what anyone said.

In reality, if Warren didn't show up by the end of the month, Deacon doubted he would.

But rumor had it that even when Reese went back to Mansfield, Reilly wasn't going with her. She was having fun at her job and, in actuality, was pretty damn safe there. None of his brothers would let anything happen to her on their watch. Which meant, she was safer in Manning Grove than Mansfield. Or back in Philly by herself.

However, he decided to stay out of that decision and let Reilly tell her big sister that news herself.

Because his momma *didn't raise no fool.*

Justice whined and nudged Deacon's hand as he pressed an ear to his office door, listening to a worked-up Reese giving someone a lesson about out-of-court settlements and why it benefitted them.

She was so fucking good at it. At both teaching those lessons and her legal expertise.

His dick was hard and heavy in his jeans from what she was saying and how she was saying it.

However, her patience was at a breaking point. He had quickly learned what that point was and what it meant to him when it came to asking her to pull up her skirt so he could give her the business.

And he wasn't talking lawyer business.

Listening in, he could tell she was approaching that tipping point at lightning speed. That meant he needed to intervene and quickly.

He tried the knob and was relieved when it wasn't locked. Pushing open the door, he blocked Justice from joining them and quickly closed the dog out in the hallway. He heard a muffled whine but having Justice in the office with him when naked body parts were flopping around within nose reach wasn't smart.

An uncomfortable lesson learned.

Eventually, Justice would get bored waiting and head back into Judge's office to hang with Jury.

He turned and Reese's narrowed green eyes practically pinned him to the door. She made a face, tucked her cell phone between her shoulder and ear, then made a strangling motion with her hands.

Thank fuck that wasn't meant for him.

"Okay, Tom, let me deal with this... Yes... I have it under control, Tom... Okay... I understand. I'll let you know once I talk to them and see what the counteroffer is..." She dropped her head and pinched the bridge of her nose. "Yes... Sure, Tom..." Her knuckles were turning white while holding the cell. "I understand. We're on the same page... Okay. Talk to you tomorrow. Bye."

She pulled the phone from her ear, jabbed at the End button more times, and with more force, than necessary and slapped it face down on the desk. She dropped her head into her folded arms and growled.

Oh yeah, she was all worked up. Her blood was pumping and now all Deke had to do was get her to focus that frustrated energy into a frenzied quickie. He stopped himself from rubbing his hands together in anticipation.

He should've told Judge to put in some earplugs or something.

She lifted her head, a few strands of her hair falling loose from her bun and framing her now bruise-free face. "They hire me to represent them. To make the best deal for their company without going to court. They should let me do what I do best and stop fucking trying to *mansplain* what I need to do. I know what the fuck I need to do, that's why they pay me three hundred an hour."

Deacon's step stuttered as he moved closer. "What?"

Her green eyes hit his again, quickly changing from annoyance to confusion. "What?"

"What was the last thing you said?"

She frowned. "My billable rate?"

"You charge three hundred fuckin' bucks an hour?"

"That's not much."

"Are you shittin' me?"

"Deacon, that's not much for an experienced civil litigator."

"It ain't?"

"Well, up here, it's on the high side. But down in Philly or Pittsburgh, it would be a basement rate. Even though my rate's at the top of the chart for this area and the area of law I concentrate on..." The breath hissed out of her and she did a slight shrug. "I'm worth it."

He stared at the woman behind his desk. She stared back. Neither blinked.

Finally, she asked, "Did you lock the door?"

"Did you want me to?"

"Isn't that why you're in here?"

"Maybe I just want to ask you to lunch."

She made a *yeah, right* face. "No, you don't."

He wasn't done talking about the bomb she just dropped. "How much did your ex make?"

"Why?"

"Just curious."

"I don't know... He was salaried. What does this have to do with anything?"

"You made more than him, right?"

"Didn't I tell you that?" She released an impatient sigh. "The harder I work, the more I make. His salary was what it was. Why does this matter, Deke? Are women not allowed to make more than their spouse?"

"For some, probably not. It emasculates them."

Her lips quirked at his use of a word she didn't expect him to know. "Would you feel emasculated if your woman made more than you?"

"Fuck no. Truth? That shit makes me hard. Powerful women like you turn me the fuck on."

"Would it drive you to work harder and make more?"

"No. Know why?"

Her lips twitched again. "I'm sure you're going to tell me."

"Because there's more to life than work, Reese. A lot fuckin' more. Our life starts the day we're born, it ends the day we die. We're supposed to live life in between those two major moments."

"I love what I do."

"Because you like control and power. But it ain't everything. We had that discussion about sometimes lettin' go. Lettin' someone else worry about the other shit. Takin' a break. Havin' fun. Why are you workin' so hard if you ain't gonna enjoy the result of your success?"

Reese sat back in his office chair and stared at him. "Why did you come in here?"

"You know why."

She stood up. "Then let's get to it. I have work to do." She shimmied up her just-above-the-knee, narrow black skirt—which was hot as fuck—and reached under it to yank down her panties. The red silky fabric fell around her high heels and she stepped out of them. "Over the desk again?"

"Reese..."

"Or, I know..." She turned, planted her palms against the wall and glanced over her shoulder. "How about this, instead?" She tipped her bare ass to the point he could see everything she was offering. And even what she wasn't.

When he didn't move, she reached back and slid her finger through her folds. He set his jaw against her tempting display.

Because... *for fuck's sake*... he had wanted to fuck her. That was his intent when he came into his office. But now...

Fuck! Was he really thinking twice about fucking Reese? What the fuck was wrong with him?

He closed his eyes for a second. They opened when he heard her jerk the desk drawer open, where he now kept a supply of wraps for all the sex they'd been having.

She threw one on the desk and assumed her position again. He dropped his gaze from her to the wrap.

"Let's go, Deke. I don't have all day."

She didn't have all day.

Hurry up and fuck me, Deke, so I can get back to work and you'll stop bothering me.

Hurry up and fuck me because I have more important things to do.

Hurry up and fuck me because that's all I want from you.

While she'd never said any of those things out loud, he could hear them in his head. She didn't have to say them, he felt those unsaid words down to his bones.

He lunged forward with a snarl, swiped the wrap from the desk, tucked it between his bared teeth, and jerked opened his jeans enough to expose his dick. He ripped open the wrapper, rolled the latex on, and moved to where she waited.

She gasped when he gripped a fistful of her hair—not caring that it wrecked her goddamn bun—shoved her cheek into the wall and dragged his throbbing dick down her crease, pausing for a second on the hole he hadn't had yet. With regret, he slid the head of his dick lower until it caught where it needed to be.

He hesitated.

He didn't like the feeling of being used.

He was more than just a dick.

The minute Warren was caught, she would leave. She'd go back to her own bubble and he'd be left behind in his.

He loved his life, but he wasn't sure if it would be enough without Reese in it.

His chest tightened as he stared at the woman he held against the wall. She hadn't fought against him being rough with her, she hadn't voiced a complaint. In fact, she was waiting for him to continue.

But, *for fuck's sake...*

His heart thumped heavily in his chest.

This wasn't what he wanted.

Yes, he wanted to fuck Reese, but he wanted more.

He fucking wanted a lot more.

Christ.

He'd lost his fucking mind. He'd never wanted more before.

Not once.

He'd always been the one to take what was offered and then move on. No lingering. No exchange of anything other than body fluids. Not even phone numbers.

Sometimes not even real names.

His chest was not only tight, it now hurt. A stabbing pain made him suck in a breath.

"Deacon..."

His nostrils flared when she tried to turn her head to look at him, but he kept her from doing so by forcing her face to remain where it was.

He waited for the odd feeling to settle. For the deep need to disappear.

He wanted to chalk it up to a case of crossed wires in his brain. A momentary misfire of neurons.

He waited.

One heartbeat.

Two.

None of it went away. On the third heartbeat, the ache moved from his chest to his gut, encompassing him. He feared it would swallow him whole.

Her flat, emotionless, very foreign words of, "You don't want me," invaded his brain.

She was wrong. He wanted her.

That was the fucking problem.

His need for her was seeping into his very soul.

Only, she didn't want to give him what he wanted. What he hadn't realized he needed until that exact fucking moment, when it struck him like a stun gun and took him to his knees.

With one hand, he ripped off the wrap, dropped it to the floor and tucked his now semi-soft dick away. He yanked her skirt down far enough to cover her ass.

"Deacon, what—" Her breath hissed from her when he used his grip in her hair to twist her around until she faced him with wide eyes. Before she could say anything else, he gripped her throat, shoved her back against the wall and took her mouth.

Whatever she wanted to say ended up muffled by the kiss. Her fingers curled into the T-shirt under his cut. They didn't push him away, instead pulled him closer.

He deepened the kiss, hoping she'd understand what he wanted—hell, *needed*—without having to say the words. Without having to slice himself open to expose that need she might not share.

He didn't want to hear her say no. He wanted to hear her say yes.

There was no guarantee on how she'd answer. Because of that, he didn't ask. He used his mouth, the intensity of his kiss, to show her how much he wanted her.

And not only for sex.

He wanted that "more" she might not be willing to give him.

Vibrations worked their way under his palm and up her throat. Stealing her groan, he mixed it with his own.

Once again, he was rock hard, but he wasn't taking it there. Not now. Not this time.

This time was a message. One he hoped she'd hear loud and clear.

She twisted her head enough to break the seal of their kiss, their lips just a fraction apart, their intermingled breaths ragged and quick.

When she whispered, "Deacon," her eyes were squeezed shut.

It was then he knew she heard his unspoken message.

His hand on her throat slid up to cup her jaw. "Reese." Her name came out as rough as sandpaper, but at least it didn't sound desperate.

Her green eyes opened. They were troubled but tinged with surprise. "I don't..." Her words faded off on a breath.

He pinned his forehead to hers and whispered, "You don't gotta say anything."

She tried again. "I don't..."

Fuck.

Fuck.

Fuck.

"Reese, don't..." He mentally cursed the desperation he was trying to hide.

And failing.

Goddamn it.

"I'm not sure I can..."

He hung on her words, worried how they would end.

"I don't—"

Her phone rang on the desk, causing them both to start. He didn't want her to answer it. Whoever it was could leave a message.

This moment was about them. No one else.

In the inner pocket of his cut, his phone beeped. A text message wasn't as important as what was currently going on between him and Reese. Everybody else could just fuck off.

He spat out a curse when they heard a pounding on the door .

The shouted, "We gotta go!" caused ice to slither through his veins. "Deacon!"

Deacon quickly stepped back and finished securing his jeans and belt while Reese hurried to shimmy her skirt back in place and tug her panties up.

She snagged her phone when it beeped at the same time Deacon's did.

Her sharp inhale of breath had him snagging her phone from her grip and reading the message on the screen.

BILLY'S HERE!

"Yo, asshole! We gotta go!"

He rushed to the door, unlocked it and faced an agitated Judge.

"Rook sent out a mass text. You get it?"

He hadn't checked his phone yet but he was sure of what the text said now that he read what Reilly sent Reese.

"Got my .40. Grab your cuffs, pepper spray and .40, too. We need to move." His green eyes landed on Reese. He frowned at her disheveled appearance but didn't mention it. "You stay here with the dogs. Gonna lock the front door and set the alarm. Don't let anyone in."

Her spine snapped straight. "No."

Judge's eyebrows launched into his hairline. "No?"

Reese set her jaw. "No, I'm going with you."

Judge shot Deacon a look that clearly stated, "Get your woman on a leash."

Right. He wanted to see his cousin try that with Cassie. Judge's deep voice would end up so high-pitched, it would shatter glass.

"For fuck's sake, we don't got time for this shit," Judge growled. "I'm takin' my sled. You want her ridin' shotgun with you, you deal with it."

Deacon knew arguing with her would just waste time. He talked as he moved. "Takin' my truck. Leavin' the dogs here." He opened the small closet in his office and squatted in front of the safe, spinning the dial. "You'll do what I say and stay out of the way, you got me?"

The safe clicked and he jerked open the door. He popped to his feet after grabbing his loaded Ruger .40 and his single shoulder holster, which hung above the safe. He shucked his cut, slipped the holster on, secured his gun and shrugged his cut back on over it.

"You carry a gun?"

"Only for self-protection. Pepper spray's usually my go-to for apprehension of skips. Not pluggin' someone with a bullet keeps me out of prison. And to do that while capturin' a fugitive is sometimes way too fuckin' temptin'."

He was still moving as he talked. He grabbed her arm as he passed her and used it to propel her out of the office. "Those fuckin' shoes are gonna slow us down. Take them off, put them back on once you're in the truck."

"But—"

"Reese. Fuckin' A. No fuckin' arguments right now. Just listen or stay here."

With a nod, she slipped off her shoes and followed quickly on his heels.

"Call your sister, find out what the fuck's goin' on. Hear me?"

"Yes."

"Put her on speaker. I need to know what went down. Or what's still goin' down."

He locked the front door, ignoring the whines of the dogs being left behind.

He didn't want to worry about them, also. Having Reese along while dealing with Warren would be more than enough. Though, the dogs listened way better than the blonde sitting shotgun in his truck.

He got that it was her instinct to argue. It was what made her a damn good lawyer, but now was not the time.

Not with her sister's safety on the line.

Chapter Nineteen

HEARING her sister's voice through the phone's speaker should have settled her nerves, but instead it made her more anxious, especially when Reilly was speaking so fast.

"Dutch was out picking up pizza. Rev was out on a test drive. I don't know where Cage disappeared to. The only ones here were Whip and Rook."

Deacon growled from the driver's seat as he drove like a maniac from one end of town, where his bail bonds business was located, to the other, where Dutch's Garage was.

He was driving so crazily, Reese had to hold the phone in her lap with one hand to avoid it going airborne, while she gripped the handle above the passenger door, so she didn't go airborne, either.

His Ford's engine was screaming as he dodged traffic. She was surprised he didn't have cops chasing him yet.

"Judge there?" Deacon yelled.

"No."

"You okay?" Reese asked, her heart in her throat and her stomach twisted.

If anything happened to Reilly...

"I'm just... Yes, I'm okay." Her sister might be in one piece but her voice shook as much as Reese's fingers.

"Where's he at?" Deacon asked.

"Who?" Reilly asked.

"Warren!" He shouted. "Christ!"

"I don't know. Whip shoved me into the office and told me to stay there."

"Can you see anythin' from inside the office?"

"No."

"Can you hear anythin'?"

"No."

"Fuck," he muttered.

"Do you want me to go out and check?"

"No!" Reese shouted before Deacon could. "You stay put. It's important you listen."

Deacon shot her a side glance, then shook his head.

She bugged out her eyes at him.

"How do you know it was him?" Deacon asked. The tires chirped slightly as he took a corner too fast.

"I saw him."

"From a distance?" he asked.

Please say from a distance.

"No. I got a weird phone call about some car part I never heard of. I had no idea what the guy was talking about, so I went to ask Whip, who was out back in the yard searching for a taillight or something. When I walked out..." She just stopped speaking.

"When you walked out what?" Reese prodded, her stomach now doing flips, and not from Deacon's driving.

"I didn't see him. I didn't see it coming."

"See what coming?" Reese asked, panic clawing up her throat.

"The baseball bat."

"What?" Reese screamed over Deacon's searing curse. "Are you hurt?"

"Luckily, Rook was hiding out back smoking... *you know*... and must have spotted him first. He tackled Billy and the bat just barely skimmed my head."

"It did what?" Reese shrieked. Barely skimmed her *head*?

"Yeah, he tried to hit a home run, but Rook took him down before he could make solid contact."

"Holy shit! Do you need to go to the hospital?"

Deacon reached over, squeezed her knee and murmured, "Reese, keep your shit together."

Right! Freaking out over her sister's head almost being smashed in by a baseball bat wielded by a psycho mother-fucker wouldn't do any good.

Got it.

She'd keep that in mind for next time.

"When Rook got him down to the ground, Whip grabbed me, shoved me inside and into the office. And then I don't know what happened after that."

"Fuck," Deacon muttered again. "Stay put. We're rollin' up now."

Reese glanced out the windshield to see he was pulling into the front lot of Dutch's Garage.

Before he even rolled the truck to a stop, he ordered, "Stay in the fuckin' truck with the doors locked 'til I see what's goin' on first. I'll get you once it's safe."

She only stared at him. He was crazy if he thought she was just going sit in the truck while her sister was inside.

But she kept her mouth shut.

He sighed as he parked the truck, shut it down and hopped out. "Stay here," he ordered again. "And lock the doors."

He slammed the driver's side door shut and jogged into one of the open garage bays. Reese's gaze sliced through the lot and spotted Judge's bike parked in front of the office. There were other cars, trucks and bikes in the lot, too. She had no idea if any of them were Billy's or just customers.

Her heart was pounding so hard she could hear the thump in her ears. She stared at the front window of the office, hoping to see her sister, but she couldn't see anything.

In her worry, she'd forgotten her sister was on the line. "Reilly?"

When she didn't get a response, she glanced down to the cell phone gripped in her fingers. The call had ended. She quickly tried to get her back on the line, but it went directly to voicemail.

She didn't like that. Not at all.

She also hated not knowing what the hell was going on.

Movement caught her eye and a plain black van with dark tinted windows sped through the parking lot and an open gate. The chain-link fence started at the right side of the garage and disappeared around back.

The yard Reilly mentioned. Most garages had a fenced yard at the back of their businesses to secure vehicles and store junk cars for parts. Dutch's Garage didn't seem to be any different.

She had no idea who was in the black van, though. Could it be someone working with Billy? Could this be some sort of ambush? Were they there to kidnap her sister?

She needed to warn Deacon and Judge.

Reese shoved open the passenger door and jumped from the truck. She ran through the open bay door, not caring she was barefoot. She didn't stop until she got to the office, only to find the door open and the office empty.

Fuck!

"Reilly!" she yelled.

Again, no response.

"Deacon!"

Fuck this!

She searched the garage for a way out back and saw a steel door. She rushed over, yanked it open, and spotted everyone outside.

Even Reilly.

Who was told to stay in the fucking office!

Deacon, Judge, Whip, Rook, Dutch, Cage, Shade and Rev stood in a circle.

She could barely see him, but Billy Warren was on his knees in the dirt with his hands cuffed behind his back. Reilly kept trying to push through the biker barrier without luck. The guys blocked her every time.

She did this while holding a blood-stained towel to the side of her head. The sight of that stole Reese's breath.

"Reilly!" she shouted, causing all heads to spin her way.

Deacon's expression instantly showed his displeasure. "Told you to stay in the fuckin' truck!"

Judge scowled and shook his head.

With a few smirks and more head shakes, the rest of them went back to staring at the man on the ground.

She rushed to her sister, pulling the towel away from her head. "Are you sure you don't need an ambulance?"

"No, it's just a surface wound."

Reese tried not to panic. She knew head wounds bled a lot, making them seem worse than they were, but still...

Billy had a damn bat. Her eyes sliced from Reilly's head to the man on the ground, who wasn't saying a word.

"No ambulances here. You wanna take her to the hospital, take Deke's truck," Judge ordered. "Whip, go close the gate for now. Rev, shut the garage doors and lock them. We don't want anyone else wanderin' back here."

The last was directed at her.

Fuck him. This had to do with *her* sister, not his. She had every right to know and be involved with what was going on.

She turned to Deacon, shooting off questions like a machine gun. "Why is he just sitting there? Are you planning on taking him into custody? Delivering him to Bianchi? What if he gets out and does this again? Will my sister never be safe?"

Nobody was doing anything and something had to be done.

Fuck this shit.

She held out her hand. "Give me your gun."

MUTTERED CURSES ROSE from every one of his brothers standing in that circle, some louder than others.

Deacon stared at the woman holding out her hand like she expected him to just hand over his Ruger so she could plug a .40 into the fucker's head.

Not on his fucking watch.

She wasn't thinking clearly, that was for damn sure. Her reaction was emotional, not practical.

Killing Warren could destroy her life. Even removing any chance she'd get caught for it, she would have to live with that decision forever.

He wasn't putting that on her.

Warren laughed and spat a wad of blood onto the dirt next to him. He was still bleeding from his mouth and nose from the fight he'd had with Rook.

Rook was a little banged up, too. He had a smear of blood under his nose and some blood splatter on his shirt and cut. The knuckles on his right hand were also torn up.

"Like you'd let that cunt kill me. I'm worth too much alive."

Deacon's gaze slid back to the piece of shit on his knees. He clenched his jaws to keep from giving the fucker a boot to the face. But then, that wouldn't be a fair fight.

Just like when Warren beat up women.

A muscle popped in his jaw when he ground his teeth.

"You ain't worth shit," Judge said before Deacon could.

"Wrong. I'm worth something to that one standing there." Warren jerked his chin toward Deacon. "The one with the girly braid and nose ring like the bitch he is. Bet his boyfriend leads him around with a leash hooked to that nose ring, then uses the braid like a handle while giving it to him up the ass."

Like Deacon hadn't heard that one before.

"Got a lot to say for someone on his knees, asshole," Rook said, wiping some of the blood from the corner of his own mouth with the back of his hand.

"You only got the upper hand once the boy joined you."

The "boy" must be Whip.

"Otherwise, that cunt bitch and you would both be dead." He glanced around the circle. "Which one of you is she giving it up to now? Or is it all of you? I wouldn't doubt she likes a good gang bang. She was a little whore who was good with her mouth. She asked me to smack her around because she liked it. Begged for it."

A frustrated scream and a whole slew of curses came from behind Deacon and Reilly rushed the circle, trying to break through. Rev caught her by the waist and held her back.

Rook stepped in front of Warren and spat a bloody hocker on his face. As it slid down the man's cheek, Warren lunged forward, trying to head butt Rook in the groin. He jumped back out of reach just in time.

Warren lost his balance and fell forward onto his face in the dirt.

Cage reached down, grabbed him by the back of the hair and yanked him back up to his knees.

"Yo!" Dutch hollered and snagged Warren's bat from Reese's hands. "Christ! This ain't the major leagues, woman."

Where the fuck had she found that?

"Hang on to her," Deacon told him.

The old man grabbed Reese around the waist and held tight, just like Rev did with her sister.

"Just let me——"

"No," Deacon barked, cutting her off. "Stay out of it."

"Deacon!"

"No. If you can't keep your shit together, I'll have them drag you out of here. You were supposed to stay in the fuckin' truck." He turned and jabbed a finger at Reilly. "And you were supposed to stay in the fuckin' office. Neither of you fuckin' listen."

Warren laughed. "This is why you got to teach them a fucking lesson. Teach them obedience. It's what they want. In the end, they thank you for it. Haven't learned that yet? Oh that's right, you don't fuck women, they probably peg you instead."

"What the hell did I ever see in you?" Reilly rage whispered, her face red and her hair wild as she struggled to escape Rev's arms.

"My big dick. You liked it in your mouth and in your fucking ass."

She was snarling while clawing at Rev's arms, her fingernails digging deep enough to draw blood, but the younger brother kept a tight hold on her. "I hope you get fucked up the ass in prison, asshole!"

Warren blew her a kiss. "I'll just find you again when I get out, baby. I look forward to getting a piece of that tight ass again. And next time you might remember the lesson I taught you about sharing what's yours with your man."

"You gotta go to prison first to get out," Deacon reminded him.

Warren laughed. "What are you going to do? Huh, pretty boy? Kick my ass while my hands are tied behind my back? Do you need that advantage?"

"Take them inside." His order was low and quiet, but it was heard.

"Deacon!" Reese yelled as Dutch battled to get her into the garage.

Reilly had stopped struggling but Rev kept a tight grip

on her anyway, most likely expecting her to make a break for it, as he maneuvered her inside behind Dutch and Reese.

"Close the door. Keep them in there."

The steel door slammed shut, cutting off Reese's loud demands and complaints.

Without looking at Whip, Deacon said, "Go stand in front of it. Make sure no one comes out."

Whip moved to guard the door without a word.

Deacon lifted his gaze, which had been locked with Warren's, to Judge. "Uncuff him."

His cousin stared at him for a few long seconds. Then his lips pressed into a thin line and he pulled a cuff key from the little front pocket of his cut before moving behind Warren.

Warren's eyes narrowed on Deacon and he smirked.

Deacon planned on wiping that smirk off his fucking face.

But he wanted to give the asshole a fair chance. Unlike Warren did with Reilly after stealing all her money and beating the fuck out of her. Unlike Warren did with Reese in the parking lot that night.

"Get up," Deacon growled. Pictures of Reilly's injuries flashed through his mind. Snapshots of Reese's face with the bruises and cuts tugged at his memory.

All that pain and damage due to the one so-called "man" in front of him. The one who would've snuffed out Reilly's life with a baseball bat without blinking an eye.

With not a care. Not a regret.

To Warren, Reilly had been only pussy and a free ride. He used and abused her.

"Get him up," Deacon shouted when Warren didn't stand fast enough.

As Cage and Judge reached for Warren, the fucker surged to his feet, stepping away from Deacon's two brothers and taking one step closer toward him.

"How's this going to be fair? It's still five to one," Warren said, glancing around the circle. He wiped a trickle of blood from his mouth.

"You worried about fair?" Deacon asked him. "You think knockin' around a twenty-four-year-old girl was fair? Ambushin' my woman in a dark parkin' lot was fair? Didn't think you gave a shit about *fair*."

"Let me do it," Shade murmured next to him. His request was soft but chilling.

"Fuck no. He's mine."

Shade would slice Warren's throat in under a second flat and it would be over way too easily. That wasn't what this was about.

Deacon's job was to take Warren alive and in one piece to Bianchi. Collect his scratch for delivering the piece of shit.

But he no longer gave a fuck about this job. It was no longer about money.

Fuck no.

It hadn't been about the money for a while now.

"He got anything else on him?" he asked no one in particular.

"No," Whip called out from near the door. "Took a pocket knife off him but besides the bat, that was it. He didn't expect much of a fight from a woman."

Right. He didn't expect to go face to face with a brotherhood.

Deacon reached into his cut and pulled his Ruger from his holster. Without taking his eyes off Warren, he held it out grip-first to Shade, who took it.

Now it was fair.

Warren widened his stance and raised his fists.

Deacon smiled and left his hands down by his sides. "I'll give you the first shot. A fuckin' freebie."

Warren's eyes narrowed, distrust plain as day in his face.

Rightly so.

The man took a wide swing and Deacon ducked, feeling the wind from Warren's arm over his head. As Deacon popped back up, so did his steel-toed boot, with a solid shot dead center between Warren's legs.

All the breath rushed out of Warren and, as he bent over due to his nuts being relocated, Deacon grabbed his head and kneed him in the face.

Warren went from bending forward to grab his junk to flying backward from the impact of Deacon's knee, his arms flailing and blood exploding from the fucker's broken nose.

Warren landed hard on his ass in the dirt, stunned but still conscious.

Good. Deacon had a few things to say.

"Sorry about that. Forgot about makin' this a fair fight." Deacon dove forward, using his chest to knock Warren completely onto his back. He straddled the motherfucker's waist, settling all his weight on Warren's gut.

"Wanna apologize for the shit you did to those women? We can pass along the message."

Warren blinked up at him in a daze, the blood coming from his mouth no longer a trickle but now a steady stream. His nose looked bent out of place, dark blood pooling in each nostril.

Deacon hoped he choked on all that blood.

"You still look better than Reilly did when you put her in the hospital. And I don't think that's fair, either. Do you?"

Warren tried to spit some of the blood out of his mouth but with Deacon crushing his stomach, he couldn't pull in a big enough breath to do so. Instead, he gurgled.

Deacon turned his head, giving Warren his ear. "Didn't hear that. Was that a fuckin' apology?"

Warren shoved weakly at Deacon's chest.

"What?" Deacon leaned closer. "Didn't quite catch that, either."

"I'll... fucking... kill those... cunts... right after... I... kill you." Each word came out on a wet wheeze.

Deacon sat up and smiled. "Yeah, fuckin' doubt that."

With a sudden burst of desperate energy, Warren surged up and began swinging wildly. One fist made contact with Deacon's temple, making his brain wobble from the strike.

Warren bucked underneath him, trying to knock off Deacon's weight, and he almost succeeded.

It was time to end this bullshit.

It was time to use the method Warren used on women to "teach them obedience."

He curled his fingers into fists and held up his right one. "This one's for Reese." He lifted his left. "This one's for Reilly."

He put all his weight behind the right hook as it made contact with Warren's cheek. As if in slow motion, Warren's head snapped violently to the right. Deacon waited for it to rebound before striking it with his left.

Then he let the training kick in that Slade had showed him when the Dirty Angels MC member came up to Manning Grove. The boxer had taught them all how to use the punching bags and MMA equipment set up in a shed at the farm. He'd been asked to help Sig and Trip find a way to work out their tempers. Everyone else who was interested got the chance to work with him, too.

Deacon couldn't walk into a ring without getting his ass kicked by even an amateur fighter with proper training, but he'd learned enough techniques in the week Slade spent with them to know how to throw an effective punch.

Or two.

Or five.

Even ten.

So many his knuckles became numb. They bled. His lungs strained. His breathing sounded like a ticked-off bull in his own ears.

A red haze covered his vision as he thought about Warren hurting Reese. Hurting Reilly.

Hurting other women and getting away with it.

Deacon lost count of how many strikes he doled out with each fist. He only knew his right one swung more often. Because that fist belonged to Reese.

Warren had touched her. Hurt her. Might have done even worse if Bambi, *thank fuck*, hadn't chased him off.

So, yeah, his right fist struck a little harder and more often. Until his hand was completely numb from the pain.

Even before the haze in his eyes and the ringing in his ears cleared, he was pulled off the lifeless body beneath him.

Only months ago, he had watched Sig lose his shit up on that mountain. He now understood how the rage had consumed him and how the club's VP had been driven to use it against Vernon Shirley, his woman's rapist and kidnapper.

Deacon understood it all now. The same rage filled him all the way to his core.

Sig had made sure Shirley would never hurt Autumn again. It wasn't only punishment, it was prevention.

Just like Deacon was preventing Warren from ever taking advantage of, or hurting, anyone again.

Not Reilly. Not Reese. No one.

Never again.

Warren was done.

But Deacon wasn't done.

Not yet.

Chapter Twenty

A BLACK BANDANA appeared before him and he wrapped it around his split and bleeding knuckles. He wouldn't be surprised if he had a couple of broken bones in his right hand.

But right now, Deacon didn't give a fuck. He wasn't feeling the pain, only fury still surged through his veins.

"Load him up." His voice wasn't recognizable, the words sounding foreign and from a distance.

But he knew what had to happen from there and they had no time to waste.

Turning to Shade, he held out his left palm. The quiet man returned his Ruger without hesitation.

"Load him in the van."

Everyone around him had stopped dead at that order, then a sudden flurry of activity whirled around him. While beating the life out of Warren had occurred in slow-motion, everything now moved at hyper-speed.

His cousin took over, barking out commands. Deacon was relieved because he was mentally and physically spent.

Whip and Cage were to stay at the garage and clean up the mess.

The bat would come with Shade and Deacon to be disposed of.

Rook dug in Warren's blood-soaked pockets, searching for keys. He was told to find the fucker's vehicle and do what he needed to do with it. The ex-con had experience dismantling vehicles, which was one reason he might've ended up in the joint a few times.

Deacon couldn't give a fuck about any of that. Rook was his brother who was standing by his side doing what needed to be done.

Just like the rest of them.

When Deacon heard the side door to the van slam shut, it snapped him out of his fog. "You cuff him again?"

Judge grunted out a "Yeah."

Deacon considered the current situation and how to handle the one to come. He dug into his pocket and pulled out his truck fob. He tossed it to Whip, who still stood guard at the door. "I'm ridin' in the van with Shade. Have the women take my truck back to the farm and tell them to wait in my apartment. I'll have someone drop me off when we're done."

When Warren was done.

When this whole clusterfuck was over.

"Make sure they go to the farm," was the last thing he said as he climbed onto the passenger seat. He glanced at Judge. "You comin'?"

"Fuck yeah," his cousin answered. "Takin' my sled. Let me go in first and see where Cassie is, yeah?"

Deacon nodded. "Yeah." Cassie shouldn't be a witness to Deacon's plans.

Judge headed out the now wide-open gate and disappeared around the front of the garage. Not a minute later, Deacon could hear the rumble of his cousin's sled, then the loud acceleration as he sped away.

Tioga Pet Crematorium was only a couple blocks west. Judge only needed a few minutes head start.

After those few minutes, Deacon told Shade to go. He took a last look at his loyal as fuck bothers still standing in the garage yard when Shade shifted the full-sized Chevy van into Drive and followed the same path Judge took.

They both ignored a low groan from the back.

Neither Shade nor Deacon spoke a word on the short trip to the club's newest business. Shade automatically pulled around back to where customer's pets were unloaded.

An area hidden from the public. For good reason.

Shade pulled the van as close as he could to the back door where Easy already waited with a large rolling cart and a folded blue tarp.

Deacon rolled down the window for some air and sat in the passenger seat, staring sightlessly out the windshield as Judge, Easy and Shade loaded a restrained Warren onto the cart.

He heard another low groan before the crackle of the plastic tarp as they used it to cover the man.

Deacon still sat there, his mind blank, his body weary, as the van doors slammed and he listened to the squeak from one of the cart's wheels as they rolled Warren inside.

A few seconds later, his cousin stood at the van door, staring at him through the open window. "You good?"

No, he wasn't good. But he would be once this was over.

"Want me to take over?"

No, this was for him to do. To settle the score. To deliver the punishment. To protect the women's futures.

"First time's the hardest," Judge grumbled under his breath.

Coming from his cousin, that comment caught Deacon off guard.

Did Judge know how many times it took until it got easy?

He'd always thought they'd been close. Like real brothers. But maybe Judge had kept secrets from him.

Maybe there were things the man never shared.

"Can't wait any longer, Deke. Sent Cassie on an errand, but she was suspicious and dug in her heels. Not sure how long she'll be gone. Don't want her seein' any of this shit." His lips became a flat line. "You get why?"

"Yeah."

Just like he didn't want Reese to see it.

To see what they were capable of when pushed.

The women might suspect, but they'd never really *know* unless they saw it with their own eyes. They'd pretend they'd want to know the truth, but deep down they wouldn't.

Deacon didn't want Reese looking at him any different, wondering what else he was capable of.

No, it was better they not know the truth.

Deacon got out of the van and followed Judge through the back door, making sure it was secured and locked.

Thank fuck he, as club treasurer, had the foresight to bring the purchase of this business to the table months ago. Deacon figured the crematorium was a good buy for two solid reasons. The first, the business finances were in the black, making it not only a good investment but a steady stream of scratch into the club account. And the second?

For the reason they would use it today.

He never expected to be the first one to use it for that purpose.

Maybe it was fate.

Whatever it was, this would be the spot where Warren took his last breath.

Easy and Shade stood near the incinerator big enough to cremate large animals. Hogs, cows and even small horses.

They hadn't used it once since taking over operations from the local vet. Their normal clientele were small animals like dogs and cats. They had three smaller furnaces for those.

But this one... This furnace was the one that had caught his attention when he did a walk-through with the vet. Deacon had seen its potential.

Just like he saw it now.

To obliterate garbage like Warren. A fucking menace to women. *Hell*, to society in general.

Shade moved to the electronic control panel, which beeped as he pushed a few buttons. Both he and Easy had been trained by the vet himself on the daily operations and use of equipment.

"Open it."

Shade unlatched the incinerator door and opened it wide, then pulled on a heavy-duty tray that was more of a metal grate set on rollers. A grate ashes would fall through and funnel into a smaller tray below.

The metallic sound of the large tray rolling out made his blood go cold.

He could still deliver Warren to Bianchi. It wasn't too late.

The interior of the furnace faded away and his vision became clouded by Reilly and Reese's injuries. The way their faces were battered and bruised.

A strong woman like Reese crying in his arms.

Warren's threat to find Reilly once he was released from prison.

Deacon's heart thumped heavily.

He ripped the blue tarp off Warren and said to no one in particular, "Help me load up this piece of shit."

"Deke, he's still breathin'," Judge warned quietly.

"Not for long."

"Want me to slice his fuckin' throat first?" Shade asked softly.

Deacon lifted his gaze from Warren, who was barely

conscious, to Shade. "You askin' me or our Sergeant at Arms?" Because, in truth, it would be Judge's decision.

"You," Shade answered without even a hesitation.

"Respect, brother, but fuck no. I hope he's conscious enough to feel the fiery depths of hell."

Shade's expression didn't change. It remained unreadable, which should scare the fuck out of them all.

Thank fuck the man was on their side. No one knew what he was capable of.

No one wanted to find out, either.

Easy and Shade took Warren's ankles. Judge and Deacon grabbed his shoulders and they lifted the dead weight onto the tray. His cousin tossed the bat next to Warren.

With a strange sense of peace, Deacon watched Shade slide the steel tray back into place inside the incinerator, close the door and latch it tight.

Shade pushed another button and they heard the door lock.

This was it.

The furnace was locked and loaded.

"You hear somethin'?" Easy whispered.

Deacon swore everyone held their breath to listen.

"What is this?" came the muffled shout from inside. "Let me out!"

"Wanna push the button?" Shade asked, not a bit concerned that Warren was now conscious.

"Deke," Judge murmured, concern etched in his face. It wasn't concern for Warren, but for Deacon.

Deacon unstuck himself and began to move forward, but the sound of running feet coming from behind them made him hesitate.

"Fuck that motherfucker!" Reilly yelled as she barreled her way past Deacon, knocking him to the side. She ran up to the control panel and slammed her palm on the big red start button.

The loud *whoosh* of the gas burners firing froze everyone in place. Including Reese, who had followed Reilly into the furnace room.

She stood as still as a statue with a hand covering her mouth and her eyes squeezed shut.

They faintly heard a single scream and then nothing.

Strangely, that was the moment he noticed Reese's feet were bare and filthy. Her hair now a loose mess around her shoulders, like she'd been tearing her fingers through it. Her mascara smeared. Her lipstick chewed off her bottom lip.

The woman who held tightly onto control had unraveled.

Her green eyes opened slowly and met his. He was afraid to read what was in them. He preferred not to know.

"Deke," her strangled whisper sounded deafening to his ears, "he was still alive."

He said the only thought that came to his mind. "You wanted him dead."

"I—" Her face turned green and she rushed to the nearest garbage can and spilled the contents of her stomach.

He closed his eyes and listened to her retch, his fingers curling tightly against his thighs.

Fuck. He didn't mean to put that on her. This had been his decision. No one else's.

Once she was done, he opened them and turned back to stare at the furnace, his nostrils flaring. "Get them out of here."

From the corner of his eye, he saw Judge jerk up his chin at someone Deacon couldn't see. Not while his gaze was locked on the furnace.

"They got away from me." Whip sounded worried. "Gonna get them back to your place and make sure they stay there."

Deacon nodded without looking at him. Unfortunately, Whip learned how strong-willed those two women were. Even so, that was no excuse for failing to do what he'd been told.

Several sets of footsteps receded behind him.

Once gone, only the eerie sound of the gas burners surrounded who remained.

Reese had simply left without an argument.

That could mean a few things. None of them good for Deacon.

"How long does it take?" he asked, his voice flat.

"Programmed it for a two-hundred-pound animal, so a few hours. It'll shut off on its own."

"You know what to do with the ashes," Judge said to Shade.

"Yeah, brother, I'll handle it."

Judge stepped in front of Deacon, blocking his locked view on the furnace. "Let's go. I need a fuckin' drink and you need about fifty, brother."

Brother.

That was what they were. Cousins by blood, brothers by choice.

"Also need a new set of cuffs."

"What just went down cost you more than a set of cuffs."

Deacon was afraid of that.

———

REESE STUDIED her sister calmly sipping on a beer she'd pulled from Deacon's fridge.

As if what just happened hadn't.

As if Reilly hadn't just killed a man. Burned him alive.

Billy deserved to suffer, but even so...

It could have been Reese who killed him instead of her

sister, if Deacon had handed over his gun when she'd demanded it. But then if he had, Billy wouldn't have suffered. His death would've been quick and easy.

Easy for Billy.

Not so easy for Reese.

It shouldn't be so easy for Reilly.

If it bothered her sister, Reese couldn't tell. Maybe the reality hadn't hit her yet. It could come later.

"We need to pack our stuff and go."

Reilly was safe now. They could leave and head back to Mansfield without worry. Put the whole situation with Billy behind them.

They could borrow Deacon's truck. Someone could come fetch it later.

Her sister took another sip of beer, then placed the bottle on the counter. She lifted her green eyes—without one tear in them—to Reese.

What Reilly had done hadn't upset her sister. Surprisingly, it had strengthened her. Made her seem more mature. That couldn't be right.

"I'm not leaving."

"What?" Reese must have misheard.

"I like it here."

No.

No, no, no. "You can't stay here."

"Why not?"

"This isn't your home."

"And where is my home, Reese? With you? Back in Philly?"

Yes! Any place but here. She tried another tactic. "You can't stay in Deacon's apartment." She'd be homeless in Manning Grove.

"Then I'll find my own place. I have a job. Dutch is willing to keep me on for now since he said I'm doing a *fucktastic* job."

A burn started deep in Reese's gut and began to rise. She couldn't just watch her sister throw away her future. "You want to work in an auto repair shop? You have a damn college degree, Reilly. One I paid for. Not so you can be a fucking secretary."

While there was nothing wrong with being a secretary, she wanted more for her sister. So much more. She didn't need a bachelor's degree to answer phones, schedule appointments and shuffle papers.

Reilly moved around the counter to where Reese stood in the center of the apartment's living area. "My degree is in business management, if you've forgotten. I'll be helping out his business. And maybe even with some of the other club businesses, if they'll let me."

A business that had done fine for decades without her. But Reese kept that to herself.

That burn now seared her throat. She wouldn't throw up. She couldn't. Nothing remained in her stomach.

She was completely empty.

Reese wanted to argue with her, force Reilly to see reality. But she knew her sister. She had raised her. Helped make her who she was. She knew if she tried to convince Reilly to leave, her sister would dig in her heels.

The same as Reese would do when pushed.

"Not everyone wants to be you, Reese. Not everyone wants to be married to their job. And only live for success. News flash: money isn't everything."

Where was that coming from? Had Reilly forgotten the struggles they had lived? How hard Reese worked to make sure they ate, had clothes, got an education? "Without it, you have nothing."

Sadness colored Reilly's face. "Sister, you are so damn smart but right now, you are very wrong. You can have a lot of things and not have money." She shrugged. "Family."

"I'm your family," Reese whispered. *Not this club.* Desperation clawed up her throat.

"You've been taking care of me my whole life, sis. Since I was born. *Your* whole life. That was unfair to you and I'm sorry you were forced to do that. I'm sorry our father decided a drunk wife and two daughters was an unwanted burden. I'm sorry our mother gave up on life and left it to you to take care of me. But Reese..." She inhaled loudly. "Let me go. Let me do this. Let me find my own path like you did. Of course I'll make mistakes. Hopefully, not one as bad as Billy. But I need to make them. That bubble you want me to live in? I'm bursting it."

"Reilly, just come back with me and we'll figure it out. Together."

Reilly shook her head. "I'm staying and *I'll* figure it out. Being in Manning Grove, I'll be closer to you than when I was living outside of Philly. I know you love me and want what's best for me. I also want what's best for you, too. Working yourself into an early grave and coming home to an empty house night after night? That's not what's best for you."

"I work hard to—"

Reilly cut her off. "Did you tell him about Minnie?"

Reese's heart skipped a beat.

Minnie.

Reilly's unexpected question deflated her drive to argue. To get her sister to realize staying here, with this club, in Manning Grove, wasn't what was best for her.

Her sister had always called their mother Minnie—never Mom—because it was a shortened version of the title Reese gave her: Minimum Mom. The woman had done the very minimum to keep her daughters alive. And when they were older, not even that.

"I told him some, but not all of it. And I kept my name for her to myself, as you should."

"Why?"

"It's no one's business." No one needed to know where they came from and how they got to where they were. No one needed to judge them for something out of their control.

"Anyone hearing it would simply think Minnie was her first name. Nothing more."

"Maybe. But that time in our life is over. No point revisiting or reliving it."

"You're right," Reilly agreed. "We both have a future to think about."

There it was. Bringing up their mother wasn't off topic. Reilly was trying to make a point. "*You* have a future to think about. Mine is already in motion, Reilly. I worked hard to get where I am and I'm not giving it up."

"No one said you had to give up anything, sis. But your future isn't set in stone. You're allowed to let it be fluid, flexible. Let people in. Grow your tribe. Not every man is like Billy or Allen. Or even our father." She sighed and grabbed both of Reese's hands, clasping them tightly to her chest. "Stop denying yourself. That detour Deacon took you on during the club run? You can also do that in life, you know. I know you have a set path but sometimes a detour is necessary."

Reese pulled her sister into a tight hug and murmured, "When did you get to be so wise?"

"I learned from my very wise, but stubborn, sister," Reilly whispered. "The one I've looked up to my whole life. She's shown me what to strive for. But she's also shown me what I don't want. I don't want to be so caught up in my own success I can't see anything beyond it."

"And you think Deacon is what's missing in my life?"

"I don't know, and neither will you if you don't let yourself explore the possibility. Maybe, in the end, he won't fit.

Your lifestyles, your choices, may be too different, but you won't know until you try."

"I just need time, Reilly. I need to be okay with what happened today. Right now, I'm not. And I'm worried for you. How this will affect you. Taking a life shouldn't be an easy thing to do. Not one of them tried to stop it."

"Neither did we."

That bothered Reese the most. When she forced from Whip where they were taking Billy, they had jumped in Deacon's truck and followed.

Reese thought her intention was to stop them, but was it? She could've easily called 911 instead. She didn't.

She might not have pushed the button, but she was just as guilty by being there.

She'd wanted justice. She just never realized how that justice would be doled out.

Hearing the scream from a man being burned to death would be seared forever in her mind. She would never forget the second Reilly's palm slammed that button or the sound of those burners igniting.

"I know this might sound fucked up, but after pushing that button? I suddenly felt free. Safe to get back on my own life's path. Fears I hadn't even realized I was holding onto disappeared. I have this club to thank for that. And you, too."

A heavy weight crushed Reese's chest. "I didn't do anything."

"Yes, you did. You once again sacrificed for me."

Taking care of her sister, wanting her safe, helping her when she needed it, was not a sacrifice. It was what family did. Real family.

Their birth mother might be blood, but that was all she was.

What Reilly saw in this club became clear. Reese understood why her sister wanted to be a part of it. And, in truth, she would only be less than a half hour away.

Reese wasn't losing her sister. She was just letting her go. Letting her grow on her own. Letting her be who she was meant to be. "My door will always be open to you, if and when you want a change. Don't ever think twice about coming home to me. For any reason. Even for no reason."

Reilly gave her a last squeeze before they released each other. "So, you're leaving?"

"Like you said, I'll only be about twenty minutes away. We'll practically be neighbors." Reese's attempt at a laugh sounded stilted. "I'll grab my things." She pushed past her sister, trying to hide the sting in her eyes.

This wasn't a forever type of goodbye. She'd see her sister often. She'd talk to her on the phone regularly. They'd still be a big part of each other's life.

They'd still be family.

Even so, it hurt. Like her life was ripping apart. Like a large piece of her was being torn away, leaving a gaping hole that had been filled the day her sister was born.

She mechanically collected her belongings from the bathroom and from Deacon's bedroom.

She could smell his presence, his familiar scent, as she moved around his room. Leather, sandalwood, smoke.

Everything that reminded her of Deacon. Of the way he lived his life.

Of how he lived giving no fucks, while she, on the other hand, gave too many.

A voice came from the doorway. "Are you at least going to tell him goodbye?"

Reese turned her head away and closed her eyes. "I'll text him."

"Reese," Reilly breathed. Her sister's disappointment was palatable.

She picked up her overnight bag off the bed and turned to her sister. "Can you drive me back to Mansfield?"

"I wish you would talk to him first."

That would make it more difficult. "I'm not sure what to say."

"Maybe you don't need to say anything."

"That's not in my nature," she said with a stiff laugh.

Always having something to say was both her strength and her weakness.

Earlier in his office, before Billy showed up, before everything went down, she had been rendered speechless.

What she saw in Deacon's eyes had stolen her words. Had destroyed her ability to think practically.

That moment had scared her because she was ready to think impractically for once. To throw everything she'd fought so hard to build out the door and just give in to whatever he wanted.

What deep down she wanted, too, but was unable to figure out a way to get a handle on.

So, yes, she needed time and distance.

And if she talked to him first, he might convince her otherwise.

She couldn't risk that.

Not yet.

Epilogue

DETOURS AND FINAL DESTINATIONS

HE DIDN'T COME RIGHT AWAY.

She thought he might.

To demand answers.

To force her to face her fears.

To face her feelings.

To face him.

Facing him would've made her decision harder.

He could've pushed the issue, but he didn't. He'd respected her need for time and space.

She had almost called him a million times. She almost got into her car and drove to Manning Grove many more.

She hadn't because she needed to be sure.

She hadn't because she needed *him* to be absolutely sure.

But not reaching out wasn't fair to him. She knew that.

Still... she waited.

Because she needed to know beyond all doubt. She took that time and space he gave her to figure out just what that doubt was. What she needed.

From him. From herself.

They were so different.

He'd never been in a serious relationship. And hers had failed.

He lived his life loose and easy, while hers was so rigid and structured.

Her home used to be her solace. Now it only felt empty.

Lonely.

A tomb that housed a life she no longer was sure she wanted to live.

Her life of living to work, working to live.

A vicious, endless cycle.

Still... she waited.

Every night she came home, she hoped he'd be there. Forcing her to face her fears. Her insecurities.

He wasn't.

Still... she waited.

Days turned into weeks which turned into a month.

Every night she'd come home to a dark house, an empty driveway. She'd open the door and head directly out to the deck.

Disappointment tugged at her when she'd find his chair empty and she was only greeted by the quiet night.

Still... she waited.

It was silly, really. A woman like her allowing those fears and insecurities—some she hadn't even realized she had—to override something she wanted so desperately.

But she needed to be sure. For him to be sure.

For them not to make a mistake.

She couldn't simply hand over her hope and her heart to someone who could crush it.

To someone who could disappoint her.

Her mother. Her father. Allen.

Each had contributed bricks to the wall she'd erected.

A wall someone she least expected had scaled.

Deacon.

A biker. A bail bondsman. A bounty hunter.

A simple man. But also, a not-so-simple man.

But would he be enough? Or would he be too much?

Would he try to control her? Change her?

She needed someone who would accept her as she was. How she'd always be.

And Deacon needed the same.

Someone who'd accept him as he was. How he'd always be.

They were so different.

Different wasn't always good. Different wasn't always easy.

But sometimes it felt right to embrace the difference.

And sometimes different just fit.

Like yin and yang. Two opposites creating a whole.

Still... she waited.

This time with her hand on the doorknob.

She took one last glance over her shoulder at the Harley in her driveway.

The house was dark. Quiet.

The knob turned easily.

She had never given him the key. He would've had to pick the lock.

Also not surprising, the alarm was disarmed since he had known the code and, since she'd been back, she hadn't changed it.

Instead, she had waited...

The recessed lighting was dimmed low, just bright enough so the kitchen wasn't completely pitch black.

Just bright enough to see the glass of wine waiting for her on the counter.

She toed off her heels and set her leather tote on the floor next to them.

Even though her heart was racing, she took her time lifting the glass to her lips and taking a sip.

He had picked her favorite.

With trembling fingers, she worked the tiny buttons on her blouse free. When she was done, she shrugged it off and tossed it over her tote.

The late May night was warm, so the lace camisole would be all she needed.

Well, it wasn't everything she needed.

She needed what waited for her on the deck.

Grabbing the wine, she moved slowly through the great room and hesitated at the French doors.

Once she opened that door, life would change.

For better. For worse. For whatever that life would bring.

She had wanted to wait until she was ready.

She still wasn't sure she was, but she could no longer wait.

Deacon deserved better than that.

So did she.

Reilly had told her she should stop denying herself.

The sister she raised was right. The sister she had always worried about was now worried about her.

The sister she only wanted the best for, wanted the same for her.

Was it Deacon?

She never expected to care so much about a man like him. It surprised her when it changed from only sex to something deeper. But would it be enough?

She wasn't sure.

However, Reilly was also right about not knowing until she tried.

Until they tried.

She closed her eyes for a second, took a long, slow breath and opened that door.

IT HAD BEEN difficult to remain in his seat. To wait.

While she drove up the driveway. While she discovered his sled.

While she found the glass of wine.

While she decided whether or not to join him outside on the deck.

He didn't bother to turn. He didn't need to look at her, he could feel her there.

Unsure.

But then, so was he.

"You never said goodbye."

"Because I couldn't say it."

He had missed the voice that swirled around him. The voice that could be hard and powerful when it needed to be, soft and caring when it came to who she worried about. Who she loved.

Her sister.

He also hoped him.

"Why not? Was it too difficult? Or was it 'cause of what happened?"

"A little of both."

"I didn't intend to put it on you."

He heard the breath rush out of her. "But you were right. I wanted him dead."

"And you weren't expectin' how it would affect you."

"No."

"He didn't die because you wanted him dead, Reese." He held up his hand.

After a moment, he heard her move and her slender fingers slipped into his. They were warm and fit within his perfectly. Her touch made the restlessness eating at him settle.

He guided her around until he could see her without turning his head. He tugged her hand in a silent request.

And was relieved when she knew what he wanted.

She climbed onto the lounge chair and straddled his lap.

He took the wine glass from her and placed it on the table next to the aluminum foil ashtray he made so many weeks ago. An unlit joint sat in it, waiting.

He cupped her face and their gazes locked, even though it was too dark to read her eyes.

"He didn't die because that's what you wanted, Reese. He was dead the second you walked through that door the night he ambushed you in the parkin' lot. His fate was sealed that very fuckin' moment I saw your face and you told me what happened."

Her lips parted and a soft breath escaped. He made the woman who could cut with her words speechless.

"He died because he touched what was mine. He hurt someone I love."

"Deacon," she breathed.

"No one will ever get away with that shit. Not ever. Know you're independent. The ruler of your own destiny. But hate to break it to you... You're mine. You belong to me."

Her eyes shut slowly, then opened just as slowly as she processed his words. "Club property."

He lifted her hand and held it over his heart. "No. You belong to me, not the Fury."

He waited. One breath. Two...

"Do you belong to me?"

If she only knew how much. "You would need to claim me."

"How?"

His lips twitched. "Tattoo my name across your ass."

She shoved at him and he captured her hands before she could escape the lounge chair.

"Just tell me you're willin' to give us a fair shot."

"I won't give up my house, Deke. Or move my practice. I'm established where I am. It's mine and I want to keep it."

He pressed his thumb against the pounding pulse in her

wrist. "Then don't. Your office is only twenty minutes away. We proved you can work remotely if you gotta. Your house is less than thirty. We can make it work."

"And if we can't?"

"It'll be fun tryin'." He held her wrists tighter so he didn't get punched in the nuts for what he was about to say. "Listen, this is how it's gonna go..."

He grinned when she groaned loudly.

"Gonna keep my place and you're keepin' yours. I'll spend a few nights a week here, and on the weekends we'll be at the farm. That means come every Friday night, you're takin' time off 'til Monday mornin'. If your clients don't understand, then fuck them. But I bet they'll stick around. You know why?"

"I'm sure you're going to tell me why," she said on a dramatic sigh.

"Because, babe, you're fuckin' worth it."

She was worth it. And not just to her clients...

"You know, you're surprisingly a lot smarter than you sound," she teased.

He smirked. "I'm sneaky like that." He got serious. "Doin' it like that will give us time to figure shit out. And one thing we have plenty of is time. But you start cheatin' me of that time, you're gonna hear about it. Just warnin' you now."

"Being with the club on the weekends will help me keep an eye on my sister."

"Don't gotta worry about that. We got that covered." They had set Reilly up at the motel temporarily. Until she could afford a place of her own. The club wasn't charging her shit since she was helping Ozzy manage the office when she wasn't working at the garage.

"Is The Grove Inn safe for her?"

"Wouldn't let her stay there if it wasn't, Reese. Ain't gonna let anything happen to her. Ozzy lives onsite and she's at the garage durin' the day. You don't need to worry about her. It's only temporary 'til she finds an affordable apartment, anyway."

"I can pay her rent."

There she went again, trying to gain control of the situation. "You know she don't want that. Wants to be on her own. You did more than your share for her, now she needs to do it herself."

"It's just difficult letting go."

"No shit." He took a breath and then released what he'd been holding onto, what had been like a knife to his chest. "Wasn't difficult lettin' me go, though."

Her walking away without a word had killed him. He understood why, but it didn't make it any easier.

"I never had you, Deke."

"You sure about that?" One of the most difficult things he had to do in his life was wait for her. Give her the time and space she needed. He had to stop himself from calling her a million times. Stop himself from hopping on his sled and driving to her house, or office, many more.

"At what point were you mine?"

He answered that easily. "The minute you demanded I get naked, shoved me onto this fuckin' lounge chair and climbed on my dick."

She snorted softly. "Yes, that was a very romantic moment between us."

"Wasn't romantic, but it was hot as fuck."

"You'll get no argument from me about how hot it was."

Thank fuck for that.

"Do you want an encore?"

"No," he answered.

She pulled her chin back and stared at him. "No?"

"Fuck no." He surged to his feet with her still clinging to him and secured her arms around his neck and her legs around his waist.

Somehow he managed to get her inside, across the great room and into her bedroom without tripping or dropping her.

And once they were there, he let her slide down his body.

"I've missed you," she whispered as he helped her get undressed.

Fuck, he had missed her, too.

Once naked, she settled on the bed. The sight of her alone tempted him, but her next words made his hands still while peeling off his own clothes.

"Let's never be apart long enough to miss each other like that again."

For fuck's sake. Hearing that might have been worth the wait.

"Woman," he growled. "Wanted to take my time and savor every fuckin' inch of you tonight. Makin' that difficult for me."

She smiled. "I'll keep my thoughts to myself, then."

He quickly shucked the rest of his clothes, dug a wrap out of his wallet and tossed it next to her. He climbed onto the bed and up her body until he was face to face with her, their eyes locked.

"Tell me again," he ordered.

"I missed you."

It was almost as good as if she'd told him she'd loved him.

Almost.

They'd get there. If not tonight, then tomorrow. And if not tomorrow, then real soon.

Because it was there. He felt it. So did she. He saw it in her eyes, too. Clear as fucking day.

But it was something neither of them would take lightly.

He never said those words to anyone other than his family.

"Missed you, too, babe. Never wanna miss you that much again."

Then he did what he had planned. Took his time and savored every inch of her.

He tasted her like she was the richest dessert. Took small bites to enjoy her sweet taste.

And when he was done stealing her breath and showing her how much he wanted her... Needed her...

Hell, loved her...

He slowly moved downward to appreciate the rest of her. From the arch of her neck, the soft curves of her tits, the hard peaks of her nipples, the slight rise of her lower belly.

He nuzzled the small patch of dark blonde hair and inhaled her familiar scent.

"Deacon," came out on a sigh.

He lifted his head and grinned. "You about to encourage me or discourage me?"

She dug her fingers into his braided hair and pushed his head lower.

No words were needed.

Because, *fuck yeah*, his momma *didn't raise no fool.*

———

Turn the page to read the sneak peek of
Blood & Bones: Cage (Blood Fury MC, book 5)

———

KEEP up with my latest news by signing up for my newsletter here: https://www.jeannestjames.com/newslettersignup

Sneak peek of Blood & Bones: Cage

**Turn the page for a sneak peek of
Blood & Bones: Cage
Blood Fury MC, book 5**

Blood & Bones: Cage

Prologue
Saying Goodbye

CHRIS SCRAMBLED AROUND HIS ROOM, stuffing whatever he could find, whatever he couldn't live without, into a trash bag. His heart raced and his thoughts twisted.

He needed to hurry.

Before it was too late.

"Mom! I'm going with you, Mom!" He hiccuped when he tried to hold back a sob.

He didn't get a response.

Quickly glancing around his room, he made sure he didn't miss anything important. But his room was a mess. His clothes were scattered on the floor. His sheets a tangled ball in the middle of his unmade bed.

His closet door hung open because he couldn't close it anymore. He had stuffed it with so much crap. Stuff he thought was important, stuff he thought he needed to keep, but not important enough to pack.

Underwear!

He scrambled over the piles on the floor to get to his dresser and ripped open the top drawer.

Empty.

He scoured the discarded dirty clothes taking up most of the floor space and found a few pairs not too holey or worn, throwing them into the black garbage bag. His eyes then landed on his most treasured possession propped in the corner next to his bed.

He rushed over to it, almost tumbling when his feet caught in a pair of dirty jeans on the way. Without a second thought, he shoved the last item into the bag and decided whatever else he'd need his mother could get him when they got to where they were going.

He had no idea where that was. He just knew they were leaving. And quickly.

His mother had had enough.

And he had no idea where his father was.

Probably at the garage. Or the warehouse. Or Crazy Pete's.

Or in some other woman's bed. He'd heard his mother yell at his father about that one too many times.

Something happened tonight, though.

Something she wouldn't explain.

When she had walked through the front door a little while ago, she shot him and his older brother a frown, shook her head and announced, "You two will end up just like him."

Right after that, she went into her bedroom. Chris had followed her, wondering why she was so mad.

What had their father done this time?

Or did Randy do something? He was always getting in trouble.

What he found was his mother packing a bag. Emptying her closet and drawers, and throwing everything that wouldn't fit into that bag onto the bed.

She didn't even hesitate when she spotted him standing in the doorway, clinging tightly to the frame. "Go get me the box of trash bags under the kitchen sink."

"What are you doing?"

"Do what I said."

He always did whatever his mother said because maybe, if he did, she'd give him a smile or a hug, or tell him she loved him.

She never did.

But he always hoped...

Maybe she would this time.

He'd taken off down the hall, found the open box of black garbage bags and ran back to his parents' bedroom.

By then she had so much stuff on the bed. Possibly everything she owned.

As he'd stepped closer, staring at the mountain, she snatched the box from his fingers.

"What are you doing, Mom?" His heart had been racing so badly, his chest became as tight as the drum he'd found in a dumpster a few weeks ago. The drum he wasn't allowed to play in the house, but only outside.

And even then, it still disappeared.

Randy said Mom had thrown it away, somewhere Chris wouldn't be able to find it, because him playing it gave her a headache.

His mother, with an unlit cigarette hanging out of her mouth, began to pull bags out of the box.

"Are you leaving?"

She didn't answer him, only kept stuffing bag after bag full.

"Randy!" she yelled. "Randy, get the fuck in here. Now!"

She was piling bags up on the floor, all of them full of her things.

"Yeah?" Chris's older brother came and stood in the doorway, his face unreadable.

His brother's eyes, the same dark brown as their father's, had swept the room. But he said nothing. He stood there casually, not caring that their mother was leaving and hadn't told them to pack, too.

"Start loading those bags there in my car," she'd jerked her chin toward the pile of full trash bags, "while I pack the rest of my shit."

"I can do it, Mom," Chris had volunteered quickly, even though at twelve, Randy was taller and stronger than him. "But I'm going with you."

"No, boy, you're staying here. Boys need to be with their father."

Boys needed to be with their mother, too. Didn't she know that? Even he knew that and he was only eight.

"But, Mom—"

"Get out of your brother's way," was all she said as she made sure Randy was doing what she told him. She turned back to the bed, shoving more clothes and other stuff into more bags.

His eyes landed on an empty trash bag that had fallen to the floor. He grabbed it and rushed back to his room and that was when he began to pack.

She was not leaving without him.

Now, with his own full bag, Chris stepped out into the hallway, no longer hearing any activity coming from his parents' room.

With the bag bouncing off his legs, he ran back there anyway to check.

Empty. His mother was gone, her bags were gone and he had no idea where Randy was.

"Wait, Mom!" he screamed. "I'm going with you!"

He rushed down the hallway, his stuffed-full garbage bag

becoming heavier with each step. "Mom! Don't leave without me!"

He dropped the bag to the floor and began to drag it behind him so he could move faster. He had to catch her before she left.

He wasn't staying here.

He wasn't.

Another hiccup-sob surged up from his gut as he reached the front living room. She wasn't there, either.

Neither was Randy.

The front door was wide open and he could see his older brother standing outside on the porch, staring out at the street.

Alone. Quiet. With both hands on his hips.

Chris dragged the bag, which held everything important to him, through the door and out onto the porch, pushing past his brother who blocked the two steps to the yard.

"She's gone, kid." He turned his head and spat into what used to be a garden in front of their small house. Before the weeds choked the flowers the previous renter must have planted and had been left to die once his family moved in.

Chris kept going, the heavy bag thumping down each step, even though her car was gone.

Even though their mother was nowhere to be seen.

No sign of her anywhere.

"Why?" he screamed. His stomach ached painfully, like it had been hollowed out with an ice cream scoop. "*Why* would she leave us?"

She'd come back for them. She had to. They were her sons. What mother didn't want her own children?

"She's a fuckin' whore."

"No, she ain't! Dad's the whore!" he shouted at his brother.

"Dad ain't a whore, stupid. Dad didn't do nothin' Mom

didn't do. Saw her suckin' dick plenty of times. And it wasn't Dad's."

What? Now Randy was just plain lying!

At the bottom of the steps, Chris dropped his bag on the narrow sidewalk and, with a roar, rushed his brother.

Before he could make it to the steps, Randy jumped down and tackled him. Chris fell backward and his head just missed the edge of the concrete.

"You're an asshole!" he screamed, grabbing Randy's hair and ripping on it.

A wild, flailing fist made contact with Chris's cheek and the pain caused him to lose his breath.

He growled and tried to roll his brother, but he was much smaller and couldn't get his weight behind him. Instead, he shoved his brother with both palms, knocking him off balance.

As soon as he rolled on top of Randy, he found himself once again on his back in the grass, unable to catch his breath. His brother was sitting on his chest, crushing his lungs and pinning his arms to the ground.

"Knock it off, you little shit. You made my fuckin' lip bleed."

"Good!" came out on a half-sob. He couldn't cry. Not in front of Randy. But he couldn't wipe the tears away while his asshole brother held him down. "Lemme go!"

"Only if you stop tryin' to fight me. I didn't do this to you. That bitch did. You think she gave two shits about you? She didn't. Her leavin' just proved it. She was just the twat used to squirt us out. That's it. Nothin' more."

"You're wrong." Why was Randy lying like that?

"Yeah, so wrong," Randy muttered and shook his head. "I'm gettin' off you. You try fightin' me again, I'm not gonna hold back. Dad will find you out in the yard when he gets home with your ass kicked. Then he'll kick it a second time for bein' a whiny-assed pussy."

Randy slowly lifted his weight and, when he was on his feet, his brother wiped the back of his hand across this mouth, smearing the blood. He spat into the grass next to Chris's head. Luckily, Chris twisted it away in time to keep from getting splattered.

"We don't need that bitch. What the fuck did she ever do for you?"

Chris laid in the grass, taking deep inhales since his brother was no longer crushing him. Anything to keep himself from crying.

With another shake of his head, Randy walked over to Chris's worn, dirty teddy bear that had tumbled out onto the dead grass, along with the rest of his things, when the bag spilled during the struggle. His brother picked up the stuffed animal, stared at it for a second, then came back to where Chris laid sprawled on the ground. He dropped it onto his chest. "I'll tell you what the fuck she's done. Nothin'. So, don't be such a fuckin' baby. We're better off without her."

Chris laid there, staring up at the late afternoon sky, and a hot tear slid from the corner of his eye. He heard his brother stomp back up the steps, go inside and slam the front door shut.

From inside the house, Chris heard a muffled shout of, "Fuck her!"

He grabbed his teddy bear, hugged it against his chest and curled into a ball around it. "She'll be back," he whispered, unable to stop the tears anymore. No longer caring who saw him cry.

Shortly after, the tears stopped.

And much later, he forgot what she looked like.

Because that night, when his father got home, he burned every damn photo of her in that house. Anything she left behind was burned, too. Then he told them never to mention her name again.

That rule wasn't difficult to follow because Chris never knew what her name was.

He'd only ever called her Mom.

Continue Cage's story here:
mybook.to/BFMC-Cage

If You Enjoyed This Book

Thank you for reading Blood & Bones: Deacon. If you enjoyed Deacon and Reese's story, please consider leaving a review at your favorite retailer and/or Goodreads to let other readers know. Reviews are always appreciated and just a few words can help an independent author like me tremendously!

Want to read a sample of my work? Download a sampler book here: BookHip.com/MTQQKK

Also by Jeanne St. James

* Available in Audiobook

Made Maleen: A Modern Twist on a Fairy Tale *

Damaged *

Rip Cord: The Complete Trilogy *

Brothers in Blue Series:

(Can be read as standalones)

Brothers in Blue: Max *

Brothers in Blue: Marc *

Brothers in Blue: Matt *

Teddy: A Brothers in Blue Novelette *

Brothers in Blue: A Bryson Family Christmas *

The Dare Ménage Series:

(Can be read as standalones)

Double Dare *

Daring Proposal *

Dare to Be Three *

A Daring Desire *

Dare to Surrender *

A Daring Journey *

The Obsessed Novellas:

(All the novellas in this series are standalones)

Forever Him *

Only Him *

Needing Him *

Loving Her *

Temping Him *

Down & Dirty: Dirty Angels MC Series™:

Down & Dirty: Zak *

Down & Dirty: Jag *

Down & Dirty: Hawk *

Down & Dirty: Diesel *

Down & Dirty: Axel *

Down & Dirty: Slade *

Down & Dirty: Dawg *

Down & Dirty: Dex *

Down & Dirty: Linc *

Down & Dirty: Crow *

Crossing the Line (A DAMC/Blue Avengers Crossover) *

Magnum: A Dark Knights MC/Dirty Angels MC Crossover

Guts & Glory Series

(In the Shadows Security)

Guts & Glory: Mercy *

Guts & Glory: Ryder *

Guts & Glory: Hunter *

Guts & Glory: Walker *

Guts & Glory: Steel *

Guts & Glory: Brick *

Blood & Bones: Blood Fury MC™

Blood & Bones: Trip

Blood & Bones: Sig

Blood & Bones: Judge

Blood & Bones: Deacon

Blood & Bones: Cage

Blood & Bones: Shade

Blood & Bones: Rook

Blood & Bones: Rev

Blood & Bones: Ozzy

Blood & Bones: Dodge

Blood & Bones: Whip

Blood & Bones: Easy

COMING SOON!

Blue Avengers MC™

Everything About You (A Second Chance Gay Romance)

About the Author

JEANNE ST. JAMES is a USA Today bestselling romance author who loves an alpha male (or two). She was only thirteen when she started writing and her first paid published piece was an erotic story in Playgirl magazine. Her first erotic romance novel, Banged Up, was published in 2009. She is happily owned by farting French bulldogs. She writes M/F, M/M, and M/M/F ménages.

Want to read a sample of her work? Download a sampler book here: BookHip.com/MTQQKK

To keep up with her busy release schedule check her website at www.jeannestjames.com or sign up for her newsletter: http://www.jeannestjames.com/newslettersignup

www.jeannestjames.com
jeanne@jeannestjames.com

Blog: http://jeannestjames.blogspot.com
Newsletter: http://www.jeannestjames.com/newslettersignup
Jeanne's Down & Dirty Book Crew: https://www.facebook.com/groups/JeannesReviewCrew/

facebook.com/JeanneStJamesAuthor

twitter.com/JeanneStJames

amazon.com/author/jeannestjames

instagram.com/JeanneStJames

bookbub.com/authors/jeanne-st-james

goodreads.com/JeanneStJames

pinterest.com/JeanneStJames

Get a FREE Romance Sampler Book

This book contains the first chapter of a variety of my books. This will give you a taste of the type of books I write and if you enjoy the first chapter, I hope you'll be interested in reading the rest of the book.

Each book I list in the sampler will include the description of the book, the genre, and the first chapter, along with links to find out more. I hope you find a book you will enjoy curling up with!

Get it here: BookHip.com/MTQQKK

CPSIA information can be obtained
at www.ICGtesting.com
Printed in the USA
LVHW090417080621
689678LV00011B/67